The wall shattered in a shock wave of splintered glass

"Get down!" Bolan ordered as he went into action, swinging the MP5 in the direction of the gunfire and triggering a short burst. His eyes were still adjusting to the gloom, but through the broken glass he could make out several shadowy forms approaching, firing as they advanced.

Equipment exploded, terminals emitting showers of sparks as the technicians jumped out of their seats and dived to the floor. Bolan got behind a console just as the next volley of rounds passed overhead, then he peered over the top long enough to deliver a sustained burst.

The Executioner had emptied his magazine and was reloading during a lull in the firing when something metal sailed through the window, bounced off a workstation and skidded to a stop near his foot.

It was difficult to see in the dim light, but Bolan recognized the shape well enough to know what it was.

Putting all fear aside, the Executioner reached for the grenade.

DON PENDLETON'S MACK BOLAN®

CRITICAL EXPOSURE

A GOLD EAGLE BOOK FROM

WORLDWIDE®

TORONTO • NEW YORK • LONDON
AMSTERDAM • PARIS • SYDNEY • HAMBURG
STOCKHOLM • ATHENS • TOKYO • MILAN
MADRID • WARSAW • BUDAPEST • AUCKLAND

Recycling programs
for this product may
not exist in your area.

First edition January 2015

ISBN-13: 978-0-373-61574-2

Special thanks and acknowledgment to
Matt Kozar for his contribution to this work.

Critical Exposure

If God listened to the prayers of men, all men would quickly have perished: for they are forever praying for evil against one another.

—Epicurus

It never ceases to amaze me what kinds of terrible things can be conjured by humans to inflict on their fellow man. But I'm here to even the odds. In spades.

—Mack Bolan

CHAPTER ONE

Benghazi, Libya

Lieutenant Commander John Falk, leader of SEAL Team Four, emerged from the murky waters off the pier at Dock 17. He lifted his goggles, disconnected his lips from the mouthpiece and withdrew waterproof binoculars from his pack. Through the enhanced NVDs he could make out at least a dozen sentries aboard the massive cargo freighter that had arrived in port early that morning.

While the freighter claimed to hail from a port of call in Capetown, Falk knew better. Military signals intelligence—MIL-SIGINT—reports claimed the raw materials such as the metals and other goods the freighter officially hauled were actually weapons to supply Islamic dissidents that had formed a local rebel group in Benghazi designed specifically to foil U.S. interests. The fighting had grown fiercer in Libya the past few weeks and the government leaders in Tripoli were screaming for U.S. assistance.

Personally, Falk didn't like the people in power. He didn't see much difference between them and the former regime headed by Moammar Khaddafi. But he knew the Islamic radicals running through the country unchecked weren't any better. They were an offshoot of

Ansar al-Sharia, with sympathizers sent in to shore up Islamic terror-group operations. Those operators were active members of the AQIM and U.S. intelligence circles knew the Al Qaeda in the Islamic Maghreb bankrolled Ansar al-Sharia efforts in Libya to the tune of millions of dollars. They were basically out of control. Many civilians and innocents had died at their hands, and this new cache of weapons and explosives aboard the freighter was only going to make a bad situation worse.

Enter SEAL Team Four to neutralize the cache by Executive order.

The mission parameters were simple. Get aboard the freighter, locate and blow the weapons cache, get out and await extraction. Simple and straightforward tactics for which they had trained time and again. Whether the mission itself would be simple remained to be seen—Falk didn't wear any blinders on that point. No mission, however standard it *might* seem, was ever without potential complications.

After one more sweep of the entire deck, Falk stored his binoculars and then reached to the laser light on his belt and keyed the button built into its base three times. A moment passed before five more figures surfaced. The alpha squad of the team would make the actual breach through the maintenance hatch in the hull while the second team provided a distraction for the sentries on deck.

"You guys ready?" Falk asked his men.

Each gave him the proverbial thumbs-up. He nodded, donned his scuba gear and they all submerged in unison. The swim through the coastal waters in the dark was nothing less than hazardous. Tides were rough and their safety margin was minimal at best. The waters in the port were horrendously dirty and rife with potential hazards. They could swim through the wrong spot and rip their bodies open on sharp scrap metal or acquire some sort of bacterial infection—or even *worse*.

Falk didn't let it faze him. There were more hazards to be concerned with; hazards such as human enemies toting subguns and harboring a distinct and unyielding hatred for any Westerner—especially Americans. Like those water-bound hazards that burned in the back of Falk's consciousness, they were without remorse and wouldn't hesitate to kill the SEAL team members if they were detected.

They swam toward the vessel, keeping to a depth of about twenty yards beneath the surface, Falk in the lead. They reached the target without injuries and Falk signaled his men to ascend. As soon as he broke the surface, he heard the shouts of men and reports from at least two dozen SMGs.

What the hell...? he thought, removing his mouthpiece.

The operation had been blown! There was no other reasonable explanation for them to be engaging the team intended to provide the distraction. Somehow they had given themselves away and it had resulted in an all-out battle on the top decks of the freighter. Falk whirled toward the heads of his men now just bobbing above the surface and was about to order them to submerge when the entire area suddenly came alive with light.

"We're compromised!" he shouted. "Evacuate! Evacuate *now*!" He gestured to his men to abort the mission.

Some of the men dipped immediately beneath the surface. He fitted his mouthpiece and whipped his body into a dive, moving toward the bottom as fast as his legs could propel him. He knew the best place for safety would be the keel of the ship.

Falk turned, headed for that point and more toward the stern so the docks would provide additional safety. His intent proved short-lived, however, as underwater lamps illuminated his position and temporarily blinded him. His instinct was to go deep, but even as he turned to do so he felt something lance his leg and a burning sensation ride a point from just above his right knee all the way to his hip.

Falk looked down toward his leg—or was it actually *up* since he was in a descent maneuver?—and in the light saw the source of the pain. A speargun projectile had gone completely through his thigh with such force that it had severed most of the nerves in his thigh muscles and nullified further use of that leg.

Before he could decide on a new course of action, someone grabbed his left arm. He sensed the body of another man in dive gear next to him.

Falk turned as he withdrew his diving knife. He was ready to plunge it into his assailant when he realized it was Cantrell, one of his own men and the team medic. They looked into each other's eyes, visible through the goggles, and Falk saw the crinkle of a smile just a moment before he watched his teammate's expression melt into horrific realization. Then the light left Cantrell's eyes and the water became cloudy with blood. Falk looked wildly in every direction trying to find the attacker, but there was too much confusion.

Then the world around him exploded into a series of lights and ear-splitting concussions, and he realized they were being bombed by a form of antipersonnel depth charges, perhaps even grenades. Falk broke free from Cantrell's grip and kicked off the body. There was nothing he could do for his friend and he had to evade capture. He gained maybe thirty yards' distance before another burning ripped through his body, this time from a point in his lower back to a point in his left upper chest.

The water around him clouded once more and Falk realized he'd just taken a bullet in the back. He spun and twisted, trying to avoid further injury as every muscle in his body seemed to scream with protest. He realized in the delirium that the screams were his own. The regulator seemed to disengage from his mouth and he sucked water into his nostrils. His lungs burned, and he knew the pain in his mouth had been from the force of his jaw clenching against the regulator stem. The burning in his lungs increased and his panic turned to terror. Stars popped in his eyes and blackness rimmed the edges of his sight.

Within a moment, Falk's sense of direction had left him and he realized there would be no escaping it. The limbs in his body no longer seemed capable of function and the initially controlled movements of swimming turned fiercely and irrevocably into thrashing as he lost control of other bodily functions. Falk never came to the realization the loss of sensation signaled something more ominous and terrifying than anything he'd ever experienced before.

Quietly and unwittingly, Lieutenant Commander John Falk slipped from life into death.

Munich, Federal Republic of Germany

ELI BRIGHTON CHEWED absently at the plastic tip of an unlit electronic cigarette.

He'd given up smoking more than eighteen months earlier; a fanfare event that had not spread beyond the boundaries of his own small and relatively impersonal world. As head of a Delta Force unit assigned to counteract terrorist activities in the European Common Union, Brighton had other things on his mind more important than self-improvement. Quitting smoking had improved his physical health, sure, but he could hardly consider it anything other than what is was: a victory over personal habits.

Oddly, Brighton hadn't been a smoker when he'd first started with Delta Force. The opportunities had come rarely, if at all, during initial training and he'd wanted to maintain peak physical conditioning. The demands of the job called for the omission of such self-indulgence. He'd taken up the habit while playing a role undercover, the byproduct of social acceptance inside the neo-Nazi group calling itself the League of Aryan Purity. When he'd first undertaken his cover to penetrate the group, he'd been amused by the oxymoron. This group boasted anything pure in body, mind or soul—they hated anyone who wasn't like them and, as in most such organizations, wouldn't hesitate to kill the racially impure.

"What's eating you, Eli?"

Brighton looked at his partner and longtime friend, Sol Gansky. The big man's shadowy outline—features marked by a bulbous nose and prominent forehead— bore out his Irish roots. His fiery red hair was subdued by a knit stocking cap, and he sat bolt upright in his usual sense of alertness. Their car sat at the curb of a run-down neighborhood in central Munich, beneath a broken streetlight.

"What do you mean?"

"You're quiet," Gansky replied.

"So what," Brighton groused. "We aren't hosting a talk show here."

"You're just usually a little more talkative."

"I like my silence sometimes, Sol."

The man shrugged. "Okay. If you say so."

Brighton returned his attention to the club they'd been staking out for the past three hours. The expected arrivals, two of the top guys inside the terrorist group headquartered in Munich, were more than forty-five minutes late for the meeting. Their contact inside the club, intelligence specialist Greg Hiram, had been doing everything he could to maintain an air of indifference.

Brighton had just about given up on the whole scenario and was minutes from calling it quits when a lone vehicle turned off a side street and made its way in their direction.

"This could be it," Brighton said as he and Gansky immediately hunkered down in the vehicle.

Brighton watched with concern as the late-model Citroën approached, icy fingers of nervousness prickling the back of his neck. At the speed the vehicle was traveling, and given the cramped space on the street, it was likely anyone driving by might spot them in the vehicle, even if both sides were crammed with parked cars. The moment passed when they saw the vehicle whip abruptly into a space just past the club entrance in a feat of parallel parking only achievable by an experienced European driver. Two men emerged from the back and Brighton immediately recognized their expected company. "Those are our guys," he muttered. "Get ready."

They waited until the pair swaggered down the sidewalk and entered the club.

Gansky pulled the stocking cap tighter on his head, climbed casually from their two-door VW and began to stroll up the sidewalk on the opposite side of the street. Brighton waited until Gansky was parallel to the Citroën before starting the engine. He could barely see the driver who seemed to scrutinize Gansky as he walked past, but Gansky played it perfectly and ambled along the sidewalk, pretending not to notice the driver. Gansky could hold his own if it went sour since he had a .38-caliber snub-nosed pistol concealed in his jacket.

Brighton waited; his gut rumbling with anticipation. This was what it had all come down to, the months of preparation and undercover work. If they could take down the two leaders of the LAP here and now, they could glean enough intelligence to dismantle the group and its operations and strike a crippling blow to the head of the organization that had spread its poisonous doctrine insidiously to like groups inside the U.S.

Brighton counted down two minutes, put the gearshift in reverse and eased back, depressing the clutch just in time to tap the bumper against the car behind him so he could stop without engaging the brakes. He cranked the wheel hard left and waited with the clutch to the floor and his right foot hovering over the gas pedal.

As soon as Gansky made his appearance and eased into view from the rear of the Citroën to come up low on the driver's side in a crouch, pistol at the ready, Brighton swung out and turned on his headlights. The light blinded the driver temporarily and Gansky made his move. The big man whipped open the door and stuck the barrel of his pistol to the driver's temple.

Brighton pulled parallel to the vehicle and screeched to a halt as Gansky yanked the driver from the car. The two climbed into the backseat of the VW and Brighton tore out of there, driving two blocks before turning into an alley.

"Wait here," he ordered Gansky, who kept the barrel of the gun to the driver's head.

Brighton killed the engine and bailed from the VW. He jogged up the street, turning up the volume on his headset as he ran. He couldn't make out the conversation between Hiram and the two LAP heavies over the dance music, and he cursed. He didn't know what was in store for him, only that they had to get the neo-Nazi leadership out of the club without creating any sort of ruckus.

Brighton got within twenty feet of the club entrance before the heavy wooden door swung out and three men emerged. Brighton immediately recognized Hiram and the two LAP leaders, one of whom had his arm around Hiram. Odds were good he also had a weapon on the intelligence agent.

Brighton skidded to a stop and reached for his pistol but in the next moment he found his arm didn't work right, most likely because of the silenced bullet that had entered the upper part of his back and severed his spinal cord.

Brighton opened his mouth to scream but nothing really came out and in that moment he registered the reason for all of these events culminated in the fact that he'd been shot by a sniper. White-hot light exploded in his sight and his breath exploded from his lungs as he pitched forward and his chest hit the sidewalk. The last thing Brighton saw was a flash where Hiram stood with the two neo-Nazi terrorists and the gory explosion of intestines and blood from Hiram's stomach.

Brighton never heard Hiram's body as it toppled forward and bounced down the stone steps—neither did he hear the explosive sound of the pistol pointed at Gansky's head through the back window of the VW.

Homs District, Syria

ON AN ABANDONED road less than half a mile outside the village of Sadad, Gunnery Sergeant Dusty Morrell of Recon Platoon, 8th Marine Expeditionary Force, waited patiently for nothing to happen. Just a few days earlier a detachment of Syrian Arab Army regulars had maintained tactical control, however loose the term, on that road but conflict in nearby areas had forced them to abandon their hold. The Marines had penetrated the region via a low-level airborne jump into the neighboring region and were now in a defensive posture designed to protect the village.

There were less than three thousand Syrians residing in Sadad, but in the past couple of weeks NATO had sent civilian workers to the village to assist the victims of a previous attack by Islamic militants in the al-Nusra Front. While it held no strategic value for the United States, or even the SAA for that matter, NATO inspectors were concerned about a possible resurgence of NF attacks if it became known the SAA had been sent elsewhere. Although the SAA commander left behind a small contingent of soldiers in Sadad, they were by no means equipped to repel any kind of significant attack.

"Holy cripes!" Morrell complained, squashing a fly

that bit his neck. "Could this place be any more miserable?"

Lance Corporal Jack Ingstrom chuckled. "Don't know, Gunney. Never been in a place quite like it."

Morrell looked at his Hummer driver. "Well, neither have I, Ingstrom, but when the recruiter told me I'd visit exotic places I sure as hell didn't have anything like this in mind. Put me back in Iraq killing insurgents. At least there I won't die of boredom."

"Aye, aye, Gunney," was all Ingstrom could think to reply.

Morrell muttered a flurry of curses under his breath and then informed his men and platoon leader in the back seat he was going to take a leak. He jumped from the Hummer, swung his Colt IAR6940 rifle across his shoulder and picked a nice, dark, secluded spot in which to conduct his business. He was midstream when he heard it, checking over his shoulder where he had a somewhat clear if not totally panoramic view of the road. There were headlights visible in the distance. But as Morrell stood there, pondering this sudden turn of events, he realized the sounds he heard weren't engines.

First, the lights on the road were much too far off for the engines to be heard already. Second, these weren't engine sounds he was hearing. They sounded more like…*choppers*!

"Yo, Gunney!"

Morrell jumped and nearly urinated on himself, catching the edge of a finger as he buttoned his fly. He turned to give Ingstrom a tongue-lashing when the area immediately behind the young lance corporal erupted in a white-orange flash. Their Hummer had been the target of the rockets from the chopper, which was now upon them.

In the aftermath of the explosion, Ingstrom got a funny look on his face and then his knees turned wobbly and he started to fall. Morrell rushed to the man and caught him before he hit the ground. Something warm and wet connected with his sleeve. He realized it was blood coming from Ingstrom's back where dozens of shrapnel fragments from the destroyed Hummer had pierced his flesh.

Morrell turned the young man over, calling his name, but the light had already left Ingstrom's eyes. Morrell lifted his head as he heard his platoon respond with audible effect, the dozen or so small arms firing on the chopper and its twin that had launched the attack.

Morrell dropped the limp body to the gravel-and-sand floor of the Syrian Desert and brought his assault rifle into play. He jacked the charging handle to the rear, thumbed the safety to full-auto and began to trigger short, sustained bursts at the choppers as they flitted about. One of the many volleys from the Marine platoon finally scored and sparks erupted from a chopper's side panel. An explosion occurred, then something seemed to flash. Morrell blinked and the next thing he saw was the chopper spinning wildly out of control and rushing to meet the ground while canting at a hellish angle. Over the brilliant explosion that occurred on impact, Morrell thought he heard the glorious shouts of victory from a number of his Marines.

Semper fi, boys, he thought.

They continued to do battle with the second chopper, but it was quickly becoming difficult as the pilot cleverly stayed high and in motion, making it impossible for them to get a bead on their target. Additionally the enemy was armed with rockets and using them with deadly accuracy, destroying two more Hummers and a five-ton truck. Morrell wanted to call for air support, but he knew there were no units within proximity—any requested assistance would arrive far too late.

The battle continued for another five or ten minutes, Morrell couldn't be completely sure, before the chopper blasted out of the area, having left plenty of destruction and death in its wake. Morrell ran toward the last known position of those vehicles that should have survived and picked up any survivors as he went, one with a leg wound and being assisted by two other Marines.

By this time the vehicles on the road were fast approaching and Morrell had only managed to collect a handful of survivors. He asked a squad sergeant named Hicks, "We got anything heavy left? Squad machine guns, crewed light artillery...*any*thing?"

"I got one .60 we pulled from our Hummer," Hicks replied. "The rocket got the front of it and flipped us on our side. Gunner got squashed, but I managed to salvage it."

Morrell nodded. "Get it set up at that high point overlooking the road. I suspect those trucks are NF, and under no circumstances are you to allow them through. I'll start collecting whatever explosive ordnance we have, including grenades and any launchers I can find. Whatever happens tonight, Sergeant, those trucks are *not* to get through. Is that clear?"

"Aye, aye, sir!" Hicks turned and ordered the man with the M-60 to find high ground and to take another man with him.

Morrell called after the young man, a private, and

said, "Listen good, Marine. Your orders are to fire for effect and prevent those trucks from getting through. Go for the equipment, *first*—especially since you got limited ammo. When you're out, it's time to start making bodies. Understood?"

"Yes, Gunney!"

"*Semper fi*, Private," he muttered as the young man turned to follow orders.

Morrell knew he'd probably just sent two Marines to their deaths, but there wasn't anything he could about it. Their mission was to protect the village and that's what he planned to do, whatever it cost.

"Sir, I don't get it," Hicks said. "How the fuck did this happen? This mission was supposed to be classified."

"I don't know the answers," Morrell said glumly. "I don't know that we'll *ever* know the answers. But I can promise you this much. If we get out of this alive, I sure as hell will get those answers—if I got to go straight to the Pentagon myself."

"If you do that, Gunney, I can guarantee I'll be right behind you," Hicks replied.

CHAPTER TWO

Stony Man Farm, Virginia

As Hal Brognola sat in the War Room and perused the reports still coming through from the Pentagon—funneled through their secure Computer Room in the nearby Annex—he felt deeply troubled. The incidents over the past twenty-four hours indicated that sensitive U.S. operations across the globe had been compromised on a level he'd seldom seen before. The Stony Man chief wondered how such a thing could have happened. Moreover, he didn't have the first clue where to begin or how to tie them together. Even Aaron "the Bear" Kurtzman's cyber team, a top-shelf unit if there ever was one, had indicated they were at a loss.

"There's no relationship between these incidents," he muttered.

Barbara Price, Stony Man's mission controller, looked up from the duplicate set of reports she'd been studying on her laptop. She tugged a strand of honey-blond hair behind her ear. "Did you say something?"

Brognola shrugged, leaned back in his chair and practically ripped the unlit cigar from his mouth. "I was just saying I don't see a link, Barb."

Price sighed as she returned her attention to the screen of her laptop. "I wish I had something to offer you, but it would only be platitudes. And I'm afraid I'm forced to agree. Three different missions by different groups of U.S. intelligence assets in three different countries. Maybe…I mean *maybe* there's a relationship we could assume between the incidents in Benghazi and Syria. But even the ties between the al-Nusra Front and the AQIM seem weak by comparison. There certainly isn't any correlation between a Marine expeditionary unit and SEAL Team Four."

"And even if there was," Brognola replied, "I don't think this neo-Nazi terror group the Delta Force operators in Munich had been following would be hooked up with Islamic terrorists."

"Agreed."

"Any word from Striker?"

"Striker" was Mack Bolan, aka The Executioner.

Price shook her head. "Nothing yet. But I've put the word out for him to contact us. I'm sure we'll hear soon enough."

The phone on the table signaled for attention and Price glanced knowingly at Brognola before she stabbed the button to answer. "Price, here."

Kurtzman's deep voice came over the line. "Morning, folks. I have Striker on the line."

"Striker?" Brognola said.

"I'm here, Hal."

"Good to hear your voice, Striker," Price interjected.

"Likewise. Your message was encoded as urgent. What's up?"

Price looked at Brognola with a wink and said, "Probably Hal's blood pressure, for starters, but that's nothing really new."

That produced a chuckle from Bolan. "I'm guessing that may have more to do with that mud Bear calls coffee."

That brought a laugh from everyone.

"We got a call from the Man this morning," Brognola said. "Some very odd incidents have occurred with the nation's intelligence operations. The reports are strangely isolated and the details surrounding those incidents even more puzzling. The intelligence is also spotty."

"Let me guess," Bolan replied. "You've had a compromise of sensitive operations around the world and the only common denominator is that there *is* no common denominator."

"You know about this?"

"I keep my ear to the ground," the Executioner said. "In fact, I just got wind of it myself. I thought maybe when I got Barb's message there might be a connection."

"Your intuition was right—as usual," Price said.

Brognola shook his head and tried to collect his thoughts. "Striker, the only thing we can tell you at the moment is that all three missions seem to have been blown in much the same way, and that all three were highly classified military intelligence ops. Unfortunately what we know is a lot less than what we *don't*."

"Anything on the hostiles involved?" Bolan asked.

"Two of the three are offshoots of al Qaeda," Price replied. "A reconnaissance platoon from a Marine expeditionary force got ambushed by choppers. The survivors managed to repel a vehicle convoy of weapons being funneled into the Syrian village of Sadad, an area that has seen a lot of terrorist activity as of late. The second attack was against SEAL Team Four in Benghazi."

"What about the third?" Bolan asked.

"A neo-Nazi terror group called the League of Aryan Purity," Brognola said. "Heard of them?"

"Vaguely," Bolan replied. "They've recently gained support from like groups here in the United States, but Homeland Security seems to have kept most of those activities under control."

"Three cheers for interagency cooperation," Brognola said as he popped a couple of antacids from a fresh roll he kept in the breast pocket of his suit coat.

"Do you think these things are related, Striker?" Price asked.

"I don't know," Bolan said. "Doesn't seem like we have enough information to tie them together logically yet. But it would seem from what I'm hearing that *you* think there might be a connection."

"The timing of the incidents would seem to point to it," Price replied.

"Okay, I'm willing to accept that in the absence of more intelligence," Bolan said. "And if there *is* a connection then the military angle seems the best approach."

"I'm curious to know how you came to be aware of this," Brognola prodded.

Bolan didn't reply immediately. While the Executioner had broken any official ties with the U.S. government long ago, they knew he still trusted Stony Man implicitly. His hesitation wouldn't have been out of mistrust, therefore, as much as his desire not to steer them down the wrong path. Mack Bolan had survived his War Everlasting this long by acting with diligence and forethought. His battle strategy—thoroughly and accurately assess the threat and determine enemy resources before hitting them where it hurt most—had remained the same for many years because it was effective. To act too soon could only spell doom for a man in his line of work.

"I helped out an old acquaintance a while back. Oz figured he owed me and contacted me by using an encoded number I gave him the last time we got together. The number goes through a series of cutouts, but leads back to the voice mail of the phone in my Stony Man quarters," Bolan said. "He oversees military intelligence signals operations between Washington and NORAD, particularly in the area of deterministic patterns analysis."

"Glad to hear *Oz* is on *our* side," Price remarked.

"Me, too," Bolan said.

"Should we pull out the stops, Hal?" Price queried. "Put Phoenix Force on it?"

Brognola scratched his chin and sighed. "Striker? I'd like to hear your thoughts."

"I think between what he told me and now your call, there's enough unrest I should get involved. It might be nothing or something big. At least let me check it out further. If an international terror group has compromised our military intelligence operations on a global scale, any major response on Stony Man's part could alert them. Better I make soft inquiries first."

"You have a lead?"

"Nothing more than I've already told you. I think it's time for me to pay a visit to my contact directly. See what I can shake out of the tree."

"Okay by us," Price said.

"How do you want to play this?" Brognola asked.

"I'll work under my usual military cover," Bolan said. "I'll need you guys to get all the background information handled, credentials and such. And I could use Jack if he's available."

"Both Able Team and Phoenix Force are currently unassigned," Price replied. "He's yours."

"Tell him I'll meet him at the private hangar, say… three hours from now."

"Destination?"

"I'm going straight to the source of all the rumblings," the Executioner said. "NORAD."

Fort Carson, Colorado

STONY MAN DIDN'T have to ask Jack Grimaldi twice.

Any time the ace flier got the opportunity to work with Mack Bolan he jumped on it with the eager abandon of an adolescent. Working a mission with the Executioner was always an adventure, and Grimaldi liked the action. The downtime between operations for the Stony Man field teams could grind on the nerves, and while Grimaldi welcomed the break, he always knew a job with Bolan would challenge his skills and provide a change of pace.

What few people knew about the Executioner was that his success drew in large part from his ability to remain highly adaptive and upwardly mobile. Bolan's alliance with his government remained largely one-sided in the sense of the terms. He took only the jobs he wanted and he set the mission parameters. Often his work required him to improvise on a level that wasn't always afforded the warriors of Able Team and Phoenix Force. When working those teams, Grimaldi had to "fly under the radar" to coin a phrase, but with Bolan he experienced a new sort of liberty.

Hence it came as no surprise to Grimaldi when he'd completed the taxi procedures at Fort Carson and came out of the cockpit to find Bolan holding up a brand-new set of U.S. Army Class A's and grinning.

"I assume those are for me?" the pilot asked with a sheepish grin of his own.

"Can't strut about as a colonel without an adjutant."

Grimaldi's eyes twinkled in the cabin lights when he noticed the insignia. "Wow—captain's bars. I'm humbled."

"Don't let it go to your head. And hurry up. We only have a few minutes."

Grimaldi grabbed the uniform and headed aft while Bolan finished buttoning his own coat. Several rows of ribbons adorned the breast pocket of the uniform jacket, a Combat Infantry Badge and blue infantry braid among them. In this case, it wasn't far from the truth. Bolan had earned all of them during his years as part of a sniper team in the Army.

When the two were dressed, they descended the steps of the C-37A aircraft, a U.S. Air Force version of the Gulfstream V business jet. The aircraft boasted advanced avionics, countersurveillance sensor packages and a hidden armory kept fully stocked with assorted pistols, SMGs, assault rifles and explosives of variable type and capability.

Bolan chose not to wear a sidearm for this visit. He could have secured his Beretta 93-R in shoulder leather beneath the Class A uniform, but he opted not to go that route. They were on a secure military installation, about to transfer to an even more secure location at the Cheyenne Mountain Complex. A full-bird colonel showing up with a concealed sidearm or even a loaded pistol in military webbing around his waist would have attracted suspicion. It was Bolan's skills in role camouflage that had kept him alive these many years, and he wasn't about to blow it out of a sense of misguided paranoia.

An airman first class saluted the two officers as he opened the rear door for Bolan. Both men returned the salute, Grimaldi opting to take shotgun. The airman greeted them respectfully but didn't say anything the remainder of the roughly twenty-minute trip along Norad Drive from the airfield on Fort Carson to the Cheyenne Mountain Complex entrance. After the security police waved them through following a close inspection of their vehicle and Bolan's orders, stamped and certified by the Pentagon, the airman escorted them into the secure communications area.

Within minutes they were seated in the office of Bolan's contact, Lieutenant Colonel Roland Osborne.

"How do you know this guy?" Grimaldi whispered.

Bolan seemed to consider the question for a moment. "I met him during my early days with the Stony Man program. I've helped him out a time or two since then."

"So he knows Brandon Stone's a cover."

"Maybe and maybe not. Actually he knew me back when I used the John Phoenix cover. When I talked to him after he left the message, I managed to convince him *that* was a cover name I used back then and that Stone's my real name."

"What happens if you ever have to change it up again?" Grimaldi asked.

"Let's hope it doesn't come to that," Bolan said. "But even if I do, Oz won't ask any questions. He's got too much style for that and he understands that what I do for the country may not always fall within strict military guidelines."

"Oz sounds like a good friend to have," Grimaldi remarked.

"Like another good friend we know?" Bolan said with a smile.

Grimaldi started to conjure a reply but was interrupted by the opening of a door and the entrance of a black man who by Grimaldi's estimates couldn't have been any less than six-foot-six. Nearly as many medals donned the breast pocket of his Class A uniform coat as they did Bolan's—probably a few more—with the most striking difference being that Roland Osborne bore the deep blue colors of the U.S. Air Force. Aside from that, he was clean-shaved with close-cropped curly black hair that was gray at the temples. He was handsome, distinguished and obviously quite pleased to see Bolan when he first laid eyes on him.

"As I live and breathe!" he bellowed, his voice deep and resonant. He stuck out a hand that Bolan rose and took immediately. "Colonel, it is *damn* fine to see you!"

"Same here, Oz," Bolan replied easily. He nodded at Grimaldi who now stood, and said, "Meet my...adjutant, Jack Gordon."

"Gordon?" Osborne said, offering Grimaldi a warm and dry handshake.

Grimaldi nodded and, noticing the almost mischievous twinkle in the colonel's eye, found himself liking the guy right off. He had a vibe that few seemed to possess.

"Pleased, sir," Grimaldi said, attempting to retain some official and military bearing. Osborne may not have been blind to Bolan's real gig, but that didn't mean

Grimaldi saw any reason to go out of his way and advertise the fact. To anybody.

"No worries, Captain Gordon, just call me Oz and let's skip all the stiff formality," Osborne said.

He gestured for them to be seated and then said to Grimaldi, "I don't believe we've ever met. Whenever this man pays a call he's usually alone."

"I only joined his staff a few years ago," Grimaldi replied simply.

Osborne nodded, obviously content with that, and then put his attention on Bolan. "So I got your message that you were flying in. I figured since you didn't say more than that this wasn't a social visit."

"Afraid not," Bolan said. "I'm here to follow up on that information you passed along to me, Oz."

"The signals thing?" Osborne raised his eyebrows. "Yeah, it's the damnedest thing I've ever seen. We still can't make heads or tails of how the signals got redirected and decoded but we're narrowing it down, closing in on the source of the hack into our systems."

"I'm not completely up to speed on these signals you're talking about," Bolan interjected. "Care to elaborate?"

"Well, you already know part of it, I would assume—at least given your background," Osborne said. "In typical standard operations, non-classified and general orders or other things, we pipe communications through the normal channels. Emails, phone calls and whatnot. But each and every military operation deemed classified requires very specific protocols be used when transmitting orders."

Bolan partially directed his voice at Grimaldi as he said, "You're talking about all orders for classified missions, regardless of where they come from, have to go through NORAD."

"Correct. We then verify the authenticity of the orders before they're sent on to whatever might be the receiving unit."

Grimaldi shook his head. "I'm sorry, sir, but you lost me. What do you mean by 'receiving unit'? You're talking a military unit?"

Osborne gave him a sharp nod. "You betcher ass, Captain. Those transmissions are coded and, regardless of origin, we have to verify the authenticity of the orders before going out. We don't want somebody, for example, to put out an Executive Order to launch nuclear missiles from a submarine halfway across the Pacific unless we know damn sure the orders were genuine."

Grimaldi emitted a low whistle as he looked at Bolan. "Even I didn't know that."

Bolan nodded. "There can't be any mistakes when you're talking about coordinating military operations at any given point."

"One miscommunication," Osborne added, "and you could spark the next world war or cause a nuclear response from a country where none was intended. To say nothing of removing America's advantage in a first-strike scenario."

"Okay, Oz," Bolan said. "That's fair enough, but how would someone intercept these transmissions? And even if they did, how would they have the know-how to decode them?"

"I can't answer that yet. But what I *can* tell you is that we found some hidden code that we can't explain. When we decompiled and refactored it we realized it was an inside job—done so well that the source is indeterminate."

"So how do you expect to find whoever intercepted the transmissions?" Bolan asked.

"The program was designed to route the transmissions through a very specific network of internal servers. Now the addresses were masked and we've hit the additional snag that the code is self-regressing."

"Meaning?" Grimaldi asked with a furrowed brow.

It was Bolan who replied. "Meaning it was designed to self-destruct if discovered."

"Bingo," Osborne replied.

"How much more time to do you think you're going to need to find this place?" Bolan asked.

"That's the tough part to estimate," Osborne said.

"Best guess?"

"Another day, maybe two. After that it won't matter if we don't have any answers because as you've pointed out, the code will have fractured to such a degree it'll be useless as tits on a bull."

"Fair enough," Bolan said. "But what if I told you I know somebody who might be able to help you speed up the process?"

"I'm open to suggestions," Osborne said with splayed hands. "At this point I see we got nothing to lose trying everything."

"Glad to hear it," Bolan replied. "Because I have just the right guy for the job."

CHAPTER THREE

"Talk to me, Bear," Mack Bolan said.

"We were able to pick apart the code," Kurtzman replied. "Akira managed to find the obligatory self-destruct codes and shut them down, so we had enough transitory information left behind. After that it became a cakewalk."

"Akira" was Akira Tokaido, one of the best computer hackers in the world, and a valued member of Aaron Kurtzman's cyber team.

"So you know where the original intercept program was sourced?"

"To within a grid about a quarter-mile square." A pause ensued and then he continued. "The transmissions were sourced from a wireless, high-frequency satellite tower in the central Rockies. I'm uploading the exact coordinates via secure link to Jack's navigation system. He can then set it from there and put you down on almost a dime."

"Unless it's heavily wooded," Bolan remarked.

"I made sure they had rappelling gear aboard, boss," Grimaldi chimed in. He'd been listening to the conversation through his own headset.

"Looks like we're set then," Bolan told Kurtzman. "Thanks again for the assist, Bear. I'll be in touch when we know something more."

Bolan signed off.

The beating of chopper blades against the air threatened to vibrate Bolan's innards down to the bone. Unfortunately the older Bell-Huey was the only thing they could get on such short notice, and the Executioner hadn't wanted to wait for something more modern. Besides, if Kurtzman's preliminary information panned out—something for which Bolan had little doubt otherwise—he wouldn't be spending a very long time aboard.

Bolan squeezed his frame out of the jump seat in back and began to prepare his equipment. He'd already changed out of his Class A uniform for woodland camouflage fatigues. He donned a web harness that held a portable medical kit, combat knife and four M-67 high explosive grenades. He whipped out his .44 Magnum Desert Eagle, checked the action and ensured a round was chambered before replacing it in his hip holster. Finally he slung an MP5K.

Under normal circumstances Bolan would have preferred something a bit more powerful in a primary assault weapon, but he figured if the terrain happened to be mountainous, he would need to carry light. His judgment had proved sound given the territory Kurtzman described. The model he carried boasted a side-folding stock, quick-detach sound suppressor and a 3-round burst mode. It chambered 9 mm rounds in a 30-round steel magazine.

Light but durable, yeah.

Bolan looked forward and saw Grimaldi twirl his finger. He donned the headset. "Go ahead, Jack."

"We're almost on point. Based on what I'm seeing,

there's no place to put down, Sarge. Looks like you'll be going in the hard way."

"Could be just as well," Bolan replied. "I don't know what I'm going up against, and I don't want to risk putting this old crate in harm's way."

"It *would* mean a long walk home," Grimaldi said. "Understood."

"I'll get the winch deployed," Bolan said. "Once I'm through, I'll find an extraction point and send a homing signal. Might want to take the time to get back and find something a little more…say, robust."

"Roger," Grimaldi stated. "Stay frosty, Sarge."

Bolan grunted an affirmation before abandoning the headset and moving to the swing-out winch. He got the rescue arm into position and locked, and then expertly deployed the take-up and belay lines through the rigging just beneath the winch head. Once that was done he quickly put his legs through the climbing harness, put the sling in place and hooked up the carabiner through the working end of the take-up and belay lines.

Grimaldi piloted the chopper with the expertise that had earned him a reputation with Bolan as perhaps one of the greatest tactical pilots ever to lay a hand on a stick. Flying talent seemed to be something that was part of Grimaldi's blood, an enigmatic and invisible element that coursed through the man's veins. Like Bolan's talents as a warrior, Grimaldi had a natural gift that not only made him a consummate flier but a solid ally in Bolan's War Everlasting.

The soldier called a last farewell and then bailed out of the chopper without hesitation as soon as Grimaldi reached hover point. He descended the rope steadily but not too quickly. Even rappelling into the woods held intrinsic dangers, and Bolan had enough experience to know it wasn't good to rush things. He could fall or slip or experience an equipment malfunction, and descending at a controlled speed under such circumstances could be the thing that saved him from a backbreaking fall.

The cards were with Bolan and he easily passed through the treetops to find the cool forest earth rushing to greet him. At the last twenty yards, Bolan yanked his arm behind him and jerked twice to slow his descent. A moment later his boots touched the ground and he crouched to absorb the mild impact. He unclipped his belt, released the lines through the carabiner and then donned the portable communications earplug and attached the throat microphone.

"Striker to Eagle, you copy?" Bolan whispered.

"Go, Striker."

"I'm down and set. Beat feet back to base and get us some modern chops," Bolan replied.

"You got it, Striker. Good luck."

"You, too. Out."

Bolan clicked off and removed the ear bud and mike before stowing them carefully in the pouch at his side. He was now in communications blackout and would remain that way until he either called for extraction or they found his bloody, battered corpse.

Bolan activated the electronic compass on his right wrist. He checked his bearings and realized Grimaldi had dropped him nearly on the spot of the coordinates Kurtzman had sent them. The soldier began to look around him, but he couldn't see the tower—not yet, anyway. The dense foliage overhead did a good job of blocking most of the sunlight, and only by the fact it was midday did Bolan have any light at all. He did one last equipment check and set off.

It took him about ten minutes of walking in ever-widening circles, using the compass as his guide, before Bolan found the tower. He made sure nobody was around before stepping into the small clearing and approaching the base. It was tall, but when he looked up he could just barely see the top of it through the trees. So that was it. They hadn't spotted it because whoever had erected the structure had managed to camouflage it so it wasn't visible from the air. Perhaps highly sensitive equipment could have detected it, like the kind found aboard an AWACS. But therein lay the problem— somebody had to actually be *looking* for the tower. Up until recently, nobody had even known there was anything wrong.

Bolan turned to study the base of the tower. He gave it the once-over with a critical eye before locating a power panel. Just visible above the forest floor was a heavy, thick cable that ran from the power box and disappeared into the woods. From that point he could see what would have been just passable for a foot trail. He considered following it, but thought better. Daylight wouldn't last forever and he didn't have time to risk moving off the target or losing the trail.

No. Better to let the enemy come to *him*.

Bolan pried the panel open with his combat knife and quickly studied the rat's nest of connections. He located the neutral and cut the thick cable of twisted-pair wires inside. If the tower was that critical to whomever had installed it here, and the Executioner bet it was, it wouldn't be long before someone came to investigate.

Bolan closed the panel and made for the woods as

close to the box as possible. He knelt behind thick foliage he found nestled between a pair of giant pines and settled in to wait. Yeah, they would definitely come to him.

BOLAN DIDN'T HAVE to wait long—about fifteen or twenty minutes by his reckoning—before someone approached the tower making enough noise to raise the dead. At first the soldier couldn't believe it, but when he saw the reason it didn't seem so incredible. The man who came through the trees to Bolan's left, just about where he'd seen the makeshift path, was fat and clearly out of shape. Even from a distance the Executioner observed that the man's face was beet red from the exertion, and he was wheezing loudly.

The man finally reached the tower and stopped to catch his breath. Droplets of sweat beaded his forehead, those that weren't already plopping onto the ground from his face and neck. Armpit stains were visible. Why anyone would have sent a guy of this girth and poor physical condition to investigate a tower on a forest mountain was anybody's guess.

Bolan stepped out of the bushes and approached the man, the .44 Desert Eagle up with sights pinned on the man's chest. The man could barely catch his breath and he seemed even less able to do so when he first noticed the big guy dressed in camouflage fatigues toting what looked like a cannon in his hand. The man did nothing to hide the surprise in his expression.

"Whoa," he said, raising his hands. "What the hell is this?"

"This is where you stop asking stupid questions and

start answering some of mine," Bolan said coolly. "That work for you?"

"Um, yeah…just…easy, man. I'm not in a hurry to get killed."

"And yet you're still talking." That shut him up. "What's your name?"

"Ah…Ducken," the guy replied. "Horace Ducken. Look, can I…? Can I put my hands down? My arms are getting tired."

Bolan almost cracked a smile. Ducken was a heart attack waiting to happen. He'd only had his arms up a moment. The Executioner thought about making him keep them up, a little incentive not to try anything, but then he nodded. Might as well let the guy off the hook. Maybe it would buy him a little good will.

"So tell me, Ducken…" Bolan began. "What are you doing up here and what do you know about this tower?"

"I just maintain the thing, man."

"Alone?"

"Alone? No, hell…*shit* no."

"Then start telling me something of substance," Bolan replied. "Or I may make you put your hands up again and keep them up forever."

"Look, I'm not doing anything wrong," Ducken said. "I lost my job with Paradine-E and—"

"Wait a second," Bolan cut in. "The electronic security firm contracted to the DOD?"

Ducken nodded.

"All right, go on."

"I was just trying to make some cash, man. My mom had to put up for a second loan on her house after I lost my job, and I couldn't afford to let her lose it."

"How did you come into this work?" Bolan asked, nodding in the direction of the tower.

"They came to *me*, man. I mean, I'm no Snowden or nothing. I didn't tell them *anything* about what I did for Paradine-E. I just got hired because I knew—"

He cut his words short and a look of horror crossed his face, as if he'd just almost given it all away.

Bolan considered what Ducken had said so far. It sounded plausible enough, and this setup was nothing he could've done on his own, especially not in his physical condition. He'd just about killed himself just climbing a slight incline to investigate the issue. Not to mention, the fat and socially awkward man in front of him didn't strike Bolan as any sort of criminal mastermind.

"The tower's not working because I cut the power. You think you can repair that?"

"Yeah, I guess. Depends on how bad you cut it."

"Not enough that any simple splice job couldn't fix."

"And then what?" Ducken asked, scratching his neck as he considered the grim visage of the Executioner.

"If you repair it, they'll be expecting you to return," Bolan said, his plan already formulated. "They *won't* be expecting us."

"Us?"

"Yeah," Bolan said. "You help me, and I'll make sure you're out of the way when it all goes south."

"Oh, shit," Ducken said. "You're about to put me out of work again—aren't you?"

"Afraid so," Bolan replied. "Fix that thing."

Ducken turned his attention toward the power box, and as Bolan suspected the young man had it up and humming in just a few minutes. Fortunately there had been a toolkit secreted in a nearby compartment that Bolan had thought was a transformer box, as it was labeled such, but in fact contained an array of tools and replacement parts. At least Bolan had some inkling he was dealing with an ingenious enemy.

But who?

The question troubled him and he pondered it as Ducken led him into the woods and down the slight hill. They proceeded for what Bolan estimated was at least a quarter mile, Ducken wheezing and panting the entire trip, until they arrived at the main facility. It wasn't impressive at first glance, mostly because it was obscured with heavy camouflage—a bunker of sorts with a low-hanging entrance and sloped dirt walls covered by brush and the tops of pine trees. Additionally there was radar-scattering camouflage netting woven into that.

Bolan grabbed Ducken by the shoulder and pulled him up short, putting his lips close to the tech's ear while he jabbed the muzzle of his MP5K PDW into a spot near Ducken's left kidney. "Hold it. Where are the guards?"

The tech shook his head emphatically. "No guards, man…no guards."

Ducken held up a card and Bolan realized at a glance it was a coded access card. "Fine. What sort of security inside?"

"Just a few guys with pistols, a sort of roving guard."

"Are they on any sort of predictable schedule?" Bolan asked.

"No," Ducken said. "They just appear every so often, look things over and then they leave. They go to some area that's off-limits."

"How many like you inside?"

"You mean workers?"

"Yeah."

Ducken shrugged. "I think there're about a dozen of us, all told. But usually we rotate in twenty-four-hour shifts of four. Each shift has a technician, a couple of data guys and a microwave tech. That's me. That's what I do."

"Fine. You'd better be telling me the truth, Ducken, because lies won't end in anything good for you. Now let's move out," Bolan said as he nudged the tech with the MP5 for emphasis.

The pair continued down the path until they reached the entrance to the bunker. Ducken looked back at Bolan, who met his gaze and nodded, and then swiped his card. The amber light turned green and Ducken opened the door. Bolan gestured for the guy to go ahead and he followed behind.

They passed through a very narrow corridor, so narrow that Ducken's girth barely managed to walk along without his arms brushing the walls. The floor of the corridor was composed of metal grating and traversed a decline path until leveling out where it opened onto a large room. The light there was minimal, most of it coming from computer workstations with large screens. Somewhere Bolan could hear the steady thrum of power generators.

True to Ducken's words, three other people were in that room, and they didn't even notice Bolan at first because Ducken obscured him. The soldier's eyes adjusted to the gloom and he spotted the empty seat that had to belong to Ducken. He shoved the guy toward it and then brandished his weapon high in two hands so all those present could see it clearly.

"That's enough," Bolan said. "Take your hands off the keyboards and put them up where I can see them."

One skinny kid with an unlit cigarette hanging out of the side of his mouth squinted. "Who the hell are *you?*"

Bolan turned toward the young man. "I'm the guy holding the hardware, so I would guess that puts *me* in charge. Is that good enough for you?"

The youth's haughty mask melted and he sat back in his chair, all signs of potential defiance fading. Meekly he replied, "Yeah, it sure is."

"Now, your pal here tells me there are a few guards in this place. Where might they be?"

"They come through there," a young woman, the only female in the group, said, pointing to a door in the corner. "About every hour or so."

"When was the last time they came through?" Bolan asked even as his ice-blue eyes flicked toward the large, tinted plate glass that spanned one of the walls.

"Maybe…maybe forty minutes?" she replied.

"Fine. You guys—"

The Executioner never finished the statement because the glass "wall" disappeared in a massive shock wave of splintered glass shards followed by a blast of autofire. One of the young men at a terminal, the only one who hadn't spoken, was the first to buy it as a half dozen rounds slammed into his lithe frame. One blew part of his head off and the impact knocked him off his rolling chair. He crumpled to the ground a bloody mess of mangled flesh.

"Get down!" Bolan ordered as he went into motion and beelined for cover.

On the move, Bolan swung the MP5K in the direction of the fire and triggered a short burst of his own.

His eyes were still adjusting, and through the one pane of shattered glass fragments he could make out several shadowy forms approaching. All were toting weapons, the evidence of that fact in the winking muzzles followed by the angry cloud of rounds pelting the opposite walls.

Equipment was shattered, terminals emitting showers of sparks as the remaining three technicians jumped out of their respective seats and made best possible speed for the floor. Bolan got behind a console just as the next volley of rounds passed overhead and then peered over the top long enough to deliver a sustained burst.

Bolan had finished spraying his magazine and was exchanging it for another during a lull in the firing when something metal sailed through the window, bounced off the wall-length tabletop that had served to house two of the workstations and skidded to a stop near his foot. It was difficult to see in the dim light, but Bolan could make out its shape well enough to know what it was.

Putting all fear aside, the Executioner reached for the grenade.

CHAPTER FOUR

Under other circumstances the soldier might have chosen a different strategy when faced with imminent dismemberment by an HE grenade at such proximity. These circumstances were different. Bolan no longer had himself to think of, but these young souls—these ignorant people who barely passed as adults—who had allowed themselves to be involved with terrorists. They were guilty of nothing more than being really brilliant at what they did and having no decent and safe outlet for their collective genius.

Such were the ideal victims of America's enemies, *Bolan's enemies*, lured by the temptress of prestige and money. When it came right down to it, that wasn't something for which any of them deserved to lose their lives.

Bolan didn't do anything as cavalier as throw his body on the grenade. He was no good to this salvageable crew under such circumstances. So he did the only thing he could—he scooped up the grenade and got rid of it. The bomb just barely cleared the frame of one of the shattered windows before it blew, but Bolan had managed to gain shelter under one of the heavy shelves serving as a makeshift desk. His ears rang from the explosion and he choked on the heavy coat of drywall dust that rolled through the darkened room, but otherwise he and the people he'd just saved were unharmed.

"Get out!" he told them, gesturing furiously toward the open door through which he'd first made his entry. "Keep on your hands and knees!"

They did as ordered while Bolan scrambled in the opposite direction, heading toward a door on the far side. He didn't know where it led but anything had to be better than playing the role of sitting duck. If he could get a little combat stretch, it would make a difference, at least in terms of buying the technical crew time to get clear while Bolan strategized a way to turn this holding action into an offense. The soldier didn't know where the door would take him, or if he could even access whatever awaited him on the other side, but he had to try. He couldn't afford to just wait there for his enemies to come to him.

Remaining crouched, Bolan reached for the knob and found that it turned. He opened the door and pushed through, keeping as low as possible. The interior had a musty smell and at first Bolan thought he'd entered a closet, which would have trapped him with no place to go. The Executioner's luck held out as he spotted yet another door to his right. He pushed through it and emerged in a narrow corridor that dipped even farther underground. Bolan looked to his right and saw the wide-open area from which his enemy had approached.

Bolan almost grinned at his good fortune, totally obscured in the deep shadows of the walkway while his enemies, three in total, moved toward the control room, apparently convinced the grenade had done its grisly work. Bolan extended his arm and leveled the MP5K. He opened up, sweeping the muzzle in a rising burst of sustained autofire. The results were devastating for the unsuspecting guards, and while they managed to bring their weapons to bear, it proved wholly inadequate under the marksmanship of the Executioner.

The first hardman fell under a double-tap to chest, the 9 mm rounds punching through lung tissue and tearing out good portions on their way out the other side. The second man tried to get cover, but Bolan dropped him midstride. The survivor managed to get off a short burst before the soldier caught him with a volley that cut across the man's guts and shredded his insides.

Bolan crouched and waited a long time—he couldn't be sure how long but it had to have been a few minutes—before rising and continuing down the walkway that ended at yet another door. He opened it to find a corridor to his right, which he followed with his back to the wall. He'd slung the MP5 and now he held his trusted friend, a Beretta 93-R in front of him at the ready. Bolan got close to the end of the walkway and one more door. Beyond that he found the remnants of some half-eaten Chinese takeout and an ashtray filled to the brim with cigarette butts and some security camera feeds.

So that's how they'd known he was coming, Bolan thought.

The soldier shook his head as he left the room and proceeded up the wide-open area in the center of the bunker. He couldn't understand what a room of this size could be used for. Was there another entrance? The place was certainly large enough to park a few cars inside. Bolan whipped out a flashlight and swept the ground around him, realizing that it was concrete. He swung the light to the wall opposite the walkway he'd first come down, but found nothing of interest. He finally swung his light upward with no expectations. What he saw surprised him.

The Executioner studied the roof over the bunker carefully for a few minutes, and then nodded and switched off the flashlight. He frisked the three bodies for ID but found nothing that gave a clue to their identities, which he had expected. Then he marched off in search of the technicians he'd saved, assuming they'd hung around. Based on what he'd just seen, he'd figured they would. Where else could they go? And even if the others split, he knew Ducken wouldn't get very far in this rugged terrain. Especially not if the large area in the center of the bunker was what he thought it was. No, they wouldn't go anywhere. Bolan needed them to help him retrieve all the information from the computers—at least the ones that were still operable—so he could get it to Stony Man Farm.

Yeah, it was turning out to be one hell of a day for Mack Bolan.

"A HELIPAD?" BARBARA PRICE repeated.

"Yeah," Bolan replied. "I noticed small puddles of what I think are hydraulic lubricants here and there, either left by the chopper or by the hydraulic doors overhead. The terrain is too rugged for any vehicles other than four-wheelers or mountain bikes. No roads in or out. When I questioned the workers, they confirmed it. Choppers bring in the new technical and guard crews every twenty-four hours and rotate out the previous shift."

"You didn't want to wait for the next chopper to come in?"

"They came in this morning," Bolan said. "I don't

figure we have that kind of time. One of them gave me a description of the chopper. Jack thinks it's an Air Force job, pretty modern."

"So whoever we're dealing with has either modified it to look like a USAF chopper or it's a real one."

"Based on the descriptions, which were quite accurate, we think it's an actual bird from the fleet."

"Okay," Price said. She reached for the printout on her desk that Kurtzman had given her minutes before Bolan's call. "Aaron disseminated and organized the data you sent. There's no doubt the codes being used are legitimate, not to mention the work is highly technical. So adding that to what we know about this chopper and—"

"You don't have to tell me," Bolan said. "There are definitely military personnel involved in this somehow."

"Right."

"Did he get anything that would indicate a source?"

Price clenched her jaw as she studied the Executioner's grim visage on the large wall screen in the Computer Room in the Annex. "According to the intelligence we gathered, all of it points to Tyndall Air Force Base."

"Florida?" Bolan asked, quirking an eyebrow. "I don't get the connection."

"You will when I remind you that the Continental NORAD Region directs all air sovereignty activities over the Continental U.S. It's the official designation of the 1AF/NORTH, which is headquartered at Tyndall."

"Sounds like that's the place I need to go next," Bolan said. "I'll maintain my Stone cover, but I'll need some new credentials. I'm thinking Defense Intelligence Agency placement."

"Done. We'll have them delivered to your present location, so please don't leave without them. What about this chopper that's expected to drop off the next shift?"

"Osborne's already indicated he can take care of that," Bolan said. "He has F-16 Falcons from the Air National Guard at Peterson AFB on full alert. When they spot the chopper, they'll send the fighters to conduct an intercept."

"And if they refuse to cooperate?"

"Knowing Osborne, he'll order them blown out of the sky," Bolan said. "But I see no point in my waiting here to find out. Assuming they surrender peacefully, Osborne said he'd forward any intelligence they got to me ASAP."

"I'd prefer you remain there to handle it," Price said gently.

"I need to keep moving, Barb," Bolan countered. "We've already had three military special ops missions compromised in the past forty-eight hours. Good men have been killed. Chances are there'll be more, and I can work best if I get in front of it as soon as possible."

Price nodded. "You're right. I hadn't thought of it that way."

"I'll be in touch," Bolan said. "Out."

The screen winked out a moment later.

Panama City, Florida

IN ADDITION TO the CONR First Air Force, two other major units operated out of Tyndall AFB: the 325th Fighter Wing, home of the F-22A Raptor and primary training site for the same, and the 53rd Weapons Evaluation Group. The latter was also responsible for training personnel that operated many of the Unmanned Combat

Aerial Vehicle programs and positional stations aboard E-3 Sentry AWACS. Much of the intelligence about the physical specifications as well as operations was considered above even Top Secret—a name so secret it didn't have a real name except that known to a few—so the base also provided technical MI knowledge training to members of the NSA, CIA and DIA.

Bolan knew he'd be viewed as an outsider unless he could imitate membership in at least one of those intelligence agencies, and given most of what had happened up to now it seemed posing as DIA would be the best choice.

Upon his arrival at Tyndall, his guess was confirmed. Straight from the airfield he was shuttled by military sedan to DIA offices adjacent to the 53rd WEG HQ. A tall man in an AF uniform with the rank of major and a nametag that read "Shoup, R." came out of his office and greeted Bolan where he'd been waiting in a chair near the secretary's desk.

"Colonel Stone?" the officer said in greeting as he stuck out his hand. As Bolan shook it he continued, "Major Randy Shoup, DIA Operations Officer. Please come in."

Shoup led Bolan into his office, offered him a drink, which Bolan politely declined, and then settled behind his desk and sat back. Bolan watched the man's eyes carefully, meeting his gaze with a striking stare that was neither friendly nor frosty. He didn't know who he could trust at this stage, since whoever had been funneling inside information to America's enemies hadn't yet been identified. Not that it would have made a difference.

Bolan didn't think he could trust anyone in this case. He'd have to play his cards close to the vest.

"Major, you've been briefed about my reasons for being here?"

Shoup shook his head. "Frankly, no. I just got a communication from B Ring less than an hour ago to expect your arrival. My orders are to cooperate with your investigation."

"Good," Bolan said with a nod.

Shoup didn't miss a beat as he continued. "And I'll be happy to do that just as soon as I know exactly *what* it is you're investigating. For example, if you're here to pick apart my unit, then I have to be up front and tell you that isn't going to happen, orders or no goddamned orders. With all due respect, *sir*."

Bolan forced his expression to remain impassive. He had a traitor to sniff out, but being rude or confrontational wouldn't buy him any love in the shut-up-and-mind-your-own-business world of military intelligence. Not to mention that if Shoup or his men thought Bolan was here to find wrongdoing on their parts, they'd close ranks as if it was nobody's business and that wouldn't help Bolan in the progress department. No, best to play it cool and be as honest as he could without compromising his identity or mission. Still, there were some things on which he'd have to play hardball if he wanted to gain Shoup's respect.

"Since you've set the tone for us so eloquently," Bolan began, "then let me get *you* clear on a few things, Major.

"First, I'm a superior officer and here at the behest of the Pentagon, so you'll follow my orders or I'll personally rip that cluster off your lapel. Second, I'm not here to pick apart your unit. There's a lot of evidence to support the fact we have a traitor in the MI community.

I'm here to expose the traitor while trying to make as little noise as possible, so if the traitor isn't among your crew you have nothing to worry about.

"Last, and I can't stress the importance of this enough, there have been a lot of good military personnel who have died in the past forty-eight hours due to the actions of this individual. I'm going to need your cooperation to make sure no more service personnel come home in a flag-draped coffin. You get me, mister?"

Shoup's face was stony and his cheek twitched as he replied, "Yes, sir."

"Fine. Now as I understand it, you may already have information on this potential traitor. Tell me about what you've found."

Shoup reached to a nearby locked filing cabinet. He inserted a key and then swiped his thumb over the cabinet and the biometric reader beeped once before Bolan heard a locking mechanism release. Shoup opened the middle of the three doors, thumbed through a number of files and finally came out with a thick manila folder labeled in red and white along its edges. The Executioner immediately recognized the top-secret labeling as Shoup handed the file to him.

"This is eyes-only, sir," Shoup said. "You technically shouldn't even see it."

Bolan nodded as he took it. "I'll take it as a sign of good faith. And don't worry, Major, I know how to keep my mouth shut."

"I hope so, sir," Shoup replied. "Because what you're going to see in that file isn't pretty."

Bolan glanced through each page, skimming most of the text. Eventually he came upon a snippet of information regarding a USAF chopper that had been transferred on loan to the 21st Medical Group at Peterson AFB. This had supposedly been at the request of the USAFSC-HQ adjutant. Oddly, the chopper had recently been reported out of service after an accident that occurred while trying to assist in a civilian air rescue operation in the forest just northeast of Durango, Colorado. Bolan continued through the rest of the information, watching as the intelligence analysts followed the trail of paperwork and odd requests.

Finally, Bolan looked up and met Shoup's waiting gaze. "Then the trail just ended?"

Shoup nodded. "Yes, sir. I mean…in a way."

"What way is that?"

"Well, a field intelligence officer with the NSA, who'd been working jointly with us, tried to pick up the trail after it went cold. That was where we decided not to catalog or record any of the information until he could get us something solid. He eventually traced those tracks to a site in the Guatemalan jungles."

Bolan nodded. It made sense, considering that terrorist groups all over the world had been using points in Central America to stage operations. Silence could be bought rather cheaply in poor countries such as Guatemala, Honduras and El Salvador. Plus, it provided terrorists with bases closer to American soil than they could ever hope to get anywhere else, and a natural pipeline for information and personnel by piggybacking onto the drug and arms trades.

Shoup continued. "Unfortunately we hit a snag. Our guy in the NSA disappeared on his last assignment into Guatemala. He hasn't been heard from in over a week. We had another guy in place, a local, actually, we tried to put on the trail but he's disappeared, too."

"Seems like whoever you're after doesn't want to be found," Bolan remarked.

"That was our assessment, as well. Fortunately we do have an informant who's been able tell us with some accuracy where both of these individuals might be found, but we're only about sixty percent confident in the accuracy of the information. I'm trying to decide if it's enough to act on."

"At least it tells you something."

"What's that?"

"You're on the right track. So what was your next move?"

"We've put a plan in motion, more of an information gathering than anything else," Shoup said. "We're hoping to be able to call it a rescue operation, but who knows if we'll get our way on that count. The devil usually deals the cards the way he wants."

"And often they're not in our favor," Bolan added.

"Right," Shoup said with a curt nod.

"Okay, I'm game to go along with this plan. But I'm going to take over the operation."

Shoup's lip twitched, but he didn't say anything.

Bolan put up a hand. "And before you go all territorial on me, you'll still be in charge of your men. All of them. And you'll call the shots in this reconnaissance. I'll handle how we act on any intelligence we find. And if it comes down to a rescue operation and we get enough evidence either of these men are alive, I'll accompany you on the op but you'll get full credit. My name need not even come into it."

"And what if it goes south?"

"Then the whole thing falls on my shoulders," Bolan said. "I'll take full blame and responsibility."

Shoup appeared to consider it for a long moment and finally nodded. "Colonel, sounds like you got yourself a deal."

CHAPTER FIVE

Istanbul, Turkey

Gastone Amocacci wasn't pleased to hear the latest report regarding their operations in Colorado.

The Council wouldn't be happy, either, although Amocacci worried much less about that than he did about how this would affect the overall timetable. So far they had only managed to counter three of the most recent special operations. So few was infuriating. He pushed down the anger that manifested itself as bile in his throat. In reality, those victories had proved no small feat. Not only had their intelligence been right about the operations, but they'd managed to conduct them at points across the globe. This proved the initial reach of the Council, but more, it proved that reach could expand. Yes, growth potential would be realized if they were able to continue to operate in secret.

This most recent incident in Colorado, however, threatened that possibility, and Amocacci knew his allies would expect him to deal with it. Swiftly and decisively; anything less would constitute a failure of a magnitude Amocacci didn't even wish to entertain on a hypothetical basis. That idiot Shoup had screwed things up royally, and now Amocacci was forced to clean up the mess. Fortunately he'd managed to provide the diversion they'd needed, so with any luck they would be able to mitigate the damage. The guy from the DIA who called himself Colonel Stone, an obvious alias, would have a very nice surprise waiting for him in Guatemala.

Yes, a nice surprise indeed.

Amocacci tossed the fake paperwork into his briefcase, shut off the lights and left his office in downtown Istanbul. His driver took him across town to the airport, where he boarded his private helicopter and made for his home in the foothills. Amocacci liked to make it look as if he were a successful, fat-cat businessman. His cover as a successful exporter of Turkish goods had served him much better than any other he'd attempted in the past because it allowed him to grease the palms of certain government officials. Unfortunately he didn't own any of it. All of his belongings, including his very personage, were community property of the Council.

The Council of Luminárii, also known as the Council of Lights, was composed of former and current high-rankers from some of the most active intelligence services in the world. It included representatives from the British SIS, Russian GRU, Mossad, Chinese MSS and the Turkish NIO. The Council also boasted informants and connections from nearly every intelligence service in the Middle East and a half-dozen in Europe.

Thus far, Amocacci had only been able to recruit support from the DIA within North America. There had been no Canadian takers at all, and the one CIA case officer Amocacci had approached had had the poor grace to kill himself rather than risk the exposure that such an organization had been operating in Turkey on his watch. Amocacci had merely shaken his head when he'd learned the news.

Amocacci jumped from the chopper and walked hunched over as he headed toward the house constructed with the funds from the coffers of the Council founders. Amocacci had contributed only a small portion, his funds limited after he'd left his position as an Italian police officer attached to Interpol. He'd been a dedicated officer until the death of his family; the net result of an intelligence operation gone very wrong. The criminals Amocacci had been trying to apprehend had discovered they had an informant inside their organization.

The informant had talked, blown the entire operation wide open, unbeknown to the task force assigned to the takedown. When the time came, there had been no criminals to be found. Many had been luckier than Amocacci, having lost their lives alongside those of their immediate family, but Amocacci had been on assignment when the criminals had killed his wife, two sons and his sister-in-law, who'd had the poor misfortune to be visiting at the time. Amocacci had immediately resigned his post and hunted down every last one of the bastards.

Unfortunately it hadn't been enough for him and that's when he created the Council of Luminárii. The Council had grown beyond anything he'd been able to comprehend, though, and although he'd started it he found himself mired in politics. The Council worked effectively, still, but Amocacci was in too deep, as were all the rest of them. Nobody left the Council unless feet-first, and nobody would dare betray them by becoming slack. There were other punishments worse than death.

But Amocacci didn't hate the Council. Far from it. In fact, he'd dedicated his life to eliminating special operations and intelligence where it would mean the compromise or death of bystanders, or create political upheaval where none need exist. The other Council members were as tired of their respective superiors creating havoc in the world as Amocacci, and they had finally reached a point where they could do something about it. These first few victories, as small as they might seem, were just demonstrations, a test bench to prove that the Council could work effectively on a macrocosmic scale, a *global* scale, and that those efforts could make a difference in the international intelligence community.

Amocacci entered the estate, dropped his briefcase on the antique table near the massive double front doors through which the housekeeper had admitted him. She tugged the overcoat from his shoulders as she advised him that the lady of the house had gone out for the evening. Ah, yes, Lady Allegra Fellini was every bit a woman as she was a consummate companion to Amocacci. They'd met while she was on vacation in Crete and Amocacci was on Council business. For more than a year Fellini had shared his table and his bed, and she'd never expected anything of him. It was a perfect match, and he'd been more than agreeable to her taking up somewhat of a permanent residence at the estate.

Amocacci acknowledged the housekeeper's notice, advised her he would be ready for dinner in about an hour, and then entered his study. He secured the doors behind him and took the access tunnel—hidden behind a full-length mirror that doubled as a door—to the headquarters of the Council. The remainder of the Council of Luminárii was already present and awaiting him. From the looks on their respective faces, they had been waiting for some time. All the rest of them had made their entrance through a hidden elevator set off a private access road that wound its way from the Eastern Thrace regional capital of Kirklareli.

It was in Kirklareli that the Council had established its urban headquarters, and only when the members needed to meet did they travel to their stronghold in the Yildiz Mountains. Their setting up residence in the region hadn't been by accident. This part of Turkey had proved a most invaluable location from which to base their operations as it allowed them proximity to both European and Middle Eastern theaters. That had paid off more than once, and they'd been allowed to operate with significant impunity and right under the noses of Turkish officials, who seemed to remain woefully ignorant. Of course, their massive infrastructure had allowed them to establish a number of front companies and a paper trail that, if inspected closely, would have led anyone straight to nothing.

And all by design, Amocacci thought with a smile as he entered the massive conference room.

The first to greet him was Mikhail Ryzkhov of the Russian GRU, a pudgy and red-faced man in his midsixties who ate too much and drank too much vodka. Not that it mattered, since he still had an uncanny mind and was a genius on the small-unit tactics of at least half a dozen countries, including the United States. But he was a staunch Communist in a time where communism had long lost favor over more modern socialism with a progressive turn, and while the Russians kept him on, they did so at a considerable arm's length.

"Well, Gastone," Ryzkhov said. "It's about time you joined us!"

"Were you worried, comrade?"

"Not so much," Ryzkhov replied quietly as he turned his attention to his drink, now feeling a bit foolish for his outburst.

"I'm sorry, gentlemen, but I was unavoidably detained," Amocacci said as he took his seat at the table.

It was massive and as round as a doughnut, again by design. The idea was that all of them were on equal ground and nobody necessarily took the head of Council. Despite that, it had become a rather unspoken edict that while Amocacci was no lesser or better than the rest of them, the Council *had* been his idea and so in that light he did act as a chair, of sorts. It was more of a figurehead title than much else, and Amocacci had never really taken to it, figuring more that it just gave all the rest of them someone to blame when things went wrong.

"I hope you weren't detained by bad news," replied a voice with a cultured but clipped British accent.

Amocacci let his gaze rest on the SIS case officer for Bulgaria, Hurley Willham. A former member of the British SAS and later a military intelligence analyst, Willham was known for his unique affiliations with agents from intelligence services. He had connections on most every continent. In fact, it was Willham who had approached a number of American agents with a proposition to join the Council, but all of them had turned him down. Still, Willham *had* managed to recruit the chief Israeli representative on the Council, Lev Penzak of the Mossad.

"I wish I could answer in the negative, Hurley, but unfortunately I can't," Amocacci said. "All three of our test operations went off without any problems. But…it would seem our potential contact in America fucked up."

Penzak, a fifty-eight-year-old man with a big nose, square jaw, wild gray hair and deep brown eyes, shook his head. "I'm not sure it's appropriate to refer to him as 'our' contact, Gastone."

"We share everything, don't we?" Amocacci replied easily with a wave. "Anyway, I've managed to mitigate the circumstances in our favor. Our operation in Colorado has been discovered, but it's of no consequence."

"No consequence?" Willham inquired, one eyebrow arching studiously. "And what leads you to draw such a conclusion? The Colorado base provided us with the only way to intercept information on U.S. special operations. Without it—"

"We are no worse off," cut in Quon Ma, a countersurveillance expert with the MSS. Amocacci and the rest of the group knew the least about Ma— something Amocacci assumed to be much by design— who had served in a number of high-ranking positions. Ma seemed almost apolitical in his views, but he was behind the Council a hundred percent and utterly trustworthy.

"You think not?" Willham asked.

Ma saw the bait his British counterpart dangled for what it was, but he took it anyway. "I do. There was no guarantee the secrecy of that operation would hold. I'm surprised it lasted as long as it did, and for this, Gastone is to be commended. However, I also think this American Air Force officer…Shoup, is it? He's become a liability we could do without. It's too early in the program to risk exposure."

"I'm forced to agree with Ma," Penzak stated. "Shoup has to go."

"I think it can be arranged," Amocacci replied, managing to keep the disdain from his tone.

It wouldn't do to be disrespectful to rebut the members of the Council. They had proved to be his greatest allies and to alienate them over such a trifle issue would have been a stroke of lunacy on Amocacci's part, no matter how strongly he might disagree with them. Shoup had nearly blown it, but now he had to tell them of this other matter.

"I'm bothered by the fact that there's another player who has inserted himself into the game now. His name is Colonel Brandon Stone and he's an officer with American military intelligence."

"Bah!" Ryzkhov cut in with a wave. "Complete fabrication…cover name, most likely."

"What makes you think so?" Amocacci said. "Even Shoup couldn't verify any falsehoods in his story."

"Would this Stone be the same man who singlehandedly brought down our, er…I meant to say *the* Colorado operation?" Willham inquired.

Amocacci nodded.

"That's very interesting," Willham said.

"How so?" Penzak asked.

"Well, it would seem that something of that nature would have gone to the FBI, or even the Department of Homeland Security. For anyone to turn over such a potential threat to one officer in the DIA, even a colonel, sounds a bit out of step for U.S. intelligence efforts. After all, they *know* there's a problem within the military intelligence circles."

"Or at least they suspect it," Ryzkhov said in an uncharacteristically agreeable tone. "So it wouldn't make sense for them to send in someone from a potential pool of suspects. They'd go to the outside."

"And so they probably have," Ma said, inspecting his fingernails. "Clearly, this Stone isn't whoever he *wants* to appear to be. I'd vote he be eliminated along with Shoup."

"Listen," Amocacci said. "Killing an American military officer is already going to draw significant attention. Killing two would bring down every American agency on us. It's too risky. I can't urge you enough to reconsider."

"There may be another way," Penzak said. He looked at Amocacci. "Didn't you say you'd planned to send them on a wild-goose chase to Guatemala?"

"That is correct."

"Well, then, why not turn the Islamic Brotherhood on to that fact? We know they're operating in Guatemala, and to score such a victory against the Americans would do their cause well. Nobody would question it if an American special operation in a foreign country met with a few dead military officers."

Willham nodded enthusiastically. "Not to mention those bloody wimps at the Pentagon would never let something like that go public. It would be too humiliating for them."

"It might be able to get done," Amocacci said. "The trouble is I have no contacts with the Islamic extremists in that part of the world."

"I think I can help with that," Penzak said. "With one phone call."

Even as nods of approval commenced around the table, Amocacci couldn't help but feel a twinge of doubt.

Tyndall AFB, Florida

"I DON'T LIKE him," Mack Bolan announced.

"Who?" Grimaldi asked.

"Major Shoup. He just rubs me wrong."

Grimaldi looked stoic. "You think he's lying?"

"I think he *might* be," the Executioner replied. "Whatever else, I'm going to have to watch my back every second. Or I could wind up with a knife in it right when I'm not looking."

"So maybe going to Guatemala with him and his team isn't such a wise thing."

They sat in the VIP quarters at the base with an array of weapons disassembled on the small, simple table in front of them along with a cleaning kit for various calibers. Bolan ruminated as he worked mechanically on his deadly hardware. "I'm really only going for the lift."

"I could give you that, Sarge."

"You will." Bolan winked at his friend. "In a way."

"Meaning?"

"You're going to take the jet down on your own. Once there, I need for you to arrange for a civilian chopper."

"A civvie job won't be of much good in a hot LZ, Sarge," Grimaldi replied. "Although I'm guessing you already know that."

"I do." Bolan ran a bore cleaner through the barrel of his Beretta 93-R before saying, "I need something small and quick. There's a lot of jungle terrain, and you won't have much in the way of maneuvering room."

"So there *is* a method to your madness."

"That's what they tell me."

"You think there'll be trouble."

"I'm betting on it," Bolan said. "It all seemed just a little too timely that Shoup and his people had a finger on this from the outset. Don't you think?"

"It does seem like heavy coincidence."

"Not to mention there weren't one but *two* agents, one working local, that Shoup said disappeared shortly after the first man. And why Guatemala? What's the connection? There's nothing down there that would pose any sort of an internal threat to USAF operations here in the U.S. And we don't have anything going on down there at present in the way of major military intelligence. Just minor CIA work keeping an eye on the drug runners."

"Weren't there rumors of al Qaeda using Guatemala as a base of operations?" Grimaldi asked.

Bolan dismissed the rumor with a wave of his hand. "Small-time. Mostly wannabes with the occasional real bad guy in the Islamic Brotherhood thrown in to gain credibility. The one thing terrorists have encountered in Guatemala is a whole lot of resistance from state terrorist groups. Basically drug gangs like Mara Salvatrucha and so forth. Local crime is the big problem there, and it's no secret that the local gangs don't like to share."

"Ah, honor among thieves," Grimaldi quipped.

Bolan deadpanned. "Really."

"Sounds like maybe you're walking into an ambush on purpose."

"Exactly. I'm betting whoever is behind the compromise in the security of American MI operations is also getting nervous. They'll want to do some damage control, and they'll want to make sure they get all the players in one fell swoop."

"Sounds like a real group of sweethearts."

"Interesting you say that," Bolan replied. "Because that's exactly what I'm thinking. We're dealing with a group here, and one that seems to have significant knowledge about special operations. At least insofar as ops by the U.S. military. So far, we've had a Navy SEAL operation compromised, intelligence signals and data to NORAD intercepted, and the near destruction of an entire platoon of special recon Marines."

"Plus the Delta Force gig in Germany."

Bolan nodded. "All military operations, all highly classified, with no rhyme or reason for specific locations. None of the groups these special units were operating against was related in any way. That means the motive *has* to be centered on intelligence or, more specifically, American defense intelligence operations."

"You definitely have your work cut out for you on this one, Sarge."

"Guess that's just how I roll, Jack," Bolan replied.

CHAPTER SIX

Istanbul, Turkey

"Please, Alara," Colonel Alan Bindler said. "*Please* let's not go into this again."

Alara Serif stood defiantly with hands on hips in their office located within the U.S. Consulate. "I will go into it again and again…and *again* until someone starts listening to me. Alan, you have to take this seriously."

Bindler pinned Serif with a cool gaze. "I take *everything* seriously my staff members bring to me, and I give equal weight to the opinions of all. Is that clear?"

Serif did her best to look properly mollified. "Yes, sir."

Bindler sat back in his chair and put his hands behind his head as he continued. "You want to know why I hired you, Alara? It's because you're diligent, because you care about the security of our nation and you give a shit about your job. Sadly, I can't say that about most of my people. And technically, you know we're not even supposed to have military personnel within our consulate, other than the Marine guard."

"I understand."

"Do you?" Bindler stood and shoved his hands into the pockets of his trousers. He went around the desk and sat on the edge of it to look into Serif's eyes.

The haughty, impetuous expression she returned almost made him want to laugh. In so many ways, Serif was like one of those little girls who's defiant and opinionated, and yet not out of spite but from driven curiosity. Serif was one of those little girls who'd been forced to grow up all too soon, if the contents of her CIA file were any indication.

The daughter of an American diplomat who married a Turkish man, Serif's entire life had been spent in embassies throughout the world. Her father, Maliki Serif, had refused to let his precious Alara go through life absent of her Turkish identity, and he'd been quite insistent on teaching her the culture, customs and language—taking her on frequent trips to the country— even when she was absent so often while her American mother made her tours of duty as an attaché at various U.S. embassies around the world.

Her background had made Serif an highly advantageous instrument to defense intelligence efforts in Turkey. Where in most ways it would have taken much training to fit a representative from the DIA into that role in this country, Alara Serif had been tailor-made for it. She could speak the language, knew the customs, and had enough of her father's genetic traits that she fit right in without a second glance. Other than her beauty, which caused a stirring even in Bindler now and again when he watched her coming or going.

Bindler forced his mind to more practical matters. "Listen, Alara. I know you're convinced this… this Council of Lights exists." Serif started to open her mouth but Bindler raised his hand. "Let me finish! I know you think it exists and *maybe* it does. But what do you have as a shred of proof beyond a series of loosely coupled theories that you can back with hard evidence but you can't actually tie together."

"Can't tie together until *now*," Serif said with a triumphant smile. She withdrew a photograph from the thick manila envelope streamed with classified red-and-white-striped tape and handed it to Bindler. "Take a look at *that*."

Bindler sighed as he stared at the picture. "Okay, it's a little grainy. What am I looking at?"

"The man in that photograph is Gastone Amocacci, a former Italian police inspector attached to the Interpol Intelligence Division."

"Great. What about him?"

"I've long believed that the Council doesn't have any leadership," Serif said, charging straight to the point as she always did. "At least not in any conventional sense. I think they operate on equal terms with one another. An effort like theirs could not survive if there was one individual in charge. One person with all the power and/or information would pose a security risk to them. That's why they've been able to operate for so long without being detected."

"So what does this…this Amocacci?" Bindler interjected. When Serif nodded he said, "What does he have to do with it?"

"I think he's a member."

"Uh-huh. And you have *proof* of this, of course."

"That photograph was taken just yesterday," she said. "I know, because I took it."

"You were in the field again?"

"Yes."

"Alara, if I've told you once I've told you a million

times…you are *not* to perform fieldwork without first my express permission and second my *knowledge*."

"I was off work," she said. "I pursued this on my own time."

"You're not *authorized* to do that."

"But—"

"But nothing," Bindler cut in. "Now I've told you before and this is the last time. One more transgression, even a minor one, and I'll pull you from duty and ship you back to an assignment in the States. Is that understood?"

Serif didn't say anything at first but when Bindler repeated the question, she finally nodded and muttered an affirmative.

"Now as to this Amocacci character, I assume—" Bindler nodded at the folder "—you have a full report in that folder."

"Yes."

"Good, leave it with me. If I think what you've put together has merit, I'll consider pursuing the matter."

Serif looked extremely hopeful so Bindler realized he'd need to put a damper on her enthusiasm. "But *only* if I think it has merit and I give the go-ahead to assign an agent to it. That won't be you."

"What? Why not?" she cried.

"Because you're too close to this thing. It's like some kind of obsession. It's causing you to disregard procedures and endanger our position here." Bindler handed her the picture and she placed it in the folder before he snapped his fingers and held out his hand.

Serif gave the entire package to him, albeit reluctantly, and then rose from her chair. "You're not going to pursue it. You're going to mothball it, Alan, just like you have all my other reports. Apparently nobody here or at the Pentagon considers this a priority."

"I've already told you—"

"And I believe *you*, Alan. But you still answer to others, and it's them I don't trust. You'll read the report, you'll forward it to them, and everyone will conveniently *forget* about it. And in two or three months when I ask you about it, you'll tell me you haven't heard anything and all will be forgotten."

"You know how it works here, Alara. We take the good with the bad."

"Yes," Serif replied. "I know how it works. It just leaves me wondering why nobody here is interested in something that could well affect the security of our nation."

"That's just not true, and you know it."

As Serif turned to leave his office she asked quietly, "Do I?"

Stony Man Farm, Virginia

"HEY, AARON?" BARBARA Price said as she walked into the Computer Room.

"Yes?" Kurtzman replied.

"What do you think the chances are that a DIA intelligence analyst would be filing reports about a secret group of former intelligence officers at the same time as this leak in military intelligence occurred?"

Kurtzman grinned as he shrugged his wrestler-like shoulders. Despite the bullet that had put him in a wheelchair, he still found time to work out a couple of hours every day. Such activities had left him in top physical condition. He may not have been able to walk but he'd never let it stop him. His physique, coupled with his booming voice and warm disposition, had earned him his "Bear" nickname.

"I'd have to say the chances are about a million to one. What have you got?"

"Pull up DIA file number 607P9."

Kurtzman returned his attention to the keyboard, punched in some codes and numbers and a moment later the entire contents of the file were displayed across three massive screens on the far wall. Kurtzman squinted at the center monitor in an attempt to make out the photograph of the key agent behind the reports.

"Alara Serif, Defense Intelligence Agency," he read mechanically. He muttered his way through the next few statistics, her physical characteristics, date of birth and such. Then he continued aloud, "Current assignment's in Turkey?"

"Istanbul," Price confirmed, shuffling through the papers she held. "She was assigned there eighteen months ago under the title of assistant to the military Marine officer in charge, Colonel Alan Bindler."

"What would the commanding officer of a U.S. Consulate Marine guard need with a DIA analyst as an assistant?"

"I'm sure the Turkish government would like to know the same thing if they had her real credentials," Price said. "Since 9/11, we've been slowly switching out standard military clerks with our intelligence analysts from various agencies. NSA works up a thorough cover for each, and the U.S. gets approval on each assignment from the host government before sending them in. Of course, those governments think they're seeing the *real* dossiers."

"But what they're really seeing are the cooked papers."

"Correct," Price said. "They forge just about everything from names to birth dates to closest living relatives."

"Naturally. So what's so special about this one?"

"Alara Serif is half Turkish," Price said. "Her father is a Turkish citizen. Married an attaché to the U.S. ambassador of Turkey at the time."

"So she knows the territory."

"More than that, Aaron. She knows the politics of the country and who's who behind every button. A lot of wheeling and dealing goes on behind the curtains in Turkey. Something few people outside the most inner circles know about that country. Of course, it's no secret to our intelligence communities, but the better part of Washington seems to want to turn a blind eye when it comes to seriously looking at the intelligence coming out of Ankara."

"Except us," Kurtzman said with a knowing wink.

Price didn't hold back a chance to smile at her friend's mock attempts to be surreptitious. "Right. We actually look at everything as a matter of policy instead of dismissing it out of hand."

"So you think something she's reporting has merit?"

"I do," Price replied. "In fact, I think it may even be related to this case."

Kurtzman gave the information some attention. He'd learned a long time ago that if Price keyed on something that seemed far-reaching, there was usually a good reason. From what he'd just read, however, he couldn't see any link to the compromise of U.S. military intelligence operations and Serif's reports.

"Okay, I give up," Kurtzman said. "What's the connection?"

"First off, there's this claim about a secret organization called the Council of Luminárii, particularly Serif's theory that this group doesn't operate with a leader, per se. She thinks this group operates well because they work in a symbiotic fashion."

Kurtzman nodded. "The ideal rules them all. It's been done before and quite effectively. Too crazy for Serif to make up."

"Exactly. And then there's the main player Serif has had in her sights practically from the beginning, a man she believes to be a member of the group, if not an actual puppet they use to do their bidding. His name's Gastone Amocacci. Fifty-six years old, citizen of Italy. Former police officer with Interpol's intelligence division."

"What's his story?"

"I checked his background and discovered he quit after an operation went wrong and most of the members in his unit were killed. He moved to Istanbul a short time later and started a business in exports of Turkish goods. The government there *loves* the guy. Guess he's made many of their diplomats a lot of money."

"Probably in kickbacks," Kurtzman interjected with a snort.

"Probably. He's also quite the jet-setter. He's been seen traipsing about Europe and Southeast Asia with Lady Allegra Fellini, who's practically Italian royalty in her own right."

"I've heard the name."

"I don't doubt it. She's the sole heir to a clothing

line empire that makes Armani look like a garment district peddler."

"Ouch."

"Yes, 'ouch' is right," Price said. "Fellini and Amocacci are an item and have been for at least a year."

"Okay, but even if Amocacci's in bed with this secret council, I still don't see what that has to do with a compromise of U.S. military intelligence," Kurtzman said.

"That's where Alara Serif comes in. Based on her surveillance and the psychological profile she worked up on Amocacci, coupled with his movements, she thinks the Council of Luminárii may be composed of people just like him."

"You mean former intelligence operatives."

"Right. And possibly even intelligence officers still currently active with multinational agencies. Can you imagine what such a group could do? And especially when you consider they're operating in Turkey. The government there would never suspect Amocacci of being involved with international espionage and even if they did, they'd never make the accusation."

"Because of his connections and the favor he's found with certain high-ranking politicians."

Price nodded. "To make no mention that he's managed to sell a lot of Turkish-made materials. That's good for their economy. And it's probably why he's allowed to move around the country freely, as well as come and go as he pleases."

"It *would* be a perfect cover for this Council of... What did you call it?"

"Luminárii," Price replied. "Serif translates it to mean 'the Council of Lights' and often references it as just 'the Council.'"

"But what's the motive?" Kurtzman asked. "And why only U.S. operations?"

Price chewed her lip as she thought on the answer. "That is, unfortunately, something I haven't been able to put my finger on. Not yet anyway."

"You'll figure it out," Kurtzman said.

"Maybe. Let's just hope I do before Striker gets into any more trouble."

Kurtzman chuckled. "Now *that's* just asking for miracles, girlfriend."

Istanbul, Turkey

NOTHING IN ALARA SERIF's DIA training could have prepared her for what happened in the seconds following her departure from the consulate.

As she turned onto the main thoroughfare that ran in front of the consulate building, a vehicle pulled up alongside her in the outside lane. At first Serif thought nothing of it but then she saw the silhouette of the vehicle as it seemed to get closer and closer to her own car. Finally she blew her horn and started to roll down the passenger-side window to communicate with the erratic driver.

The body of the vehicle made contact with her own before she could open her mouth, forcing her to turn her attention to the looming rush of oncoming traffic.

Serif stomped on her brake pedal and swerved into the opposing lane, but instead of staying there she continued across until her vehicle bounced onto the sidewalk. Drivers in the oncoming vehicles leaned on their horns, a small price to pay to avoid slamming into them head-on. She would have most definitely occupied the losing position of any such an encounter.

Like an expert, Serif downshifted and applied her brake until the engine stalled, then threw her gearshift in reverse and tromped the accelerator. Most occupants on the sidewalk had already moved out of the danger area when Serif had first jumped the sidewalk, so there weren't many in her way as she backed half the distance of the block before swinging the nose of her vehicle in the opposite direction, *now* moving with the flow of traffic.

The low-profile sedan nearly bottomed out as Serif came off the high curb of the sidewalk and entered the lane. The drivers were now giving her plenty of room, but it didn't make a whole lot of difference. Even as she passed the intersection onto which she'd originally turned, she saw the headlights of two more vehicles swing tight on her tail. Serif wondered where the police were at the time she needed them. She thought about circling back and making a break for the consulate, but that would be the first thing they'd expect her to do and more than likely she'd walk right into their waiting arms.

Serif chewed at her lower lip. She couldn't go to the consulate and she sure as hell couldn't go home. She needed some running room, and she wouldn't get that in Ankara. She'd have to get clear and onto a highway, go south and circle back.

First, however, she would have to lose her pursuers and that wasn't going to prove easy. Apparently she'd stepped into something much bigger than she'd originally anticipated. She slammed her fist on the steering wheel as her eyes flicked continuously between her rearview mirror and the twin pairs of headlights now close on her tail.

"Damn it," she muttered. "How could I have been so *stupid*...?"

She never finished the thought, so distracted by her self-flagellation that she didn't notice another vehicle come off a side road and smash into her. The lateral impact caused her to lose control of the steering and simultaneously her hips went one way while her head went another. The breaking of glass as her skull smacked into it was the last sound in her ear, coupled with the rushing wind through the shattered window.

By the time her car had veered onto a nearby sidewalk and smashed into a storefront, Serif had completely lost consciousness, totally unaware that her enemies had just seized the upper hand.

CHAPTER SEVEN

Somewhere in U.S. airspace, the Executioner watched the shimmering, blue-green waters of the Gulf of Mexico in silence.

He sensed such tension in the air that it seemed nearly palpable to him, and he could feel the occasional boring looks from Shoup and his men. They were treating him like an outsider and not making any secret of it. That was fine. Technically, he outranked all of them and he could take charge of the unit at any time. He didn't want do that, though. Playing it more as a neutral party and letting the major run the show would allow him to keep one wary eye on Shoup.

On paper, the guy was a first-rate officer. He was a highly decorated veteran of several combat posts as well, and his superiors spoke nothing but the best of his command abilities. Chances were good, in fact, that Shoup would be up for promotion to lieutenant-colonel before the year was out. Bolan still had his reservations. He had been at this game a long time, and he knew trouble whenever it came his way. Yeah, he'd definitely have to keep his eye on this one.

Bolan's phone vibrated. He whipped it out and saw the special code that told him it was Stony Man. He looked around to make sure nobody was paying him any attention—not easy to do onboard a sparse plane where they were basically forced to face one another—before he answered it. At least being a pariah among this crew bore out a few privileges.

"Yes?"

"It's me." Barbara Price's voice greeted him like a warm rush in his ears. While they had a rather unusual arrangement as it went among most, Bolan never got tired of hearing from her. "Are you secure?"

"As can be expected."

"Should I call back?"

"I don't know that an hour or two from now will be better," Bolan said. "So you talk and I'll listen. How's that?"

"As it should be," she replied, and that brought a chuckle from the Executioner. "Anyway, we came across some interesting information and I thought you might want to hear it. There's a DIA agent serving with the U.S. consulate in Istanbul, named Alara Serif. She's been filing reports through her superiors, hounding the Pentagon or anybody who will listen to her, really, about a secret group she believes has formed in Istanbul.

"Under normal circumstances I would have just filed it away, but she's drawn some rather atypical conclusions and I thought it worth a closer look at her background and theories. She has some very interesting insights. Quite unusual really."

"Such as?"

"Well, for one thing she's convinced that this group, which may go officially by the name of Council of Lumnárii, is composed of members from a variety of intelligence organizations. And she thinks the group operates in a sort of symbiotic fashion, where every decision is agreed upon by all or none."

"It's an interesting theory," Bolan said. "But how does it tie into our problem?"

"According to Serif's reports, the movements of the guy she's been tailing have increased significantly in the past couple of weeks. A lot of visits to his home in the Yildiz Mountains."

"And she thinks what? That maybe he's meeting these other agents there?"

"Precisely. She's never been able to acquire any tangible proof, mind you, which is why I don't think the Pentagon's acted on the information much beyond giving it a cursory note. But it seems with these recent events, we should probably take it seriously. I've started working the angles at our end to see if I can gain some additional intelligence."

"All right," Bolan said. "Let me know what you find. If you hit something significant, I'll be happy to check it out when I'm through here. I don't want any loose ends."

"Agreed. We've hit a snag, however, and that could make it more difficult."

Bolan sighed tiredly. "Lay it on me."

"She's been nabbed," Price said. "Information came over the wire less than a half hour ago. I thought you'd want to know up front, which is why I decided to call."

"That would definitely be a game changer," Bolan replied. "Okay, intel is noted and thanks."

"Any time," Price said. "And Striker?"

"Yeah?"

"Jack called, told me about your suspicions regarding Shoup. I dug deeply into his background and didn't find anything. He's clean as clean can be."

"Too clean?"

"Maybe. But I trust your instincts over sketchy facts. So do me a favor and keep listening to them."

Bolan grinned into the phone as he replied, "Always."

THE SUN HAD not quite set beyond the rolling hillsides of Guatemala as the small, retrofitted USAF cargo plane streaked below radar level. They would make their jump at just below twelve-hundred feet. Bolan would have preferred a HALO entry if he'd been given a choice, but he hadn't and he'd promised to let Shoup conduct the operation as he saw fit. Besides, being in the air that short a period reduced the risk that any traitor among them might attempt to shoot him out of the sky.

Not that the Executioner had left the idea to chance. He'd decided to cover his upper torso in a Kevlar vest, something he didn't wear under normal circumstances. He supposed it wasn't the smartest thing. These days, he could only dodge bullets if they came real slow. As he'd been fond of telling others in his line of work, "It's not the bullet with my name on it that concerns me. It's the one addressed 'To whom it may concern.'"

Despite Bolan's concerns, the jump went off without a hitch, and in just a few minutes the entire team of a dozen combat special operatives was on the ground and assembled by their assigned groups. Shoup moved out immediately, letting the two point men take the lead as they advanced deeper into the jungle. Bolan stuck by Shoup's side, allowing him to keep one eye on the officer while he watched for a betrayal from a squad member with the other.

Bolan didn't know if any of the men under Shoup's command were dirty. Maybe they were just nervous because they were itching for a fight, or maybe it was just a measure of uncharacteristic paranoia on Bolan's part. In truth, the Executioner couldn't be sure Shoup wasn't anything but a first-rate officer. He had an impeccable record with many good recommendations from his superior officers. Then again, he could be fooling them all.

So far, Bolan hadn't seen or heard anything that would point to this particular location as the place where the agent disappeared. In fact, he couldn't understand what evidence Shoup had that would even have led him to Guatemala. The connection between the compromise of U.S. military intelligence operations and a terrorist group operating in Central America seemed thin at best. Moreover, he didn't know the exact location in which they'd be operating, so he hoped Grimaldi could maintain a signal on the tiny GPS transmitter the Executioner had stowed in his gear.

Bolan had asked for the operation details just prior to their departure and Shoup had refused to tell him.

"Under the circumstances, sir," Shoup had said, "you'll understand if we don't disclose any details before absolutely necessary."

"Even to me?"

"Even to you, sir."

In one way, Bolan had been able to understand that—he admired it, in fact, so he didn't bother to press the issue. Besides, he could find out if he really wanted to know badly enough, but he figured if he circumvented Shoup it would only make the guy more defensive and even less willing to share information. Bolan couldn't blame him—there had been a lot of strange happenings the past few weeks, enough to put every secret operations agency in the U.S. on full alert. And somewhere in that mix Bolan knew they had a traitor—possibly Shoup and possibly someone else.

Something else bothered Bolan, though. This new information about a DIA agent in Turkey and some random intelligence about a possible secret ring of operatives. While he had to admit there was something definitely off about the timing, he also knew Stony Man had no evidence tying them to any of the compromised military ops. Of course, like any good soldier, he couldn't afford to believe in mere coincidence. In a situation such as this, they had to pursue every possible lead and if this did have something to do with his mission, Price would sniff it out.

Minutes passed, then a half hour, then an hour. The jungle got darker and they were nearly at the two-hour point of their journey by the time they had reached the target. Bolan could only make out the shadowy outlines of his team members when the point guys brought the entire team to a halt.

Shoup's whispered order came through the ear buds of every man on the team. "Disperse."

The Air Force combat controllers did as ordered, each taking his assigned position. Shoup turned to Bolan. "It's your show from here, Colonel."

"My show?"

Shoup nodded. "You said you called the shots on any intelligence we find."

"And this is it?" Bolan gestured to dark jungle terrain ahead of them.

Shoup nodded. "Perimeter of the camp is just beyond this tree line."

Bolan felt something cold settle in the pit of his stomach. Was this the point Shoup planned to make his move? If Bolan pressed forward with investigating whatever lay beyond them, would he find answers or only death? The Executioner decided to call Shoup's hand, knowing that if there would be any time now was it. He wouldn't get a second chance.

"Okay, I'll go ahead of the rest of you." Bolan shed his small pack and retained the M-4 ACC-M he'd brought. He also had his trusty Beretta 93-R in shoulder rigging, and the .44 Magnum Desert Eagle rode in military webbing at his right hip.

Bolan turned and made his way toward the rear of the squad, moving in the opposite direction of the perimeter. He could almost feel Shoup's eyes on his back. The guy hadn't planned for this move at all. Bolan wasn't going to just walk right into the trap he suspected lay waiting for him, giving Shoup the satisfaction of knowing he'd outwitted his enemy. Instead the Executioner would circumvent his plans and make entry to this alleged camp on the far side. He knew, just as his enemy did, that if Shoup offered up any protest to Bolan's change in plans he'd be showing his hand.

Bolan disappeared into a dense part of the foliage. Once he'd proceeded far enough to be out of the view of Shoup or any of the other squad members, he crouched and withdrew a thin, cylindrical object just a hair larger than a pill. The device contained a high-frequency micro-transmitter that would pinpoint his exact coordinates to the dedicated GPS satellite maintained for Stony Man's use. The codes were strongly encrypted, not to mention there would only be one man looking for them.

Bottoms up, Jack, Bolan thought as he downed the pill with a swig from his canteen.

Bolan unslung his M-4 carbine, wrapped the strap around his wrist to prevent the sling from making noise, then got to his feet and continued circling the perimeter of the camp. He moved with measured strides, catfooting his way through the dense brush with hardly a sound. Most men his size would have been unable to move with such sure-footedness while simultaneously remaining whisper quiet in their course.

Mack Bolan wasn't most men.

Bolan ventured a good hundred yards before circling back toward the camp. Something caught his attention—a low thrumming sound reached his ears and forced him to stop in his tracks in an attempt to identify it—enough to heighten his sense of alertness. It took him a minute or so but finally he identified the sound: some type of generator. Probably belowground given the dampened noise. If he'd been stomping around the jungle floor, he might not have heard it until he was on top of the enemy.

So there *was* some kind of encampment here. At least Shoup hadn't been lying about that.

Bolan thought at first about keying his communications transmitter and advising Shoup he was about to make entry, but then he thought better of it. The smarter thing to do would be to create a little stir. He could then see how Shoup and his men reacted to the situation. If they came charging in to his rescue, he'd know they were legit. If they turned tail and ran, well…he'd deal with them when the time came.

Bolan crouched and moved in closer to the perimeter, his senses attuned to the hum of the generator. The progress seemed agonizingly slow, but his patience paid off because he eventually located the generator. At first

he found the camouflage tarp and then he realized that
it covered a hard surface. They had obviously covered
the generator well with a wooden plate vented to prevent a buildup of fumes. Bolan could barely detect the
smell of spent diesel. A generator of that size would
probably run an hour or two before it needed to be re-
fueled, so he'd have to work quickly. Someone might
come to check the fuel level at any moment.

The soldier reached to his combat harness and withdrew an incendiary grenade. He didn't want to make
a lot of noise, but he also needed to make sure they
wouldn't be able to use the generator again. With luck,
he'd be able to place the grenade as low as possible
in the generator well, and the covering and generator
would mask most of the sound of the blast. At least it
sounded good in theory.

Bolan yanked the pin and dropped the grenade
through an open slat in the makeshift cover. He then
crashed through some nearby brush until he made sure
he was well clear of any flashback.

Contrary to lore, incendiary grenades of that military grade did not explode, per se, but rather ignited and
began to burn until they reached a peak temperature
of approximately two thousand degrees in a matter of
seconds. The internal thermite mixture, a combination
of phosphoric chemicals and molten metal, would burn
through practically any surface in no time. In this case,
the fumes of diesel not being flammable, the fuel would
merely burn. Contained within the pressure of a tank in
the generator, however, coupled with the covered area
that had only slats to leak oxygen, would provide the
catalyst needed to generate an actual blast.

The explosion didn't provide as much damage as it

did a distraction, which is exactly what Bolan sought. The mix of noise and heat would provide the pandemonium necessary to get him inside the camp to see if there really was a mission to be accomplished—Shoup would use to his advantage if he was really on the up-and-up—such as the rescue of one or two of these mysterious agents that had been allegedly working this case the entire time. Conversely, if it was all a setup, Bolan had already formulated a proper response for that, too.

The thunder of a half-dozen boots and the swish of branches worked to signal Bolan it was time to move. The warrior pushed into the camp and found exactly what he'd expected to find: an open bivouac site of maybe a fifty-yard radius with a few small outbuildings ranged around it. Emerging from those openings were the silhouettes of men with varying styles of small arms, probably sourced off the black market. These were mercenaries, perhaps drug-runners or even terrorists, but they weren't terribly organized. If nothing else, however, Bolan knew they weren't friendly to the U.S. or his mission here.

Bolan whipped his M-4 into action and triggered a trio of short bursts. The 5.56 mm NATO rounds found their marks, the first a target who had just leveled his own weapon in Bolan's direction. The bullets perforated his gut before the enemy gunner could get off a single shot and he crumpled to the damp, muddy ground. Another enemy gunman caught a round in the throat, followed immediately by a second that tore away part of his chin and cracked bone. The last one to fall under the Executioner's marksmanship was driven back until he connected with a tree before the impact pitched him onto his face.

Bolan dived for cover even as a new group of a half-dozen gunners burst from the largest of the several outbuildings and opened up with sustained fire on the position he'd occupied a mere heartbeat earlier. Varying degrees of intersecting autofire burned the air and the acrid stench of fresh cordite permeated Bolan's nostrils. The battle had been joined and so far, he couldn't tell if he was getting any support from Shoup or the other combat controllers. What he *did* know was that there seemed to be a lot of fire coming from the camp, and none of the enemy numbers seemed to be dwindling.

The Executioner unclipped a grenade from his combat harness, this one an M-67 fragger. Bolan yanked the pin and tossed the bomb into the group firing on his position, and then crawled through the dense foliage to find cover behind a tree trunk. While the M-67 had an average fifteen-foot kill radius, it could send shrapnel a significant distance. In this terrain, however, seeking solid cover was the best option and Bolan knew it. Unfortunately for his enemies, they didn't, and having not seen Bolan actually toss the grenade due to the dark, most of them caught the blast full-on. Three were killed instantly, two mortally wounded, and the survivor thrown far enough by the initial blast that it knocked the fight and sense out of him.

Bolan scrambled to his feet, located his next two targets and raised the M-4 to his shoulder. One of the most advanced of the dependable Colts, the ACC-M—Advanced Colt Carbine-Monolithic—featured a true free-floating barrel due to the single-component architecture of the upper receiver. Combined with the burst mode, it provided a very high first-hit probability—a consummate death-bringer in Mack Bolan's hands.

Bolan dashed from his position to another cluster of thick foliage wrapped against tangled, gnarled tree trunks. The jungle environment was one of the least hospitable but one that the Executioner had become quite accustomed to. He'd operated in a combat role on most every terrain, traveled to every continent, and fought in nearly every type of environment. From the urban jungle to the icy plains of the Arctic, Bolan had perfected his deadly skills and these foes were learning that lesson hard.

Bolan still couldn't see any support from Shoup's unit and, given his current predicament, felt quite certain he was alone on this one. He couldn't understand why they had abandoned him, though. Surely Shoup's entire unit wasn't bad. If he'd chosen to retreat when the fireworks started rather than provide covering fire and support, somebody in the unit would have questioned him. Still, the Executioner wouldn't worry about that right at the moment. This situation demanded his full attention and he planned to keep fighting until the fight was done.

Three more hardmen came up on his left and Bolan thought they were trying to flank him. Quickly he realized they were part of the team that had gone to investigate the fire in the generator pit and were now returning to assist their comrades. They didn't see him until they were practically on top of him, at which point it proved much too late.

Bolan flicked the selector switch to full-auto and swept the muzzle across their ranks, cutting down the three enemy gunners with firm resolve. In one respect, it truly proved to be like shooting fish in a barrel since he couldn't miss at that distance. But somewhere in the heat of the moment—the sounds of violence and bloodshed that always accompanied a close-quarters battle scenario—Bolan felt something prick the back of his neck and then something hard strike him in the side.

Vision blurred…sounds became muffled.

Bolan had experienced the sensation a few times before and knew it for what it was immediately. He'd been drugged with a heavy dose of Thorazine or some sort of derivative. And even as that thought passed through his mind and he cursed himself for letting his guard down, his eyelids fluttered and the world around him went black.

CHAPTER EIGHT

Bolan's subconscious yielded to the steely consciousness of his mind, clearing the blanket of darkness like the parting of a murky veil. He sucked in precious oxygen as the black-red haze that brimmed his eyes gave way to a dim light. His tongue felt thick and dry in his mouth, and his head felt as if a little man on the inside were beating at his brains with a claw hammer. They were all the classic symptoms of post-tranquilization with a sedative, so Bolan didn't let it concern him.

The Executioner had been doped before.

More frustrating, however, was that by attempting to circumvent the trap he thought Shoup had been setting for him, he'd managed to allow his enemies to capture him. At least he had the GPS micro-transmitter he'd swallowed, which gave Grimaldi a pinpoint location on his position. It didn't tell the Stony Man pilot that Bolan was in trouble, but at least he knew where to find him. No matter, since Grimaldi had instructions to come calling if Bolan failed to make the rendezvous at either the primary or alternate pickup point.

Rough hands grabbed the Executioner by his arms and sat him upright. Bolan had thought at first, through his drug-fueled haze, that he'd been confined, but that didn't seem to be the case. Light blasted his eyes in the next moment and he raised his hand to shield them. As his environment became clearer, he realized that he was seated in an old wooden chair at a table and that he'd been lying across the seats of two of them. That's probably why the ribs on his right side felt stiff and sore.

"Who are you?" a voice demanded.

"You first."

"Don't give me any lip, friend, or I'll just have you taken out and your throat cut." The speaker followed that with a weighty silence and then continued. "Now, who the hell are you? And while you're at it, tell me who sent you."

Bolan couldn't see his enemy due to glare, but he forced a smile despite it. "You don't need me to tell you that. Supposedly you have all the intelligence already. You're the traitor in the DIA."

"I'm not with the DIA," the man said, snorting. "I'm not with any U.S. military organization, actually."

"But you're an American."

"Perhaps I am, perhaps I'm not. And so what if I am?"

"So," Bolan said, turning the conversation to his advantage, "tell me what you know about the operation in Colorado."

The man produced a snort of derision followed by a scoffing laugh. "That wasn't me. In fact, that *was* a military insider."

Shoup. Bolan didn't even have to ask a name to know who was behind it. The guy had set up this whole operation, probably a pretext to cover his ass if anyone official from the DIA or CID came sniffing around. If too many bodies started to disappear around Shoup back in the States, he'd have a lot of explaining to do. But if an officer died here on a mission, or the occasional straitlaced enlisted man died there, who would question it? Covert operations performed by military personnel were typically the most secret, since the press didn't have prying eyes in every combat sector.

Bolan started to open his mouth but his words were cut off by the contact of something hard and unyielding to the side of his head. The punch felt like it had some sort of reinforcement behind it, perhaps a leather glove with metal or plastic shivs in finger pads. Bolan couldn't tell where the punch had originated, but he knew his assailant hadn't put everything behind it. They wanted him to talk and they were going to make him talk by employing whatever methods they had perfected. Bolan had been at this game for a long time. It had never ceased to amaze him exactly what kind of terrible things might be conjured by humans to be perpetrated against their own kind.

Bolan tasted the salty hint of blood and it felt as if his lip may have caught on a tooth. He spit the offensive matter away and shook his head. "I've been through a lot worse than that. I'm not going to tell you anything, no matter how hard you beat me."

"That was only a sample of what you'd get," the voice said. "You could avoid anything worse if you were just more forthcoming."

Throughout the conversation Bolan had been using a tried-and-true method of stalling while he thought about what sort of cover story he could tell. He saw no reason to resist, since it would most likely be just as this guy had said and buy him nothing more than beatings and worse. He couldn't move forward with the mission if he let them perform unknown torture on him, weakening his mind and body. Better to find something with which to divert their attention; keep them occupied checking out his story. Yeah, the more complicated and convoluted his tale, the longer he could stall them until he figured a way out of his predicament.

"Okay," he said, spitting more blood. "Okay, I don't see any reason to hide the truth. The fact is, I'm actually with the NSA and I'm working undercover as an officer with the Defense Intelligence Agency, Pentagon division."

"But you're not military."

Bolan shook his head. "Ex-military. I was attached to the unit that attacked you."

"Why?"

"They were on a mission to find undercover agents who allegedly knew the identity of whoever was behind the operation in Colorado."

"Stop there a minute. Why would that tiny operation in Colorado draw any interest from the NSA?"

Bolan did his best to produce a mocking laugh. "Really? Are you that stupid?"

"Careful, pal! I'm anything but stupid."

"Then why the stupid questions? That operation in Colorado was intercepting encrypted transmissions containing orders that were eyes-only for NORAD's covert military operations. That all boils down to signals intelligence, so it would be of interest to the NSA above any other agency."

"So why the pretext?" the interrogator interjected. "Why not just come right out and say you're NSA? Why have you posed as part of the DIA?"

"It was a better way to get cooperation, for one," Bolan replied. "Second, we didn't know if anyone in the DIA could be trusted on the local levels. This seems to go pretty high up."

"So none of this explains *why* you are *here*." The man's face moved into the light now.

Bolan searched his memory but couldn't place the face. Beady eyes held Bolan's icy stare with resolute skepticism. The guy had cropped, brown hair and a dark complexion. He also looked to be as tall as Bolan, perhaps taller, and easily outweighed the Executioner by seventy pounds or so.

"And why you brought an entire party of military special operators. We saw your plane as soon as it hit Guatemalan airspace, and we knew your flying below radar could only mean a low-altitude jump. That has the makings of a military operation, so don't bother denying it."

"None of this was my idea," Bolan said. "The head of the group led me around by the nose."

The man folded his arms and smirked. "You don't look like you just fell of the turnip truck, uh…wait. You still haven't given me a name." The guy looked at some unseen force and nodded; the same unseen force punched Bolan again. This time, however, the blow was toward the back of the head and not as hard as the last.

"Why did you do that?" Bolan asked.

"Because you're not answering my questions."

"I *thought* we had a dialog going here."

"You're telling me half-truths. Or maybe you're not telling me the truth at all. Maybe you're just stalling. In any case, we're going to check out your story to the last letter. And in the meantime you're going to answer my questions directly or, as I said, we will subject you to some very nasty motivations. Now let's begin again. What…is…your…*name*?"

"Stone. Colonel Brandon Stone is my cover name. Matt Cooper is my real name. I'm an analyst with NSA, a covert field operator sent on a mission to infiltrate whatever group may have been responsible for intercepting the intelligence signals at NORAD."

The man looked at the subject behind Bolan and delivered a curt nod. Bolan braced himself for another blow but it never came. Instead he heard the shuffle of feet as someone left the room. That was the other thing he'd noted. The walls around them appeared to be concrete and the place had a damp, musty smell that made Bolan's nose itch. Obviously they'd transported him from the campsite. But to where?

"We'll look into your story. But if you're lying to me, I'm going to find out." The guy rose and folded his arms, his giant shadow dwarfing Bolan in the single harsh light. "And if I find out you lied to us, my return won't signal anything pleasant in your future."

"That's a drag," Bolan challenged. "Since up to now it's been a peach of an experience."

The man didn't say anything for a moment, instead watching Bolan, and then he turned and left the Executioner alone.

Bolan sighed in relief, glad his stall tactic had worked. Of course, Stony Man had that entire workup of his profile handled and if they had any connections at all, the dossier they pulled on his fallback cover identity would bear even the most intense scrutiny. That didn't help him as far as his captors were concerned, since it didn't buy him any good will either way. After all, he'd killed a lot of their men and he doubted they would find any knowledge he possessed worth keeping him alive. So it was just a matter of time before they did him in.

His thoughts turned to Grimaldi. The Stony Man flier would soon be darkening the doorstep of Bolan's captors and likely would be ill-prepared for what awaited him. While Grimaldi was certainly a capable fighter, he didn't have anywhere near the Executioner's talents or combat expertise. He could very well walk straight into the middle of an unwinnable firefight or, worse, be captured by the enemy and occupy a cold, damp cell right next to Bolan. Short of an execution, neither of them would ever be heard from again.

The GPS transmitter in Bolan's gut would undoubtedly send a fix on his exact position, to be sure, but it didn't mean whomever came to his rescue—it wasn't beyond reason Stony Man would send Able Team or Phoenix Force to bail Bolan out if Grimaldi's initial attempt to locate and rescue him failed—would be prepared for whatever waited outside the walls of this prison.

No, that would *never* do, which meant Bolan, who for some reason his captors apparently felt didn't pose enough of a threat that they even bothered to bind him, would have to make sure that never happened. He couldn't allow his friends to put themselves in a situation that could compromise the mission. So Mack Bolan would just have to find a way to turn the tables on his enemies.

Livingston, Guatemala

IT WAS WELL rumored among pilots who'd traveled as extensively as Jack Grimaldi that the best place for information in Central America could be found in the tourist towns. It didn't imply that the natives of Livingston's highly unusual cultural mix would necessarily cooperate with outsiders. But when that particular individual happened to be a ruggedly handsome and quietly unassuming type like Grimaldi—whose solicitation of those with a cooperative and talkative nature had a hell of lot more to do with his ready wad of cash than a charming nature—information *could* be had by certain tongues.

Of course, money or alcohol had a profound effect in loosening the tongues of some. In part, the "some" included those individuals who were really more about personal gain or self-preservation than following some obscure code of silence. If one got caught talking, he or she could wake up to find his or her throat slit, but for the most part information flowed freely for the right bribe delivered to the right place.

Grimaldi knew those places frequented by the more talkative denizens of Livingston, and so it didn't take him long to find his way into a seedier establishment near the shores of the Caribbean Sea. He'd opted to put his plane down in Punta Gorda, a district capital in southern Belize, and travel by boat to Livingston. The city had once been the largest port in Guatemala and still enjoyed a rather rich tourist trade. Entry to the port was relatively casual, although they still went in for the formality of declaring oneself and presenting a passport for inspection at customs.

Still, Grimaldi had learned how easy it was to operate in the liberal town with little to no interference from outsiders, and that's exactly the situation he found himself most in need of now. According to the homing sensor in his cell phone, Bolan's GPS transmitter had activated and was sending coordinates from a location about ten miles from Livingston. That location seemed to be some sort of obscure town according to the satellite photos Stony Man had sent him.

Grimaldi had no idea what he might be getting himself into. While he didn't have the resources to go up against a force of unknown size or capabilities, neither could he stand idly by and let his friend die. He also had some questions for Shoup, who had apparently disappeared into thin air. In fact, his entire unit was listed as MIA, and if they didn't report in soon Grimaldi knew it would blow the whole lid on the operation and they could no longer keep this thing a secret.

So his mission was simple in the most academic sense of the term. Gather intelligence on the site from where Bolan's GPS homing signal was transmitting and determine the feasibility of a rescue attempt. Barring that, he'd have to get information back to Stony Man and request assistance. In fact, he already knew he'd get it despite the fact the Executioner preferred to work alone. Brognola had made no bones about it: he'd activate Phoenix Force in a heartbeat. The Stony Man chief had done it before and he wouldn't hesitate to do it again, despite however Bolan might feel, if Grimaldi requested it.

But first Grimaldi meant to try it on his own to see where things went. He'd agreed to a meeting with someone at the suggestion of Stony Man, which had a score of information brokers in the area.

He didn't know exactly what his mark looked like, but he did know he'd recognize him on sight. Or *her*, as it proved to be in this case. She wore a red bandanna across her forehead, which teased her dark, wavy hair in odd directions. She had on a black T-shirt with some sort of abstract symbol on it and well-worn jeans that tugged seductively at her hips. She moved with a swagger that indicated part practiced movement and part confidence.

Keeping his mind on business, Grimaldi immediately left the bar with a pair of ice-cold beers. The bottles sweated in the tropical heat and the cool water dribbled down the backs of his hands. A veritable puddle formed when he finally set them on the table, shoving one toward the new arrival and keeping the other for himself.

She snatched it up, looked at him with a cock of her head, and then smiled when he offered his own bottle for her to clink gently in a toast. Her grin transformed into more of a knowing smile and appeared to relax now that the ceremony of that recognition signal had passed.

"You're Jack?" the woman asked.

Grimaldi had walked on most every continent and piloted myriad craft to points all over the world, but he couldn't quite place her accent. "That's me."

"Cretia," she said, tapping her chest. "I was told you have questions about a certain village upriver."

"I do." Grimaldi glanced over his shoulder surreptitiously to make sure nobody was listening, and then took a long pull from the bottle before he continued. "But not here. Isn't there someplace more private we could talk?"

"The gentlemen I deal with usually don't want something more private for...*talk*." Another disarming smile. "If you know what I mean."

"I'll admit my curiosity, but unfortunately I don't have time right now to satisfy it. I have a friend who's in trouble and the numbers are running down. I was told by reliable sources you could help. But this place may have ears."

Cretia nodded. "Which is why you suggest perhaps someplace else is better."

"Right."

Grimaldi smiled.

Cretia smiled.

Both smiles faded when four men came through the front door of the dark, cramped bar toting machine pistols.

Grimaldi saw the movement by the flickering change of light in the woman's eyes followed by her expression of surprise. He immediately sprang to action, getting to his feet and upturning the table to provide cover while simultaneously yanking the lithe form of his companion out of her chair. The flimsy table wouldn't stop the bullets, but it would provide a point of deflection while Grimaldi got to his belly and crawled toward a curtain drawn over an opening in the back.

The screams of surprised patrons were drowned by the unmistakable chattering reports of the submachine guns toted by the enemy. Even as Grimaldi and Cretia made it through the makeshift doorway unscathed, which opened onto a large stock room that apparently doubled as living quarters for the bar's owner, Grimaldi knew the arrival of these men was anything but coincidental. Somebody had ratted them out—somehow knowing Grimaldi's purpose for being in Livingston— with orders to terminate the pilot's life.

Grimaldi didn't take kindly to the thought and he began to wonder who might be to blame. Not that he had any reason to ponder the thought at that moment.

There were other more pressing matters demanding his attention, and keeping himself and his companion alive was inarguably at the *top* of the list.

Grimaldi turned to Cretia as they scrambled to their feet. "Listen up!"

"I'm listening."

"Are you packing?" She shook her head as Grimaldi produced a pistol. "All right, then you need to make yourself scarce."

"But what about you?"

Grimaldi heard genuine concern in her voice, something that both surprised and touched him, but he couldn't afford distractions so he went for stoic. "No time to argue."

She nodded. "Okay, listen then. Two blocks from here you'll find a man named Miguel who runs a boat tour and rental called *Los Flotantes*. Tell him you know me and he'll give you directions to a backup location I use."

Grimaldi nodded. "Get."

She had barely been gone a minute when two of the four armed men burst through the curtain with their weapons leveled. They had apparently made the assumption that their targets were helpless and unarmed, and that's why they had chosen to run. What they *didn't* know was that that was exactly what Jack Grimaldi had wanted them to think.

The first gunner never saw it coming as Grimaldi, waiting in deep shadows provided by an alcove to the right of the curtained doorway, extended his 9 mm Glock and squeezed the trigger. The bullet entered the right rear portion of the target's skull and blew out a section at the forehead. Gore sprayed the man's companion, who whirled and triggered his weapon reflexively. The shots went wild and didn't come close enough to Grimaldi to even cause the pilot concern.

Grimaldi triggered two more rounds, both hitting the man's chest. The impact drove him back and he smashed against a collection of dusty shot glasses and empty bottles that had been neatly stacked. The man's weight overturned the flimsy table and as he crumpled to the ground, the bottles and shot glasses rained upon him.

Grimaldi waited, but the other pair didn't show. If he had to venture a guess, they had probably doubled back to try to catch anyone who came out the back. Hopefully Cretia had managed to evade them.

The Stony Man pilot found the rear exit, stuck his head out the door and looked along both sides of the alley. Empty. He crossed quickly to the dense line of trees on the opposite side and slipped into the concealment and comparative shade of the heavy, tropical foliage. For the moment he'd managed to hold off the enemy—whoever that enemy might be. Now he would have to find this Miguel to see if he could reconnect with Cretia.

Hang on, Striker, he thought. I'm coming for you.

CHAPTER NINE

"Would somebody *please* explain to me how the hell something like this could happen to one of our operatives?" Colonel Alan Bindler demanded.

Nobody in the conference room at the consulate spoke a word, and the steady hum from the couple of window-mounted air-conditioner units seemed thunderous in the dead silence.

"I need an answer from someone," Bindler added as he dropped into his chair at the head of the table.

One of his junior officers finally spoke up. "Sir, we just didn't see anything like this coming. She's an analyst and a civilian, and she really doesn't possess any intelligence about military operations."

"I'm aware of her *official* capacity, lieutenant." Bindler shook his head. "And all of the bullshit we put into her dossier for the Turkish government's dissemination. But she's been operating on other cases outside normal channels, and apparently she ignored my orders to drop her conspiracy theories about this mysterious Council of Luminárii. Now she's been taken and our operations here compromised."

Again, nobody said much and with good reason. They knew more than anything that Bindler was just ranting. He truly did care about his people, however, and right now he was just trying not to show his anxiety for whatever awful circumstances might have befallen Alara Serif. It's not that he blamed any of them. In fact, chances were good he blamed himself more than anything or anyone. If there was anything that people who knew him well could say, it was that Alan Bindler never sloughed his responsibilities onto someone else. He was large and in charge, and he took responsibility for everything that happened.

"Okay," Bindler said after a deep sigh. "Let's put aside the potential *why* someone would want to kidnap Alara and focus on the *whom* for a moment. Is anyone aware of materials she had or something she was working that could help us?"

"Well, I did set up a surveillance package for her," one of the technicians stated.

"I didn't authorize any surveillance." When the guy looked sheepish, Bindler said, "Never mind that. I won't take any negative action against your record as long as you come clean with what you know."

"She…she told me you approved it," the young man protested.

Binder tried to maintain his patience. "I just said I wasn't going to bust you for it, Karsten. Just start talking."

"I'd have to go back and look at more details, but I do recall one of the main subjects was a local businessman named Gastone Amocacci. Some sort of small-time exporter of clothing and raw materials like linens and silks. Stuff like that."

"I remember that name in her reports," Bindler said. He turned to his intelligence man, a cryptanalyst named Sargent, who had short red hair and a face full of freckles. Some had remarked he looked like Archie from the comics, and in fact the resemblance was so striking it had earned him the nickname during his service years and "Arch" had stuck with him to this day. "What do we know about Amocacci?"

"Not much more than I've already explained," Sargent explained. "He and Lady Allegra Fellini are an item."

"Is this the same Fellini as the Italian clothing designer family?"

"Yes, indeed," Bindler's adjutant interjected.

Nestor Maxwell had served as Bindler's right-hand man for the past three years. He was tough, reliable and a consummate officer on many levels. Bindler had the utmost respect for the guy. He appreciated Maxwell's honesty and no-bullshit command style. Maxwell got things done; Bindler liked people who got things done.

"But before you ask," Maxwell said, "there's no connection we can find between Lady Fellini and this Council of Luminárii, or even between the Fellini family and anything past or present related to Amocacci."

"The relationship between Fellini and Amocacci, while profoundly convenient, looks to be legit, sir," Sargent concluded.

"So in fact," Bindler replied, "what you're telling me is that we have diddly-squat on any of these people. And yet we have a missing analyst who may or may not have been onto something when she came up with this Gastone Amocacci's connection to the Council of Luminárii, an organization that may or may not exist."

"This obviously sheds some legitimacy to Ms. Serif's theory, sir," Maxwell said.

"It would seem so, Major." Bindler shook his head for a minute and was lost in thought. He knew every eye in the room was trained on him. One of their own had been grabbed, and the entire team expected *him* to do something about it. He was their commanding officer and he was supposed to be their protector as the CO of the Marine guard assigned to this consulate.

Finally, Bindler spoke, casting his first glance at Sargent. "Okay, let's start pulling out all the stops. I want to know everything about Amocacci, and I want it yesterday. No detail is too small. Where was he born, where did he go to school, what's his background. Got it?"

"Yes, sir," Sargent said as he furiously jotted down what was required.

Bindler turned to Maxwell. "Major, you'll lead the rest in putting together a three-man tactical team for special detail. They'll need to have creds as civvies, but I want the top three men in our detachment. Find me guys who are smart, preferably with some sort of intelligence background. Out of twenty-five Marines or so, it shouldn't be hard to get three good candidates."

"Aye, sir."

Bindler took a deep breath and let his eyes rove the room at his people. "Listen up and listen good, folks. We're going to find Alara, and we're going to get her back. And we're going to make sure that whoever's behind her disappearance gets a clear message that you can't just go around kidnapping Americans without us doing something about it. Am I clear?"

At various nods and assents, Bindler dismissed them.

The officer was barely out of the briefing room and down the hallway when another junior officer, this one the head of the clerical staff, rushed toward him. She tossed a quick salute that he returned smartly. "Sir, you have a telephone call from Washington. Priority One channel."

Bindler didn't even break stride as he replied, "Pentagon?"

"No, sir."

Bindler stopped midstride. "I thought you just said Washington on the Priority One channel, Lieutenant."

"That's correct, sir."

"Well, then, if it isn't the Pentagon it could only be the White House. Secretary of Defense or Chief of Staff?"

"Neither of them, either, sir."

"Are you trying to be funny, Lieutenant?"

"No, *sir!*"

Bindler studied the impassive face a moment. No quirk of the lips, no faltering in the seriousness of her expression. No, Lieutenant Hodgkin was quite serious. And since it wasn't close to Bindler's anniversary or birthday, this wasn't some surprise party in disguise. He turned and continued down the hallway, ordering Hodgkin to put the call through to his office in one minute.

BINDLER GRABBED UP the extension handset and pressed the flashing red button. "Colonel Bindler. This is a secure line. May I help you, sir or ma'am?"

"Colonel Bindler?" a pinched, almost nasal voice greeted him. "Please hold for the President of the United States."

Bindler was so taken aback that he jumped to his feet and stammered, "Yes, ma'am."

A moment later the voice of the President came on the line. "Alan?"

"Yes, sir."

"You know who this is?"

"I do, sir. Of course, sir."

"Very well, then we'll skip the whole authentication BS. What I'm about to tell you is to be treated with the strictest confidence. You are *not* to disclose anything I'm about to say and you are not to reveal the name of the man you're about to speak with. That's an order from the Commander-in-Chief. Is that clear?"

"Crystal, sir."

"In a moment I'm going to patch you through to Harold Brognola. Among other things, he's an official with the U.S. Justice Department. You are to cooperate with him, answer his questions and do whatever you can to facilitate his mission up to and including placing secondary considerations on all other operational objectives save those that would jeopardize the safety of the consul and staff. Understood?"

"Aye, sir! It's understood."

"Thank you, Colonel. Please stand by."

There was a minute of latency and then a gravelly, no-nonsense voice resounded in Bindler's ear.

"Colonel Bindler, this is Hal Brognola. You've been advised of my capacity as it relates to your command and resources?"

"I have, sir."

"Good. Then let's get right to it. Tell me everything you know up to now about the disappearance of Ms. Serif."

Bindler's jaw almost hit the ground. He'd only just put word through official channels maybe four hours before. While word traveled pretty fast through certain parts of the Pentagon upper echelon, Bindler wouldn't have thought such information would reach the Oval

Office so quickly. He certainly didn't think something such as this would attract the attention of the most powerful leader in the free world. But then, none of what had transpired to this point could be viewed as conventional.

Without skipping even the most minor detail, Bindler began to describe everything he knew to Brognola.

The man listened patiently until Bindler finished. For a long while Brognola didn't say anything, and Bindler thought at first they'd lost the connection. But then Brognola finally produced a satisfied grunt. "Everything you've just told me fits with the reports your superiors at the Pentagon received as it pertains to this Council of Luminárii. Moreover, Ms. Serif did an excellent job tracking the one man who might be the key to solving this puzzle."

"I'm afraid I don't understand, sir," Bindler said. "What's this all about, if you don't mind my asking?"

"I don't mind," Brognola replied. "In fact, I'd say it would be unfair to ask you to extend resources to people you don't even know without at least filling you in on what I know to this point. But we don't have time for a lot of chitchat, so I'll be concise.

"In short, everything Alara Serif has reported so far seems to be true. There *is* a Council of Luminárii and it *is* overseen by Gastone Amocacci. At least, we know he's involved with the group. Our own analysis would seem to point to the fact that this group does operate in a somewhat symbiotic fashion, just as Ms. Serif's analysis suggests."

"But to what end would a group like this operate, sir?"

"You're aware of the recent signals intelligence briefs

issued by the Department of Defense indicating a potential compromise in the security of military operations abroad."

"I scanned the briefs that were sent, yes, sir," Bindler replied. "But I cannot see what correlation they have to anything as it concerns this alleged Council of Lumínárii. And it seems odd the DIA would let this group concern them even if they did exist. How much harm could they do, given they seem to operate at only a local level—?"

"On the contrary," Brognola interjected. "That's the very point, Colonel Bindler. They're not operating at a local level, they are operating at very much an *international* level. And we have good reason to believe their members include assets from a half-dozen intelligence agencies, at least."

"U.S. agencies?"

"No, fortunately. In fact, we don't believe there are any members from the United States that would belong to such a group. But there are other foreign agencies that could profit by significant disruptions in U.S. military intelligence efforts throughout the world. For one, they would be able to disrupt our efforts to control international terrorism and prevent it from reaching American shores. There are also the ties that could be broken between our agencies and other friendly intelligence services such as the British SIS or Israeli Mossad."

"I think I'm beginning to understand the far-reaching interests of a group like this."

"That's precisely the point," Brognola said. "And it's why I had to get the President's permission to reach out to you in this way. We *never* had this conversation. You get me?"

"I get you, sir," Bindler said.

"We're using you to get to them. You can put eyes and ears on the ground, and your people are most familiar with the social geography of the Turkish landscape. Amocacci has an office building. His corporate headquarters, supposedly, are there in Istanbul. But we think he's also conducting operations from an estate in the Yildiz Mountains."

"I already have boots on the ground, sir," Bindler said. "In fact, I have my adjutant putting together a three-man team of sniffers now."

"Where are they from?"

"Part of my detachment for consulate security. Officially, that's what I oversee here, although you probably don't need me to tell you that. I would assume you might be able to tell me what I had for breakfast three weeks ago Tuesday."

"I might, but I couldn't tell *you* that," Brognola replied with a chuckle.

The quip put Bindler somewhat at ease. "So would you like me to proceed as planned?"

"I would," Brognola said. "But only in the role of gathering information. You are *not* to execute a rescue operation of any kind until our man arrives."

"I'm sorry, sir, did you just say you were sending someone here?"

"Yes. His name is Colonel Stone and he's part of the DIA."

"And perhaps a bit more?"

"I said I'd shoot straight with you, Colonel Bindler," Brognola said in a steady but warning tone. "I didn't say I'd give you the entire playbook. Any decision to rescue Alara Serif or to conduct any other offensive action against those you sniff out will be Stone's decision. You'll operate at his discretion and you will give him your full cooperation."

"Yes, sir. But…Hal—may I call you Hal?"

"Of course."

"Wouldn't a fully equipped staff of U.S. Marine special operations be a better choice? Even if we find Alara, we may not have a lot of time to act on the information. They might move her or, worse…well, I don't have to spell it out for you."

"Look, Bindler, if it comes right down to it and you have no other choice, you're authorized to go in and get her out. But if it appears there's no immediate threat to her life, then you are to wait until Colonel Stone gets there. Trust me when I tell you there's nobody you'd rather have for a delicate situation like this.

"Now are there any other questions?"

"Just one, Hal. I'd like to know why somebody didn't jump on this before now. I mean, you…or…*someone* has had this information awhile. Why sit on it if you knew it was legit?"

"I can't speak for the bureaucrats in Washington or your superior officers at the Pentagon," Brognola replied truthfully. "We only became aware of it about thirty-six hours ago. And right now we're waiting for Stone to get back to us regarding another lead he's pursuing. But trust me, we didn't sit on the information. As soon as I was told what we might be dealing with and Ms. Serif's analyses flagged our systems, I was on the phone arranging this meet."

"Okay, thank you. I believe you."

"That's most appreciated. Now if you don't mind, I need to get going. We're sending a coded communication your way, along with a cypher for decryption. Use the standard dual-authentication methods for decoding the message. It contains clear instructions on how to report back to us with any findings your people make. You are not to communicate that information to any entity other than us, and you are to keep all the regular reports flowing out of there just as normal."

"In other words, keep the status quo so as not to alert the enemy we may be on to them."

Brognola chuckled. "I can see why you were chosen for that post, Bindler. You're as sharp as they come."

"Thank you, sir."

"Good luck, man," Brognola said and then hung up.

Bindler stared at the receiver for a moment before placing it quietly in the cradle. This wasn't at all the call he'd expected. One low-ranking DIA analyst had disappeared, maybe kidnapped and possibly dead, and the White House and some black ops group get involved. Not that it mattered to Bindler, since he was a Marine and Marines followed orders. Plus, he cared a lot about Alara. The thought that something bad might have happened to her on his watch didn't set well with him at all.

Sure, he was responsible for the security of the consulate and intelligence was not his first standing order. But he also cared about the entire staff and regardless of who they worked for, they were American citizens and they were under his protection. Someone had violated that protection and he'd been either too blind or too stupid to see it.

Well, no more, because he planned to do everything he could to facilitate Alara's safe return. He owed her that much. He'd violate his orders if he had to. There was no way in hell he'd leave his coworker and friend at the mercy of a bunch of terrorists. And while he had every plan to obey Brognola's orders, he wouldn't hesitate to pull her out of a scrape if he could find a practical way to do it without risking the mission objectives.

She was an American and she was a friend, and Bindler saw himself personally responsible for her. The enemies of freedom and democracy had violated the most basic tenets of what it meant to be an American citizen. He wouldn't put up with that—he *couldn't* put up with it. To turn a blind eye to what had happened was nothing less than a dereliction of duty. No, one way or another, Bindler would find a way to get Alara Serif back.

He would do it out of a sense of duty. He was a United States Marine, part of a group whose motto was *semper fi*—a shortened form of the Latin for "always faithful." And come hell or high water, he would honor that motto to his dying breath.

CHAPTER TEN

Istanbul, Turkey

Alara Serif's head felt as if someone was beating against it with a hammer. She hadn't remembered blacking out after the accident. Accident… As if that's what it had really been. In fact she knew the impact had been a purposeful act, although she also believed they had done it only to stop her and not kill her; otherwise, she'd be dead by now.

The words of her boss came back to her, echoing in the recesses of her mind. He'd warned her to drop the matter and leave it alone. But as usual she had her father's curiosity and her mother's stubbornness. Those might have been great traits for an investigative journalist or foreign correspondent, but in the intelligence trade they could be deadly. Her current situation bore out that fact.

Serif had no rescue fantasies. This wasn't good, and she didn't bother telling herself otherwise. It was a matter of practicality. The sooner she accepted what had happened the sooner she could get on with planning her escape. Her training would take over, and she was glad for the many refresher courses through which the DIA had put her. Serif recalled what her instructor had said. "Your first duty if kidnapped is the same duty of a soldier. You must view yourself when you've been taken by a hostile force as a POW. Once you've done that, your priorities are escape and evasion. You all have secrets you must keep, and if you fall into enemy hands, then those secrets potentially fall into enemy hands. Because sooner or later, you'll talk. Sooner or later, everyone talks."

Serif had never forgotten that lesson, and she ran it through her mind again even as the sound of metal scraping against concrete yanked her from the dream-like state she'd been in. A soft, reddish light came from the open steel door and silhouetted the figure that entered. Serif couldn't make out his face but as her mind played through all the possibilities of identity, she noted the man had about the same height and physique as one Gastone Amocacci. And when he spoke, she picked out the Italian accent almost immediately.

Yeah, it was Amocacci, all right.

"Well, Miss Serif," Amocacci said. "Imagine seeing you here. I trust they've treated you well?"

Serif kept her mouth closed, bent on not speaking to him unless he forced her.

"What's the matter? Cat got your tongue or are you simply employing the silent treatment?" Amocacci let out a chuckle and shrugged. "Okay, have it your way. You can remain silent as long as you'd like, in fact."

Amocacci took a seat in a chair bolted to the concrete floor just inside the cell door. He crossed his legs at the ankles and rested his hands in his lap, and a very casual air clung around him.

"I suppose I should begin by telling you that I have no intention of making you talk. About anything. We aren't going to torture or hurt you, but I'm afraid we can't let you go, either. At least not until I've finished what's begun."

So she had been right—Amocacci was involved in some grand scheme and it most likely had something to do with the Council of Luminárii. He'd used the term "we" after all.

A large number of people had insisted Serif was crazy to even posit the existence of such a group. She'd never been able to understand why her colleagues and superiors had always been so quick to dismiss her ideas. She'd provided them with plenty of evidence, and yet even when her reports were sent up the chain of command, they always seemed to get squashed when they reached the Pentagon. Well, now maybe her smashed car and subsequent disappearance would generate some action. That assumed, of course, they weren't ordered to deny the entire incident outright. If they wanted, they could wipe out her very existence and deny she ever existed.

Serif decided to remain silent would be a foolish and useless gesture at this point. Better to see what additional information she could get.

"I don't know what you're up to, Mr. Amocacci, but I can guarantee my government won't let you get away with this. Or whatever it is you have planned."

"Actually, there's very little they can do about it, I think. What we have in mind is already well begun. And I'm sorry if I disappointed you by not being surprised you know my name."

"I'm not disappointed."

"How nice. You see, I've known for months you had me under observation. Everything you've seen or heard has been by design. And it's all been to throw you off the real scent. Your reports about an alleged council, the, uh...what did you call it? Ah, yes, the 'Council of Lights.' It's all a ruse, intended to divert you from the true goals of my associates."

"Is that right?"

"It is. Would you like me to prove it? I could quote you directly from some of the more colorful and dramatic passages of your reports to Washington, DC, but then I don't see much point to it. I can tell just from the look on your face that you know it's true."

"You're crazy."

"No! I am not crazy!" Amocacci slammed his hand against the side of his chair.

His very reaction indicated he was, however. Serif had been trained in the underpinnings of psychological warfare, and one of the first things she'd learned about megalomaniacs and crazies was that they got irate when someone called them megalomaniacs and crazies.

"It might interest you to know that some of the people you work with colluded on getting copies of your reports to us. Does that surprise you to hear?"

"Not really," Serif replied with a shrug. "Mainly because I don't believe you."

"I'm many things, Miss Serif, but a liar isn't one of them. I believe honesty is next to godliness, in fact. And your refusal to believe that your own people could betray you is exactly what makes my point."

"I'm not listening to this anymore."

Amocacci produced a snort of amusement. "You don't have any choice. And you might change your mind if I told you I actually empathize with your current situation.

"You see, such treachery isn't unique to the U.S. intelligence community. It's pandemic! They will smile in your face while cutting your throat and they won't lose a wink of sleep over it."

"Who's 'we'?"

"Who isn't?" Amocacci shook his head. "Every such act is perpetrated by an individual or collective, but they pose as the insidious and faceless enigma of such acts. The acts themselves are the concrete results of governments and terrorist powers operating abstractly against one another. And it is the innocents who die."

"American intelligence isn't perfect, I'll admit. But neither is any other intelligence agency."

"I completely agree!"

"And neither is the Council of Luminárii."

"I've already told you, my dear, the Council of—"

"Please!" Serif raised a hand. "Spare me your feeble attempts at denying it. I've been on to you much longer than you think. You see, you've only been in Turkey for a short time, Mr. Amocacci. But I lived here for years, and I know this culture and these people."

"Odd, your file doesn't indicate that."

"The file you have probably doesn't," Serif replied. "But that doesn't change the fact that the government of the United States knows all about you and your activities here, and I can guarantee they're going to stop you. And whatever you're up to."

"I can see that despite the fact your own people have betrayed you, you're resolute in your views. Nothing I say is going to change them."

"You're probably right."

"Then I guess there's really little reason for us to continue this conversation." Amocacci stood. "You will be fed and treated humanely for the duration of your stay.

And no one will touch you because you are under my protection. If you cooperate and don't make trouble for the guards, you will be released when this is done. But I cannot afford to have you running around Istanbul right now following me or any of my people."

"You do realize that my people are already looking for me. You won't be able to keep me here indefinitely."

"I have no need to keep you here indefinitely. I know my timetable down to the minute. I wish you a pleasant stay, Miss Serif. If you would care to change your mind at any point, please let the guards know and I will come and speak with you."

Amocacci inclined his head with a polite smile, turned and left the cell. A moment later the door closed behind him.

There was no reason to worry about it being open while he spoke with her. She'd already figured out any hope of escape through the door was nothing short of impossible, given her left leg had been affixed to a metal ring stamped into the concrete. A thick, leather restraint encircled her ankle and was attached to a cord just long enough for her to reach the stainless-steel toilet in the wall at the foot of the cot on which she now sat.

After Amocacci's footfalls diminished, Serif considered the information he'd given her. Actually, he'd told her more than he probably realized—maybe even more than she realized. First, his immediately bringing up the Council of Luminárii as a ruse told her that it was anything but. Moreover, he'd spoken out against not only U.S. intelligence but the intelligence community in general, which meant those entities were key targets in whatever he had planned.

In fact he'd said the plan was already under way, and

Serif bet the recent compromises in select military intelligence operations, something that had recently gone over the alert wire, may well be Amocacci's people at work. When she'd first heard of the breaches, Serif had tried to determine commonality among the ops. Unfortunately, she hadn't managed to come up with much of anything. All of the compromised ops had been in disparate sectors, and they had all involved different agencies. The only common thread among them was that they had all been against terrorist organizations, and those organizations had links to al Qaeda. Then again, that wasn't much of a surprise—most Islamic terrorists were connected to that body in one fashion or another.

Whatever was happening, Serif couldn't see someone like Amocacci allying himself with Islamic extremists. No, there was a lot more going on here than met the eye. Serif saw it as her duty to find out what.

And that began with objective one: escape and evade.

As GASTONE AMOCACCI left the hideaway, a house set in a quiet and unobtrusive neighborhood at the southernmost edge of Istanbul, he contemplated his predicament. This hadn't gone exactly as he had planned.

Originally he'd thought to lead Alara Serif around by the nose and let her provide them with a nice, quiet cover story. After all, if the DIA or other U.S. intelligence units wanted to play it that way, Amocacci was more than happy to oblige them.

What he hadn't expected was for someone, anyone, let alone a lone woman in America's junior spy division, to uncover so many details regarding the Council. He'd lied to her, of course, but she wasn't biting. That meant tailing him hadn't been her only source of information. He'd known about her surveillance practically from when it began, and he'd fed her information one delectable morsel at a time.

Since Amocacci hadn't leaked it to her, that could only mean one thing. The former Italian Interpol intelligence officer waited until he was in his car and headed toward his home in the heart of the city before dialing a number on his secure satellite phone.

"Yes?" the voice answered.

"It's me."

"What can I do for you?"

"Our little fox would seem to know a lot more than I suspected. She got close somehow."

"Somehow?" Silence followed that statement before the voice continued. "We both know that's a generalization you're making because you really don't want to voice the alternatives."

"I suppose."

"You have a leak."

"Perhaps."

"Just because you don't want to believe it doesn't make it any less true."

"I don't need a lecture."

"Not at all my intention. I'm simply pointing out the fact we knew this might happen. It wasn't as if you could keep such a thing a secret forever. Working with individuals in the intelligence world to overcome other assets was highly risky to begin with."

"I understand."

"So how do you propose to deal with the situation?"

"I thought that's what you were paid for," Amocacci said in a borderline snarky tone. "Do you have a specific target in mind?"

"If I had to venture a guess, I think the chips would fall on your friend with the MSS."

"That's an unusual choice," Amocacci said. "Are you sure it's necessary? In very many ways, he's been one of my greatest supporters."

"None of them are your supporters, my friend. And none of them can be trusted. If I were in your shoes—"

"I don't mean to sound pedantic, but you aren't in my shoes." Amocacci sighed. "I really could do without platitudes or advice."

"You asked me who I thought the most likely culprit and I gave you my answer. As per contract, only you have the authority to make the final decision. But once made, you cannot reverse yourself."

"Meaning?"

"Meaning I would think very carefully on it. If you have a stronger alternative, you're obviously welcome to name the party selected."

"My concern would be if you're wrong that we would be losing a powerful asset. And if it gets out too soon, suspicion could well fall back on me."

"I've already given you my full assurances that you cannot and will not be even remotely tied to it. In fact, given the back stories of these individuals, any of them has acquired more than enough enemies over the years that you would be able to remain safely above reproach."

"You've obviously been thorough in your research."

"As I always am. So what would you like to do?"

"Go forward with the target you originally specified. How long will it take?"

"Forty-eight hours from the point we verify the funds were transferred securely via the route specified and in the amount agreed."

"It will be done shortly."

"And remember—?"

"You don't need to say it," Amocacci cut in.

"What was I going to say?"

"That once it's done there's no going back."

"I'm impressed. It's nice that you make a point to understand our position. Of course, we will get to work as soon as possible."

"Just make sure it doesn't come back on me," Amocacci replied.

CHAPTER ELEVEN

Livingston, Guatemala

It didn't take Grimaldi any time at all to find Miguel. He sat on a stool just outside one of the several boats for rent arrayed along the dock—marked by a sign identifying the place as *Los Flotantes* and promising tours up the Río Dulce—and polished some sort of wooden piece that looked as if it belonged to one of his small craft. Miguel was short and squat with massive shoulders. He had a shock of long, dark hair coated by a fine layer of dirt that gave it a dull sheen in the sunlight. Basically, he looked like a black lab that had rolled in some mud that had since dried.

When he smiled, Grimaldi saw a row of teeth stained by tobacco and who knew what else. One of the front teeth looked as though it was made from gold, and that surprised Grimaldi. The man had a piece of metal in his mouth that might well have exceeded the value of some Guatemalans' annual income. Yet for all Miguel's seeming shortcomings he came off as agreeable and friendly.

Grimaldi liked the guy right off. In Spanish, Grimaldi inquired, "You're Miguel?"

The man studied Grimaldi a long moment, squinting against the sun although a large camouflage boonie hat was covering his head, and then spit a giant wad of tobacco juice into the water nearby before nodding.

"Cretia sent me here," Grimaldi said, figuring it was best to press forward and be honest. While guys like Miguel were known for their shady dealings, they were also known for their candor. They didn't mess around with anyone and preferred to deal with others in a no-bullshit fashion. Especially in a community such as Livingston where things were loose and somewhat liberal.

"What do you want with Cretia?" Miguel asked in a voice so quiet Grimaldi thought maybe at first he was hearing things.

"We were meeting each other and ran into some trouble. We had to separate and she told me that you would know an alternate location where I could meet her."

Miguel swatted a mosquito away from the back of his neck and then nodded. He set down the wood he'd been polishing and gestured for Grimaldi to enter one of the boats. The pilot reached the edge of the dock and was about to step in when Miguel, who'd already entered the boat, cleared his throat and held out his palm.

Cretia hadn't said anything about giving Miguel or anyone else any money, but that didn't mean anything. That's just the way they did things in this area, and this was definitely not the time to be arguing for what was fair. Grimaldi gave all of that only a moment's consideration before he reached into his pocket and withdrew a wad of cash. He peeled off two fifties and slapped them into Miguel's waiting hand.

Grimaldi never really saw what happened to the bills other than they disappeared very quickly. Next thing he knew, Miguel had turned to head for the pilot's hatch and Grimaldi gingerly stepped into the boat. Within a minute a short cloud of oily smoke puffed into the air as the engine sounded. The water gurgled to life and seconds later the boat slid from the dock.

The Stony Man pilot watched the area behind him as they gently and smoothly made distance from the shore, intent on locating anyone who might be observing them. Nobody seemed to be close to the boat dock and he heard no shouts for them to stop. The boat made a sudden turn and before he knew it they were passing beneath the shade of overhanging trees that marked the mouth of the Río Dulce.

Miguel kept the boat at a steady but slow pace. Grimaldi tried not to become impatient, but time was beginning to run short. The longer it took him to find Bolan, the less his chances of finding his friend alive. He had no idea who'd taken the Executioner; he only knew the GPS transponder signal had him at a fixed point upriver.

Grimaldi was about to point out to Miguel that he didn't have much time and to consider a different pace when he suddenly realized how clever the decision had been. If Miguel had gone blasting down the river in a tour boat, a sight that had to be pretty uncommon among the local residents, that could have potentially attracted some very unwanted attention. Instead, Miguel had taken a more leisurely pace so that anyone who saw them wouldn't think anything of it.

Grimaldi smiled to himself. It was obvious Cretia knew her business and how to choose the right allies.

THEY HAD TRAVELED roughly thirty minutes upriver before Miguel slowed to a crawl and pointed the boat toward shore. At first Grimaldi didn't see anything, but then he could spot the almost imperceptible opening in the dense trees and brush and what appeared to be a man-made path. As they got closer to the shore, a small and familiar figure emerged from the trees.

She'd changed from her beat-up jeans and T-shirt to a khaki shirt tied at the midriff and tan shorts. Brown hiking boots and a boonie hat similar to that worn by Miguel completed the ensemble. She'd tied up her dark hair, but a small braided tail danced from the hat and down the left side of her neck until it came to rest just over the rise of her left breast. Her skin was dark, almost exotic, a point Grimaldi hadn't noticed before in the dim lighting of the bar. She was even more beautiful in the rugged jungle terrain, and Grimaldi found it noteworthy that the natural but dangerous beauty of the environment seemed to suit the natural and dangerous beauty of the woman he knew only as Cretia.

"How do I look?" she asked with a beaming smile.

"Like you've done this before," Grimaldi said. He looked her up and down, adding, "And that getup gives you sort of an animal attraction."

She cocked her head. "What are you trying to say?"

"That you got me thinking."

"Good."

As soon as the nose of the boat came close to the shore, Miguel tossed a rope and Cretia grabbed it. She towed the boat until it bumped against the muddy shoreline, her small but shapely arms straining as she pulled hand over hand. She then stepped back, tied the rope loosely around her waist, made two long strides and jumped into the bow of the craft with the ease of a pole-vaulter.

Cretia disengaged the rope from her waist before

coiling it onto the deck in much the same condition it had been. Apparently, Grimaldi had been more right than he'd known about her experience. She seemed to know just where things were supposed to be and how they worked, and it came as even more of a surprise when she sidled up to Miguel, hugged his neck and planted a kiss on his cheek.

As Cretia moved aft where Grimaldi stood waiting, she seemed to notice the shocked look on his face. "Why do you look so surprised?"

"Huh?" Grimaldi shook himself. "Oh…nothing, I guess."

"You think he's not my type?" Cretia asked, tossing a thumb behind her to indicate Miguel.

"No, I wasn't thinking anything of the sort."

She cocked her head again in that way Grimaldi found so irresistibly cute and said, "For a man in your line of business, Señor Jack, you're not a very good liar."

"That right?"

Cretia nodded. "And, anyway, you're thinking of it all wrong. He's my papa."

"Your dad?" Grimaldi's eyebrows rose involuntarily and he wondered why he was acting like a jealous schoolboy. More bothersome was that she could obviously read the relief in his face. "You mean your *real* dad? So this is a family business."

"Yes."

"Makes much more sense now," Grimaldi said with a grin intended to charm her.

"So what's the story?" he asked as the boat eased out of the shallows and Miguel backed them from the shore. "You were about to tell me you had information regarding my friend."

She nodded, taking a seat next to him on the boat once they were clear of the shallows. She had to raise her voice to be heard above the hum of the motor.

"Yes, we made some inquiries as soon as your people called us."

Grimaldi knew what that meant: any information Cretia gave him could be trusted implicitly. Although you never trusted anyone implicitly as a general rule, Stony Man had apparently used this team before and so the intelligence had to be solid. Besides, Cretia and her father didn't seem like the type who had a thing for terrorists or drug smugglers, or whoever was tied to the military intelligence leak. And they *certainly* didn't seem like the type to rub elbows with turncoats and criminals.

Cretia continued. "There's no question your friend was captured by members of the Islamic Brotherhood."

"Terrorists? Operating here in Guatemala in such an open fashion?" Grimaldi shook his head. "Seems like a bit of a stretch."

"It would be under normal circumstances. But this group has had relatively good success with keeping the drug and weapons pipelines open, and in return they acquire significant resources."

"What sort of resources could a poor and meager country like this offer the IB?" Grimaldi asked. "I mean, I can see by your expression you're a little offended, but that's not my intent. I like this country and its people. But from a strictly conventional sense, there isn't much in the way of money flowing through here. And they can get all the weapons and dope they want. So how does it help them?"

"The same way it helps *you*," Cretia said. "And no offense taken."

Sunlight danced across her long, tanned legs as she leaned over to the side of the seats they were on and reached into a cooler. She withdrew a couple of bottled waters that had been set in ice and handed one to him.

"Information," Cretia said after taking a long pull from the bottle and licking her lips. "It's as valuable to the Islamic terrorists operating here as it is to your people."

"Okay, fair enough," Grimaldi replied. "But what about Stone? Is he still alive?"

"That information wasn't available to us, and believe me when I say we definitely inquired deeply into it. A lot of people made a lot of money, even for us to find out what we did. All we can confirm is that after he was captured, he was taken to a prison camp deep inside our territory up the Río Dulce. That's where we're headed now."

"And how do you plan to get in?" Grimaldi asked. "I mean, I don't think you're hiding any sort of army aboard this boat."

"We don't need an army," she said. "Only the two of us. We have ready access into and out of the camp. They're concealed well in the jungle, or at least they think they are. They haven't bothered to protect their position on the river since they believe nobody knows of their location. It will be a simple matter of just getting inside under cover of darkness, finding Colonel Stone and getting him out."

"And what about weapons?"

"We have more than enough," she said.

She tapped the floor with her foot and gestured for

him to stand. When Grimaldi had complied, she flipped back the cushions she'd been sitting on, opened a hatch and stuck her hand way down into what looked like the top of the engine. She pulled on something and suddenly the floor panels seemed to shift and give where they had otherwise appeared seamless just a moment before.

Cretia smiled as she lifted one of the panels. Nestled in what was obviously a waterproof container were half a dozen Kalashnikov assault rifle variants accompanied by plenty of spare magazines loaded with 7.62 mm ammo. Grimaldi's eyes appraised them quickly and he realized they were AK-47 assault rifles. They looked to be practically brand-new. There were also a few canvas satchels that he assumed contained some sort of ordnance and a couple of flak vests that added a somewhat legit touch to the entire cache.

Grimaldi let out a wolf whistle and remarked, "Nice…very classy."

"I thought you might appreciate it."

"I can see that you're into more than just information brokering."

She smiled. "We're not without good connections. In this day and age, we find it's more profitable to be flexible, to adapt to the ever-changing need of our customers."

"I like the way you think," Grimaldi said. "Although it can be a pretty dangerous business."

"Danger is how we make our living, señor."

"Why don't you call me Jack?"

"Okay, if you prefer."

"Now what else can you tell me about this camp?"

As Cretia restored the hatches and seating configuration to its former state, she began to explain. "There are three separate holding blocks. Two are aboveground with one below to hold the high-value detainees."

"Which they will most likely consider Stone to be."

"Exactly our thought. Maybe a half-dozen guards at any one time, two teams of two on staggered perimeter patrol."

"So roving guards," Grimaldi interjected. "That's going to make it a little more difficult."

"There are also other considerations," she said.

"Such as?"

"Such as the fact they are heavily armed. As I noted before, the IB is well equipped here. They maintain a significant drug and weapons pipeline for the gangs in the cities, and in return they're fed a lot of intelligence. Some of it is bad or old, if it was even legit to begin with, but most is accurate. The one thing the terrorists here don't realize is that the same information they glean is the same information that runs through our own internal networks."

"Meaning you know about the same time as they do what's up," he concluded.

"Sometimes even ahead of them. More often than not, in fact."

"You know something else?"

She nodded. "We weren't paid for it by your contact, but I'll tell you, anyway, as a gesture of good faith. And because I think you're cute."

Grimaldi smiled and winked. "Likewise."

Cretia took a deep breath. "We've been led to understand that Colonel Stone wasn't the only prisoner taken. It's possible that a number of the other men on your insertion team may also have been captured. We know with certainty that at least some were killed."

Grimaldi felt as if his heart had fallen into his stomach and settled there like a cold knot of meat. His head began to hurt. Had they been walking into a trap from the beginning? Had Shoup actually been on the side of the good guys or had he planned for Bolan's demise from the start and got his own head lopped off in the process because he'd been a liability? Not to mention that he might have been one of the ones captured and was in the same predicament as the others.

"Any way you look at this," Grimaldi finally said, "we're going to be at a disadvantage. We have to get Colonel Stone out, sure, but we also have to consider the lives of the others. Those are American POWs, and we won't leave them behind."

"While I understand your concern," Cretia said, "I have to point out that rescuing multiple persons was not a part of the plan. We were only prepared to get Colonel Stone out of there."

"Those men that were taken put their lives on the line for their nation," Grimaldi countered. "There's no way in hell we're going to just leave them there."

"I gave you that information as a courtesy, Jack. I did not expect you to use it as a weapon against me."

"I'm not trying to use it as a weapon," Grimaldi said as gently as he could manage. "And I'm glad you told me. But now that I know, I have a duty to take them out—*all* of them. Surely you can understand that."

"I can." She smiled. "And I suppose I was aware of this. But you must also understand that this boat has weight limitations. If there are too many of them, we may not be able to get all of them out."

"Then we just merely need to plan some alternatives."

"Such as?"

Grimaldi thought a moment. "Any chance you have some sort of map of the area? Particularly one that shows terrain?"

"Of course." Cretia rose from her seat, walked to a nearby trunk that seemed to be bolted to the frame and opened the combination lock. She dipped her hand inside and rummaged around before producing a topographic map covered with a plastic film. She secured the trunk before bringing the map back and handing it to him, then she sat on the seat next to him as he unfolded it.

"Okay. Let's see…"

After studying the map a minute and having Cretia point out the approximate location, Grimaldi removed the GPS homing device from his pocket.

"What is this?"

"It's called a Geo-Caching Terrain Mapping Device, or sometimes just a T-mapper for short. It uses a satellite to home into a micro-transmitter planted on Colonel Stone we can then scan into this map. Like so." Grimaldi ran the scanning portion over the map of the area and then punched in the coordinates as noted by the mapmakers. He continued his explanation. "What this will do is create a three-dimensional overlay of the surrounding terrain. We can use this to show us all the access points for the camp and it will tell us if there are alternative ways out."

"I don't understand how this information will help us. We already know we will evacuate using this boat."

"Ah," Grimaldi said, raising his finger. "But we also need to know if there are alternatives in case we have too many. And look here. See this line?"

She squinted at the screen of the small device he held up for her inspection. "Yes."

"That's a road if I've ever seen one. And it looks like it's in pretty good shape, which means this camp can be accessed by vehicle. I'd bet there are one or two vehicles on site, otherwise it would be difficult to get supplies into and out of the area."

"Maybe they use boats."

Grimaldi shook his head. "Boats moored along the side of the river in an area remote as this would draw attention from either river patrols or just general tourist traffic. An access road off one of the few roads leading in-country, however, might be innocuous enough that people would pay it scant notice. And if it provides a very narrow right of access into and out of the camp, it would be relatively easy to secure from outsiders."

Cretia nodded. "It seems you have come up with an alternative, after all. I'm impressed."

"I'm glad we agree," Grimaldi said.

"Now we must hope we find your friend alive," Cretia said.

"Yeah."

CHAPTER TWELVE

Of all the things Mack Bolan had expected to see, the head of Major Randy Shoup hadn't been one of them. And yet there it was, dangled in front of his face in the fists of Bolan's chief inquisitor.

"You knew this man?"

"I knew him," Bolan said.

"Then you would do well to remember him just as he is now and not as he *was*."

"And why's that?"

"Because this was his just punishment for lying to us."

That eliminated any doubts Bolan harbored about Shoup. He'd either been involved with this group from the start, or he'd associated with a traitor inside his own organization. In any case, they had clearly seen him as a liability and eliminated him. The whole thing had smelled of a setup to begin with. Bolan just hadn't realized that it was Shoup who'd been set up, even though he'd thought it was *he* who'd been setting up Bolan the entire time.

"We checked your story," the man continued as he tossed the head aside as casually as if it were the remnants of an eaten apple. The dull thud of the head hitting the floor echoed sickeningly in the confines of the small cell. "It seems you've told us the truth. Shoup did not, and that is why he's dead and you're still alive."

"Am I supposed to be grateful?"

The man inspected his fingernails and Bolan could now make out his face well. He searched his memory but still couldn't place the guy. "Not at all. It's just our way of showing you that we keep our word. We are men of honor, after all."

"You don't even know the meaning of the word."

"So be it," he said with a nod.

The punch came just as it had before, hard enough to rattle his brains inside his head but not enough to cause any permanent damage. He also noticed this time that the striker hadn't supplemented the punch with anything like the plastic-sheathed gloves used before. This was more of a punch toward the back center of the skull to remind Bolan of his place. It was a psychological move above all else, and the Executioner knew that game well. He would not let them intimidate him.

"Now, we can make the rest of your stay here a bit more pleasant," the man said, "or we can make it doubly *not* so. How would you like this to go?"

Up to this point the Executioner had been willing to play along in the hope of stroking the guy's ego and stalling. He knew sooner or later Grimaldi would arrive with the cavalry. But now, seeing the pointless murder of a U.S. military officer—whether Shoup had deserved what he got was another matter entirely and not something Bolan would debate in moral ambiguity under these terms—he wasn't about to let this man get the better of him.

"You can torture me and play your psychological games with me," Bolan said. "I've already figured out what you're up to. I think you know it, too. Which means that I'm no longer of any real value to you. If you keep me alive, it's only because you think it will benefit you or your organization in some way. And if you don't, then I'll wind up just like Shoup. Right?"

The man gave Bolan a frosty smile; a death's head leer like that of a grinning skull. "I see that you're a learned man if not very bright."

"Just what is it you're hoping to gain by all of this?" Bolan said. "You've killed a U.S. military officer, kidnapped another, and who knows how many of our men you've already butchered. Do you really think my country will let that stand? Eventually they will come for you and in force. And you won't have enough guns or wits for them, and they'll overrun your entire cause as well as your position. And you'll be dead, just another pawn sacrificed by some lunatic who cares nothing for you personally."

"You speak sure words for a man who claims to know nothing about me or our mission here."

Bolan decided now was the time to go for shock factor since he had the guy visibly off balance. "What part did you play in the compromise of recent U.S. military intelligence operations? Are you a member of the Council of Luminárii?"

A long, weighty silence followed and the man's former aura of cockiness and arrogance vanished. The blow had just the effect Bolan had hoped it would. With that one simple question, he'd revealed he knew exactly who he'd been dealing with the entire time but also that this man had a direct relationship with the people Serif had uncovered. It told him all he needed to know in that moment. Not only was the Council of Luminárii real, they did in fact have some direct relationship with the recent compromise in American military intelligence. Somehow they were tied into the base in Colorado and they had gotten their hooks into Shoup.

And they were likely behind Alara Serif's disappearance.

It all just left Bolan with one unanswered question. Where the hell were they getting their information?

"You should have played out your original ruse a little bit longer," the man said, standing. "With those words you've just spoken, you have signed your own death warrant."

"I'm shaking in my boots," Bolan replied calmly.

"We'll see if you are so confident when we pour oil over you and set fire to it."

The man said something to one of the guards and, while Bolan didn't understand the words, he did recognize it as an Arabic dialect. That meant his captors were probably a terrorist group, although he couldn't be sure which one. Somehow, Islamic terrorists had compromised U.S. military intelligence, and they had done so with the assistance of this mysterious council. But how and for what purpose? What did they hope to gain by it?

And with the Executioner now facing a horrific death, who would figure it out in time to stop them to avert an all-out disaster?

DARKNESS BLANKETED THE river as the boat bumped against the shore.

Miguel tied off and then deposited the equipment bags on shore as Grimaldi and Cretia jumped from the boat. They were geared up with everything they could possibly carry, including one extra weapon each for any captors they managed to rescue. Grimaldi had also secured extra grenades and a satchel of ordnance. The plastic explosives looked old but more than capable of doing any job Grimaldi assigned to them.

Once the pair was on shore and had secured their other equipment, Cretia bid her father a whispered farewell before turning.

Grimaldi was certain he heard the old man reply, *"Via con Dios,"* before he fell into step behind her.

They moved through the woods with surprising quiet despite the fact they were on unfamiliar terrain. Cretia seemed to have a natural affinity for it while Grimaldi had training and experience in such environments. It wasn't the first time he'd moved through the nighttime jungle carrying the tools of war, and he was pretty sure it wouldn't be the last. Having navigated and fought on such ground many times before, in fact, Grimaldi thought of it much like learning to ride a bike.

They proceeded for what Grimaldi estimated to be less than half a mile and eventually came to a stop. Cretia knelt and Grimaldi checked their flank before joining her. She whipped out the map and put it on the ground, then shone a red-lensed flashlight on it. Grimaldi took the T-mapper from his pocket and double-checked the coordinates of their position as it related to the map. He was surprised to find Cretia had brought them within a mere fifty yards of the camp. The signal coming from Bolan's transmitter was still going strong.

"Nice job," Grimaldi whispered.

Cretia nodded and indicated he should now take point. He agreed with a nod of his own—he'd have to call the shots from here out. The actual rescue was his show, they had agreed, since he was the one who could pinpoint Bolan. Rescue of his friend had been the first priority for them. The plan was simple. Cretia would create a distraction as far from Bolan's location as possible. Once the guards headed to her position, Grimaldi would slip inside, find Bolan and liberate him.

If time permitted, they would then search for survivors.

Grimaldi took point and continued on the path toward the camp. When they got to within striking distance, he signaled for Cretia to do her stuff. She quickly disappeared from view through the brush.

It didn't take the woman long to get the show started. She'd grabbed a couple of grenades from the satchel, leaving the rest with Grimaldi. She would have to be able to move quickly and being burdened with all of that equipment wasn't going to help on that count. Once enough time had passed to facilitate Grimaldi's rescue efforts and the pilot gave the signal, Cretia would head back to the boat and wait for their arrival. If nobody showed after thirty minutes, she and her father were to get the hell out of there and return to Livingston without being seen—if possible.

The blast came a bit suddenly, despite the fact Grimaldi was expecting it, and somewhat closer than he'd preferred. Still, it did its job; he could hear the shouts in the aftermath of the explosion. The hammer of boots seemed to move away from him and Grimaldi took the opportunity to break cover. The Stony Man pilot entered the encampment and found it contained nothing more than a couple of rickety structures, one large and another somewhat smaller. Well, a place with only four guards probably didn't need much outside the most basic accoutrements. And it wasn't as if the place had occupants all the time. It served more as a way station, the way Grimaldi understood it from Cretia's explanation.

He moved quickly through the camp until the blip that signaled Bolan's location went solid red as Grimaldi came to a stop in front of the smaller of the two shanty-like buildings. If he'd attempted to breach the building immediately, he would have missed the light that spilled from a hole in the ground to his left. Grimaldi went to the sliver of light and realized it emanated from a door in the ground. He grabbed the makeshift, lever-style handle, turned and then pulled. The door flung open to reveal a very steep stairwell. Grimaldi descended the steps that terminated inside a narrow, bunker-like cell with cracked concrete walls slick with moisture.

Bolan sat with an almost demure expression on his face. It looked as if he'd taken a beating but not so much that he was unrecognizable.

"Took you long enough," Bolan said.

Grimaldi grinned. "You get what you came for?"

"I did."

"And?" Grimaldi asked.

"Terrorist group, probably sourced from al Qaeda."

"Islamic Brotherhood, actually," Grimaldi interjected.

Bolan stood, flexing his neck muscles and jaw, making sure he didn't have any broken bones or other injuries that would prevent him from making his escape.

"All good?" Grimaldi inquired.

"Fine," Bolan said.

Grimaldi passed a Beretta 93-R pistol to the Executioner, followed by a fully loaded AK-47. Another explosion sounded and a raised eyebrow from Bolan made him say, "Distraction. I think it's time to leave. Our luck won't hold out much longer."

"Agreed."

As they began to leave, Grimaldi suddenly noticed the head in one corner of the room. "Shoup?"

Bolan nodded. "Long story. Now let's get out of here or you won't get to hear it."

"Are there any other prisoners here?"

"What?" Bolan asked.

"Any other prisoners here?"

"I don't know. Shoup's the only one I've seen."

"Our contact said there might be others."

"We'll check on the way out," Bolan said. "Now let's shag it. You know the layout better, so you got point."

Grimaldi nodded as he turned and ascended the stairs with his friend on his heels. They emerged from the underground cell, and Bolan immediately checked the shack near the cell door. He shot the lock from the door with a well-placed round from the Beretta, opened it and pushed through, weapon held at the ready while Grimaldi covered his flank. The sight sickened him. The bodies of the rest of Shoup's team were piled up in the cramped spaces. They had been stripped naked and left to rot.

Bolan looked at Grimaldi. The pilot could not recall the last time he'd seen the Executioner's face set with such grim and iron resolve. "Those explosives in that satchel?"

Grimaldi nodded.

"Hand them over."

"Sarge, we should move."

"Jack...hand them over."

Grimaldi didn't see any reason to argue the point. He

let the satchel fall from his shoulder and Bolan snatched it. The Executioner knelt, reached inside and found the detonator cap he'd been looking for. He set the cap into one of the blocks, attached the other end of the wire to the remote receiver and turned it on. Bolan then removed the arming switch from the satchel, tossed the primed explosives inside and closed the door.

"Let's go!"

The pair burst from the scene and headed toward the perimeter, Bolan triggering the switch on the run. At first there was nothing, only the distant sound of a lone automatic rifle somewhere in the distance resounding. Then the blast came, sending a fireball high enough into the air that it could be spotted for miles. The explosion was something that would not only obscure the identity of the fallen soldiers but double as a funeral pyre.

The Executioner would make sure every one of the men on that team received a hero's burial back home, but for now he would not allow them to be disgraced as their flesh rotted in the jungle. Better to be consumed by the flames of honor, to be burned to ash in a funeral pyre fit for men of such courage, than to waste away as a stinking corpse. Such was the honorable thing to do in Bolan's mind, and Grimaldi knew it.

And he also knew from the look on Bolan's face that the perpetrators of such an atrocity would pay dearly. The Executioner had been liberated and all had gone as planned. Now it was time for the offensive to begin.

"THANKS, JACK," MACK BOLAN said, clapping his hand on his friend's shoulder. "Thanks for coming after me."

"You know thanks aren't necessary." Grimaldi waved at Cretia and Miguel. "But it is these two you really owe for it. Without them I never would have known what we were up against."

Bolan stepped forward and offered his hand. "Then I guess I owe you a debt of gratitude, as well."

"So now that you have the information you were looking for, what's next on the agenda?" Grimaldi asked.

Bolan sat and reached into the cooler. He scooped up a handful of ice and held it to his bruised face. "First we get back to the plane. You brought transportation, I assume."

Grimaldi nodded. "Left it parked in Punta Gorda. But, yeah…we're good."

"Our next stop's Istanbul," Bolan said. "Now that I've positively connected this terrorist group with the information coming out of Turkey, there's no question the incidents are related. Someone is pulling the chains of the terrorists at this end. Those are the same people who infiltrated Shoup's people in Florida, and also who set up the base of operations in Colorado."

"So why Istanbul?"

"Well, it took me a while to pull it out of the guy interrogating me, but he balked when I mentioned the Council of Luminárii. Apparently a DIA analyst at the consulate in Turkey has been sending reports for some time to officials at the Pentagon advising of this group operating in Istanbul. She believes the group is led by, or at least has a member who is a former Italian intelligence officer at Interpol. At first, I wondered if there was a connection, and I wasn't sure how far to play my hand after I avoided the initial ambush. It wasn't until I realized they were trying to capture me and not kill me that I knew the theories of this analyst had merit."

"Wait a minute," Cretia cut in. "You're saying that you *allowed* yourself to be captured by these men?"

"It just worked out that way."

Cretia exchanged glances with Grimaldi and Bolan, and a smoky ember of distrust suddenly glinted in her dark eyes. "That's why Jack knew your location this entire time. You weren't in any real danger at all."

"Well," Grimaldi began, "that's not exactly true—"

"Isn't it?" Cretia demanded. "I put my reputation at risk, not to mention my papa. We only agreed to do this because we thought Colonel Stone was in real trouble. But instead you had this planned."

"We didn't have it planned, lady," Bolan said with a swipe of his hand. "And you can just cut the righteous indignation. You did this because you were well paid by our people to do it. You're mercenaries and in it for the cash, first. Maybe you feel some allegiance to the United States or those you perceive could be in trouble by your shared mutual hatred for an enemy. But please don't pretend that the very large compensation you get doesn't come into your decision on who you will and won't help. Okay?"

Grimaldi was taken completely aback by the exchange—Bolan could tell just by the way he continued to look back and forth between them. He couldn't be sure, but he almost had to wonder if they hadn't shared some sort of intimate moment somewhere along the way. Jack being Jack, it wasn't as though it would have come as any surprise to Bolan.

The look on Cretia's face, however, made it clear that Bolan had called it correctly. They had done what they had for the money. First and foremost, that's what it had all been about.

"So can we cut the crap and get back to business?" Bolan asked Cretia.

She nodded slowly, not meeting Bolan's penetrating gaze.

CHAPTER THIRTEEN

Kirklareli, Turkey

Quon Ma had a reputation among his peers as being tough and resourceful. He was also known to possess a keen intelligence. All of these qualities would make it more difficult to kill him.

Heinrich Wehr checked his watch: the luminous display indicated it was nearing six o'clock. Ma would be arriving home from his office at any minute, totally unaware that he'd been marked for death. When the order came through from Savitch, who was apparently detained in Guatemala with the American special ops team sent from Florida, Wehr had already been prepared for it. The only thing he hadn't been able to predict was the target.

He had to admit the selection of Quon Ma for execution had definitely surprised him. In fact, he couldn't help but wonder what the point of killing the guy even was. In his earlier observations Wehr had never seen anything to convince him Ma could be a traitor to the cause of the Council of Luminárii, whatever the hell that cause might be. And the idea of killing one of their own seemed to go against the very fabric of what made the Council so successful in its efforts. The system worked because they worked together, with no party having the upper hand on any other party.

Then again, maybe that was the entire point. Savitch had convinced Amocacci that Ma was the leak within the group, and they couldn't have that. It gave Ma and the Chinese Ministry of State Security the upper hand. They couldn't have that in a group that relied on operating symbiotically with each other.

Not that Wehr gave a shit about it one way or another. He was just supposed to be a hired gun and, as a professional assassin, he killed who he was paid to kill. His profession didn't necessarily allow for scruples or conscientious objection. Of course he wouldn't cross certain lines. He wouldn't kill children or female civilians, and he wouldn't pull the trigger on the elderly. He'd been raised to respect those groups, and there were certain things that were sacrosanct in his business. Those were just some of them. An assassin totally without scruples or a sense of morality was little more than a functional psychopath. Wehr had run into a few of them over the course of his career, and he held no respect for them. In his line of work they were considered little more than hacks.

Wehr checked his watch again and then smiled when he saw the headlights of Ma's car swing onto the street on which the spy resided. Wehr adjusted his body so his shoulder nestled comfortably against the stock and then put his eye to the high-powered scope. The rifle was an Accuracy International L115A3 AWM. It included a combination sound-and-flash suppressor, 25×56 night-scope, adjustable bipod and folding stock. Weighing in at just over fourteen pounds, the British-made rifle chambered the .300 Winchester Magnum cartridge with an effective range of 1,100 meters.

Wehr had used the rifle on a few previous jobs and come to like it for its versatility and precision. He watched through the scope as Ma's car pulled into the drive and waited for it to make its entry through the wrought iron gate. The vehicle proceeded up the drive to the double front doors. The house couldn't have been called a mansion exactly, but it had a bit of acreage to it and that wasn't uncommon in this part of Turkey. Only the affluent or upper class could afford to live in an area such as this. So while the homes along this route weren't palatial, they were most certainly nicer than most of the offerings in the city and surrounding areas.

Wehr readjusted the nightscope to provide a more focused sight picture. He aligned the crosshairs of the illuminated sight on the driver's door of the vehicle. Wehr closed his eye a moment when the red flare from the taillights came on to prevent it from blinding him, and then settled to wait. Only a few seconds elapsed before the door opened and Ma's shadowy form emerged.

Wehr grinned at what a cakewalk this would be even as he depressed the trigger with steady, even pressure while making sure he didn't involuntarily anticipate the recoil. The weapon's report was hardly more than that of a firecracker as it punched against the padded shoulder sewn into the lining of Wehr's coat. He kept his sight picture long enough to verify the bloody spray of the head shot and watch the body tumble from view. He lowered the barrel of the weapon to maintain the picture as he followed the body to the ground, then squeezed off a second round to ensure the kill.

Wehr didn't wait for any sort of response. He pulled

the rifle from its perch, slapped the bipod into a re-
tracted position and then headed for the rooftop access
door that would take him down the back steps of the
tenement building and out a rear exit. The hallway was
dimly lit and Wehr hoped he wouldn't run into anyone
on the way down the four flights that led to the ground
floor. It was a busy time of day with many people returning from work, but Wehr figured that might serve
to cover his escape.

And, anyway, he didn't have to worry about anyone
who saw him because it would be the last thing they
saw. He couldn't risk anyone seeing his face and reporting his presence to authorities. Once word got out about
Ma's assassination, the place would be crawling with
cops and MSS agents—plus this activity would most
certainly bring down heat from the Council.

Wehr managed to get to the first floor without encountering anyone and pushed through the door that led
onto the back lot. He dumped the rifle in the appointed
brush. Someone would come to retrieve it in a day or
two when it was safe. There was no way he could be
caught toting it around with him in the vehicle. As a
foreigner in the Republic of Turkey, carrying a loaded
weapon of any kind on his person or in his vehicle was
highly illegal. The government viewed weapons and
the drug-running trade as activities that fed off each
other, and anyone caught with weapons without a permit faced stiff penalties and fines.

Wehr climbed into his car and took a few deep
breaths to calm himself. He then started the engine
and pulled out of the lot. He'd gone half a block when
two vehicles suddenly pulled up on either side of him.

Wehr looked at the black sedans with tinted windows and in a moment he knew his situation had gone hard.

Impossible! How the hell could they have been onto him so quickly? Wehr started to panic. He had no weapons with which to defend himself and no place to go. This wasn't overly familiar territory to him since he'd only been in the city for a few days waiting for word from Savitch. Had he been set up? And if so...*why*?

Well, now wasn't the time to worry about questions like that—better he take some action to try to even up the odds. Wehr jerked the wheel hard to the left just as they approached a T intersection to force the vehicle on the driver's side onto the sidewalk. He then made a hard left turn at the intersection, blowing the stop sign and risking a collision with the heavier traffic. Fortunately he managed to avoid such impacts since the other drivers seemed alert enough to avoid crashing into him. The driver of the sedan on his right wasn't so alert and ended up clipping a minivan taxi. Both vehicles spun out of control, but the sedan righted itself and the driver got back in a pursuit course, now hugging Wehr's tail.

There was too much traffic on this undivided four-lane road for his pursuers to gain the advantage, and Wehr used that to keep one step ahead of them. He couldn't afford to be captured or impeded. If they attempted to take him alive, then his orders were clear. It was suicide or die fighting his captors—anything less was totally unacceptable. He knew too much, and he couldn't even begin to imagine the untold damage it would cause if his enemies were able to take him alive and make him talk.

Wehr swerved in and out of traffic, expertly keeping his pursuers at bay and gradually increasing the distance between them. If he could just get into the main part of Kirklareli, he'd be able to lose them for good. His worst fears were realized, however, when he saw another vehicle approach from the opposite direction—this one sported lights, sirens and the unmistakable emblem of the Turkish police.

Wehr held his breath but the vehicle buzzed past him without even slowing, and as he watched the lights fade in his rearview mirror he deduced that whoever pursued him had no ties with law enforcement. He still had a chance to escape if he acted quickly. Wehr pressed on the accelerator and poured on all the speed he dared without risking an actual crash. As he came up to a major intersection and the lights changed, he knew he couldn't make it through before the vehicles in front would stop.

Wehr swerved onto the sidewalk at the last minute and took a right turn that put his vehicle on two wheels. He thought he'd lose it but the car came back to ground at the last moment. Wehr looked behind him and saw that the sedan was no longer in sight. Just as he'd suspected, they'd been unable to pursue him. He'd gotten away with it, and he knew now his survival depended on him getting rid of his vehicle and making a hasty exit out of the country under the cover of night.

Those arrangements had already been made. As soon as he ditched his car and reported success to Savitch, he'd be on his way. Free, clear and significantly richer!

QUON MA STOOD over the body of his driver and aide as blood ran from the man's still form. His dark eyes smoldered and his security team had given him a respectful berth. While Ma was thankful that his man had died and the assassins hadn't succeeded in killing him, he couldn't help but wonder who would have attempted such a bold move.

Ma's other assistant and head of security, a former Chinese army officer named Shunang, shook his head. "I don't understand it, sir. I don't understand who would want to do this."

"Who would want to do it doesn't interest me near as much as who has the *capability* to arrange it. I think if you point your inquiry toward finding that out, the identity of the party or parties will evolve naturally."

"I must apologize for this, sir," Shunang said. "We utterly failed to protect you."

"It's not your fault," Ma said. "It's *my* fault for not seeing this coming sooner. It's no secret that I've made quite a number of enemies over the years given my activities for the State. But it's even more interesting this has happened in light of recent reports that there is a leak among my associates."

"You speak of—"

"What I speak of must never be spoken aloud!" Ma said, raising his hand. "*Never*. Is that clear?"

"Of course, sir," Shunang said with a bow.

Ma sighed. "It's enough that we both know of what you refer to, and that's sufficient. But you cannot direct your investigation that way. I must pursue those avenues on my own. I will pull them out one at a time, and eventually the culprit—if it is one of my associates—will give himself away. In the meantime, you should start looking at more conventional reasons. As I noted previously, you should pursue those roads that lead you to answering the question of what agencies and individuals that might bear me a grudge would have the resources to make an attempt on my life."

"Yes, sir." Shunang looked Ma in the eyes. "You realize, of course, that it would be better if for now the assassin or assassins believed they had succeeded."

"Of course. That goes without saying." Ma smiled. "It's all just part of the larger plan I have to track the ferret straight into its lair. And when we have found them out, I will make them pay."

Istanbul, Turkey

"I THOUGHT MY orders were clear!" Colonel Alan Bindler snapped as he dropped his fist on his desk.

Major Nestor Maxwell jumped in spite of himself. He stood at attention in front of Bindler, eyes focused straight ahead. "They were clear, sir."

Bindler shook his head and came around the desk. He stood about three inches shorter than Maxwell, but he had a commanding air and intensity about him that could intimidate most others regardless of size or even rank. Bindler had seen action on five separate continents and spent more time in a hot LZ than the average combat Marine. It was this experience that had seen him promoted through the ranks so quickly, and his unswerving abilities to command in even the most inhospitable regions with great promise that landed him a premium position of the Marine guard detail at a major consulate.

"So then maybe you'd care to explain why our people were involved in a high-speed pursuit of some unidentified party in Kirklareli instead of being here in Istanbul looking for Ms. Serif!"

"You asked us to investigate and that's where the trail led, sir."

"I ordered you to operate under the radar!" Bindler said. He began to pace around the room. "You assured me that you'd select guys who could be subtle. Chasing assassins through crowded Turkish streets is *not* subtle, Major Maxwell!"

"Sir, our latching on to this guy came quite accidentally. We were pursuing the one lead we had, and it just turned out that somebody got to that lead first."

"And what lead is that?"

"It was one that Serif had noted in her reports. Just a notation, really, but we thought it had enough merit it might give us some answers as to her whereabouts."

Bindler stopped pacing and stared at his adjutant. It wasn't really Maxwell's fault, but the shit rolled downhill. He'd promised Brognola that he'd let Stone handle any such operations, and the men under his command had unwittingly caused him to break that promise, not to mention their efforts could have caused an international incident if they'd been caught and detained by local authorities in Kirklareli.

"At ease, Max." Bindler gestured toward a chair. "Take a seat."

Maxwell did as ordered and then Bindler dropped into the other chair directly across from him. "Okay, so relax and speak freely. Tell me what you found out."

"Well, Serif had mentioned the possibility that the Council of Luminárii could be composed of representatives from multiple intelligence agencies."

"So why Kirklareli? What lead were you pursuing?"

Maxwell reached down to the attaché case he'd brought with him and withdrew a candy-stripe-edged file folder. Bindler took the classified file, opened it and saw a large black-and-white photograph of a lean Asian man in his early forties.

"That picture was taken a few months ago when Ms. Serif was on an excursion in Kirklareli."

Bindler shook his head. "I never authorized any trip to that city. How did she manage it?"

"Vacation time, apparently."

Bindler thought on that for a moment and nodded. Of course, Serif had dual citizenship, so she could move easily around the country without any problems. She spoke the language, knew all of the customs, and was the daughter of a Turkish citizen in good standing. In fact, it was Serif's ties with her father—a former government employee within one of the ruling political parties—that many had viewed could be a potential liability to consulate operations. Bindler hadn't seen it that way. He'd considered it to their advantage and had even recommended extending Serif's duty assignment because of that fact. Her intelligence and connections in the country had more than once proved invaluable to maintaining diplomatic security.

"Okay, so I admit to remembering she took vacation at that time," Bindler said. He shook his head with regret. "She told me she was going to tour some of the country with her father."

"Which she did," Maxwell said.

"But she was always the rebel and a consummate analyst."

"I wouldn't get down on yourself, Al," Maxwell said, feeling a bit more comfortable now and more casual. With a horrific afterthought he said, "I mean 'sir.'"

Bindler smiled. "Forget about it, Max. And forget

about what I said before. Just consider that you stepped on your dick and you took your ass-chewing for it. Far as I'm concerned, it's now forgotten and we should concentrate on damage control."

"Thanks, sir." Maxwell shook his head and shrugged. "But there really wasn't any damage done. The team is safely back in Istanbul now and nobody's the wiser. And we have a lot more information than we did before, something that might actually put us closer to blowing this thing wide open."

"So tell me about this character."

"We've identified him as Quon Ma, a high-ranker inside the Chinese Ministry of State Security. Serif's notes, which I've provided along with that picture, indicate that Ma could be a member on the Council."

"Analysis?"

"Well, Sargent believes that if Serif was right about Amocacci and Ma being a part of this group, and they both have professional experience with intelligence groups, the Council could well be composed of members in other international intelligence agencies. Specifically, she included China, Italy and the Russian GRU."

Bindler swore under his breath. "That's bad."

"It's *real* bad if true."

"But even if Serif's right and there is something to all of this, it still doesn't explain to what end. If the entire purpose of this group is to disrupt U.S. intelligence efforts, as we've been led to understand, in what way does it benefit them?"

"Well, it does strengthen the intelligence assets of anyone who's involved with the Council. It would also give them a better tactical advantage. Nearly every one of these intelligence agencies employs less than legit means to create hostilities in foreign countries. That sort of instability can make a country a hotbed for intelligence-gathering efforts."

"Assuming something about the country poses some credible threat to the parties in question," Bindler replied. "And now we have an intelligence group involved in this that I'm guessing doesn't even exist."

"What do you mean?"

"It's nothing," Bindler said. "At least nothing I can talk about, which brings me to let you know about something else. We're going to have help from Washington arriving shortly to take charge of the operation to find Serif. And when we've located her, *if* we've located her, they'll be the ones to actually do the extraction."

Maxwell didn't look happy at that announcement. "Okay. So I take it someone in DC passed this down. I don't suppose you can tell me who?"

"You're correct. Suffice it to say that the orders were…not open to interpretation. They were very clear, very direct, and I was led to understand in no uncertain terms the consequences of being creative about them."

"No wiggle room?"

"Not one inch."

Maxwell clenched his teeth and sucked air through them. "Okay, I get the picture. We'll cooperate fully with them when they arrive."

"Not them—*him*."

"*One man?*"

"That's right, and he's a full bird with the DIA, so you're to give him the same courtesy you would show me. He has full authority in this matter."

"But…this is *your* command, sir!"

Bindler waved it off although it made him swell with

pride to know that Maxwell had his back. "This consulate is actually a delegation of the State Department. At the end of the day, they run the diplomatic show. And to tell you the truth, I'm actually a bit relieved by it. This is really is the kind of job that's better handled by someone with the expertise in special operations. I'm just in charge of Marine security."

"Yeah, a job that's vitally important to continued smooth operations at this consulate. We're on United States' soil. We've all seen what can happen when security breaks down at a U.S. Consulate. Has everyone forgotten Benghazi?"

"That's entirely different and you know it," Bindler replied. "Now I'm telling you, Max, my ass is riding on the line with this one. You will extend full courtesy to Colonel Stone and you will follow his orders to the letter just as if they were my own. Are we clear?"

"Clear, sir."

The intercom buzzed on Bindler's desk.

"Yes?"

"Sir," the secretary announced, "Colonel Stone has arrived."

CHAPTER FOURTEEN

"Colonel Stone? Alan Bindler." Bindler extended his hand and Bolan shook it. Bindler then pointed to Maxwell and introduced him. "My adjutant."

Maxwell saluted smartly, which Bolan returned with equal deference, and then the pair shook hands. "It's a pleasure, sir. Welcome to Turkey."

Bolan nodded. After all three had taken a seat, the Executioner began, "I want it clear up front I have no desire to interfere with whatever you've got going here as it concerns security, Colonel Bindler. This is your show and it remains your show. My only concern is the safe return of Alara Serif. I feel she's the key to cracking this recent breach in our intelligence network and the upper echelon in Wonderland agrees."

"As do we," the colonel replied. "In fact, Max here was just telling me about something we stumbled upon recently. Max?"

The major handed Bolan a classified folder and as Bolan opened it to leaf through the contents, he said, "Ms. Serif may have been on to something. The man in that photograph is—"

"General Quon Ma," Bolan said mechanically. "Former Chinese military and now a top foreign intelligence agent with the MSS."

Maxwell made a show of trying to keep his jaw from dropping.

"I see you're informed," Bindler said, seeing Maxwell's reaction.

"Yeah," Bolan said. He looked at Maxwell. "And I apologize for cutting you off, Major, but I didn't want to waste your time by having you tell me something I already knew."

"No problem, sir," Maxwell said.

Bolan saw the brief silent exchange of knowing looks that passed between Maxwell and Bindler. He said, "Colonel, I assume by the fact you're in possession of this photograph that your people may have inadvertently overstepped the parameters of your orders from Washington not to pursue this matter above a cursory investigation."

"It's possible we might have tripped a trigger or two, yes."

"Then let me be the first to assure you that I don't care about that," Bolan said. "The way I see it, you're more familiar with this territory than I am, not to mention with whatever else Serif might have uncovered."

"What are you trying to get at, sir?" Maxwell asked.

"I'm telling you that I'd prefer to use your extensive resources to help me with this case rather than risk us working at cross purposes. I just came from a very bad situation in Central America… I can see from the surprise on your faces you didn't realize it went that deep."

"How the hell could anything that far away tie back to what's going on here?" Bindler asked.

"Because this Council of Luminárii would appear to have that kind of reach," Bolan replied. "I was told you read the after-action reports of all three of the missions in question. Those ops occurred all over the globe. That's a pretty significant reach. They even used a faction of the Islamic Brotherhood to sucker a U.S. military unit into a trap. Every man in that unit was killed. I saw the bodies with my own eyes. These people are responsible for the murder of a lot of U.S. service personnel. These were *good* people. I plan to make sure someone answers for that."

"Well, it would seem somebody is one step ahead of you on that count, sir," Maxwell said.

Bolan frowned. "Meaning?"

"While we were following up on Serif's lead to this Quon Ma, somebody tried to assassinate him."

"In fact, they didn't try—they *succeeded*," Bindler added. "And now we're trying to figure out who and why."

"I may have the answer," Bolan said. "Or at least why it came about. I ran into somebody that seemed to know everything about the Council. They even managed to capture me while I was trying to sidestep the trap their connection inside the U.S. military arranged. It didn't pan out well for him, either. As soon as they captured me, they killed their military insider. Tying up loose ends. I knew by virtue of the fact they didn't kill me outright that they had to be informed I wasn't really part of the DIA."

"So you got them to play along," Bindler said. "Nice work, Colonel."

Bolan nodded in way of thanks before continuing. "Once I got inside and allowed them to interrogate me, I put my alternate cover in place. That cover was verified. It was a cover as a spy with the NSA and, near as I can tell, it remains solid."

"But you managed to escape," Maxwell said. "How does that help us now?"

"Since the cover remains intact and since they know I know about their operation, it only makes sense I'd try to approach them. I figure the information is going to get back to the Council. Now that I've escaped, I become a liability to their operations."

Clarity seemed to fall upon Bindler as his face lit up. "Unless you can convince them you're actually worth more to their efforts alive than dead."

Bolan grinned. "Right."

"So...you're saying that you planted that whole story from the beginning," Maxwell said. "But how did you know it would pay off?"

"I didn't," Bolan said. "I was only playing a hunch. The way I saw it, if they were setting a trap for me with the intent of killing me, they had plenty of opportunities to do it. Instead, they went out of their way to capture me at some significant cost. And they even threatened to terminate me once I revealed my knowledge about the Council. But whoever was running the show in Central America didn't have the authority to just kill me outright. That bought my people enough time to get inside and extract me."

"But if they were planning to kill you," Bindler said, "wouldn't contacting them now just give them an opportunity to try again?"

"Under other circumstances, yeah," Bolan replied. "But in this case I'm guessing this is the break they've been hoping for. You see, up until now, it's obvious they haven't been able to turn a U.S. intelligence asset. Their group is incomplete. I think they're trying to destabilize U.S. military intelligence operations. So far, they've managed to pull off a few small-time jobs. But imagine how much more impact they could have if they actually knew someone high up with inside secrets."

"We'd considered that," Bindler said. "But what we haven't been able to figure out is why they want to do it at all. What does it buy them?"

"That's simple. Power. Consider the purpose of U.S. military intelligence. It's to provide our armed forces with a tactical advantage over its enemies. Any way they can find to weaken that network would give their own countries more power and a greater footprint in the military community. They could predict our moves and countermoves, and adjust their own military strategy accordingly."

"But why would countries like Italy or China want to risk all-out conflict with the United States?" Maxwell said. "That's suicide!"

"It's not about making open war with the United States. It's about making U.S. military might less effective. Imagine the advantage it would give other countries if they were able to predict with some certainty our most secret military operational capacity. Military intelligence is more than just the keeping of military secrets. It's about signals intelligence, new technology and capabilities within the defense industrial complex, and increasing our protective force capabilities against terrorists. Compromising military intelligence weakens the effectiveness of our nation as a whole on a grand scale. It reduces our political influence, as well, leaving gaps these other countries can step into."

"But why would the particular countries choose to work together? For example, there's no benefit in an alliance between Italy and China."

"Maybe not one we can see or understand," Bolan said. "But that doesn't mean just because we're blind to them they don't exist."

"Let's suppose there are other intelligence agents from a variety of countries involved. Each would have something significant to gain by just such an alliance. And it would give them a way to weaken the U.S."

"So this could be about retribution of some kind," Bindler remarked.

Bolan splayed his hands. "Possibly. Why not? It's no secret the general opinion about the U.S. these days isn't terribly favorable. They view us little more than thugs for the United Nations, as the world police that go unchallenged because of our significant fiscal and international resources. To destabilize our military might is to destabilize our country, and gives others the chance to slide into the number-one slot."

"And, unfortunately," Maxwell interjected, "if the U.S. loses its influence in some of the areas it could well spell doom for our allies and put some of those dangerous countries back on the map in terms of their military capabilities."

Bolan nodded. "It would be almost like a reset of the Soviet war machine and the cold war."

"Global consequences," Bindler muttered. "It's unthinkable."

"That's why it's important we stop it. Now I have a plan to get inside, but I'm going to need your help."

"What can we do, Colonel?" Bindler asked.

"I understand you have eyes on Gastone Amocacci?"

Maxwell nodded. "Yeah, we got him under twenty-four-hour surveillance."

"Then listen up," Bolan said. "Because we can use that to get me an introduction."

International Airspace

WHEN DEREK SAVITCH heard Wehr's report and received news that the American had escaped Central America, he realized their plans were coming apart.

Somehow, Amocacci had managed to screw it up, and Savitch had no idea where to begin to try to fix it. His first thought had been to call for the immediate elimination of Gastone Amocacci and his woman, but he recanted the idea. It would serve no purpose, and it would especially create more problems than it would solve. It hadn't occurred to him that it might be Amocacci himself who was the leak in the Council. If that were true, to kill him would only bring potentially worse consequences and a whole shitload of revenge onto Savitch's head. He didn't need that.

Savitch had never been crazy about the whole idea of the Council of Luminárii when Hurley Willham had first brought the idea to him. In fact, he'd thought maybe the crazy Brit had let his time in the SIS and his shit assignment in Bulgaria drive him to desperation. But when he'd seen the money it could make and the other potential benefits to such an alliance between various intelligence groups, he'd begun to understand the long-term profits to be reaped. This thing was a cash cow, and Savitch had only begun to make money.

Amocacci had wired a quarter-million dollars into their secure account. After Wehr's cut, that left a fifty-fifty split between him and Willham. A cool fifty-thousand dollars of untraceable cash. And for what?

To order someone to pull the trigger on some spy. And there was no way any of it could be traced back to Savitch. He could disappear back to his home territory in Montreal and nobody would ever be the wiser.

Only one problem: it wasn't enough.

It wasn't nearly enough to live the lifestyle to which he wished to become accustomed. He supposed he could have stiffed Willham out of his money, but it was Willham who had the upper hand and the inside line to the Council. Willham knew how to manipulate each of his colleagues whereas Savitch didn't have a clue. And it wasn't Savitch's way. To be sure, he believed in keeping a legitimate face to all of his business dealings. There was no point in pissing off men who had the potential to make him lots of cash, and Willham definitely did at that, even if he had to take a circuitous route to attain it.

Now, soaring above the Atlantic aboard a private jet courtesy of the Council of Luminárii, Savitch considered his next move. The death of Quon Ma would most certainly result in some sort of retaliation. It wouldn't be long before Turkey was crawling with a veritable army of MSS agents, if not men who were loyal to the MSS cause. They wouldn't take the death of one of their most able men lightly, and they would want to make certain that someone paid. And they would succeed in making a public example of the individual or group they deemed responsible. For the Chinese, it wasn't about revenge or even about honor. It was about making a statement that warned everyone else who might want to seize the advantage from the situation.

Given the terms of his contract with Amocacci, Savitch knew he needed to get to Istanbul and do some damage control before it all came apart on him.

The personal phone aboard the jet rang and he picked it up gingerly. "Hello, Hurley."

"Don't hello *me*," Willham replied. "What the bloody hell is going on with you? I give you one simple task and you can't even pull that off."

"What are you going on about?" Savitch asked. "We got the job done."

"The hell you did! You dumb, stupid, bloody prick!"

"Careful, Hurley," Savitch said. "I'm quite fond of you and our arrangement, but don't think to take it so far that I'll stand idly by and let you hurl abuses at me for no reason. Now calm your ass down and tell me what's going on."

"Ma's still alive."

"What do you mean 'alive'? He's dead. I have complete assurances he's nothing more than a corpse."

"Well, then, someone's lying to you because I just got wind an hour ago that one of my people saw him alive and well. Your little errand boy failed."

"Wehr isn't my little errand boy. He's a complete professional with a one hundred percent success rate. If he says he killed Quon Ma, then I believe him."

"So what are you trying to say? My man's wrong? That my contact—who I can assure you I've known for more bloody years than I care to count and relied upon time and again—is seeing ghosts?"

"If Ma's still alive, why hasn't he contacted you?"

"Because he's safer if whoever it is who tried to kill him knows he's dead. It doesn't take a fucking genius to figure that out."

"Okay, let's suppose for a moment that your people are right and Ma *is* still alive. What can we do about it? Will Amocacci ask for the money back?"

Willham was quiet for a moment, and his lack of an immediate response told Savitch those wheels were turning. Willham had an utterly convoluted mind, and Savitch admitted that at times he had difficulty keeping up with the British agent's intuition, let alone his keen intellect.

"He won't."

"How can you be sure?"

"As long as Ma is able to maintain the legitimacy of his alleged demise, Amocacci and the rest of the Council will have no reason to doubt it."

"It will, of course, create a delay in our plans since Kirklareli will soon be overrun with MSS agents looking to capture the assassin."

"I don't see that happening."

"Why not?"

"Ma knows just as well as we do that if the Chinese government believes him to be dead they will respond in force. Ma can't let that happen since it would risk exposing him before he's conducted his own search for the assassin. No—until his people have the opportunity to learn everything they can about the reasons behind this incident, Ma will keep his government at bay. He will tell the upper echelon, and he will most assuredly keep them at arm's length."

"I hadn't thought of that," Savitch admitted.

"Well, that's why I don't require you to do any of the thinking."

Asshole, Savitch thought.

"So what are you currently planning to do?"

"I'm heading to Istanbul. It's time to do some damage control with Amocacci."

"Fine. Just make sure he isn't aware you're in the

country. He may want to meet with you and we can't have that," Willham stated.

"Understood. So who's next on the list?"

"Let's allow it to die down first. Then we'll get to work on determining our next step. And, Savitch?"

"Yes."

"No more fuck-ups or any future deals are off. Understood?"

"Yeah."

With that, Willham hung up. Savitch would have liked to reach through the phone and choke the pompous jackass to death, but he knew he *had* to work with Willham as long as possible. It was important to stroke the guy's ego and keep him on Savitch's side. Eventually, Willham would probably be like all the others and outlive his usefulness, and Savitch would have to deal with him in the same way he'd dealt with those who'd come before him. But until that day, Savitch would collect as much of a payday and as often as possible.

After all, there was still so much money to be made.

CHAPTER FIFTEEN

Istanbul, Turkey

Mack Bolan sat in the taxi as rain hammered the roof. The driver had stopped at the curb in front of one of the city's fancier hotels. According to the Executioner's intelligence, Gastone Amocacci was known to frequent the hotel because of its excellent restaurant. Apparently the food and drink in this place was some of the best to be found, and Amocacci was known to avail himself of places just like it after a long day in his front job.

Bolan had been waiting outside the hotel for the past twenty minutes. He could see the driver was beginning to get impatient, and he wondered if maybe he should let the guy drop him a few blocks away and rendezvous with Maxwell and his men.

As if fate had read the warrior's mind, Bolan felt the vibration of his cell phone. He withdrew the device and put it to his ear. "Yes?"

"We just spotted his car passing us, sir," Maxwell said.

"Good eye," Bolan stated. "I'll take it from here. We'll go just as planned. Fifteen minutes and you park in front of the hotel as conspicuously as possible."

"Aye, aye, sir."

Bolan paid the cabbie with a hefty tip and exited the vehicle.

Once inside the hotel, Bolan trolled the lobby until he found a plush wing-backed chair that afforded him an unobstructed view of the front doors. He removed his drenched overcoat, sat and took a complimentary magazine from a nearby coffee table. He crossed his legs casually and began to thumb through it. He knew the ruse wouldn't work with a guy like Amocacci. The former Interpol intelligence agent would spot him as a phony the minute he laid eyes on him. Good. Bolan hoped to play on Amocacci's natural paranoia and use that to get inside his guard.

Bolan didn't have to wait long. Amocacci came through the front doors a minute later and the Executioner locked eyes with him only a moment before returning to his magazine. Amocacci didn't even break stride and Bolan smiled as if he'd read something amusing, when in fact he knew he'd played his cards right. Amocacci had definitely made Bolan for being more than just a casual observer or guest of the hotel. Now all Bolan had to do was wait.

Amocacci went to the front desk, which Bolan found a bit odd. Intelligence had it that Amocacci only availed himself of the restaurant. For all they knew he'd never rented a suite at the hotel. Not that he couldn't afford it.

Bolan began to sift through the possibilities. Amocacci might be checking for messages, or he might have some sort of connection with the hotel staff. It was possible he was doing this because he'd spotted Bolan. A guy with Amocacci's background would definitely have alternate plans in place should he think he'd come under observation.

Bolan wondered if what transpired now was something similar to the events that led to Alara Serif's disappearance. Of course, they had plenty of evidence to indicate Serif's captors had tailed her vehicle and then attempted to spring their trap at the most opportune time. But for them to do that they would have to have seen her as a threat. For her to be a threat, Amocacci would have known she'd been tailing him to begin with. The most disturbing aspect of that thought was the viability of Serif's analysis. If Amocacci *had* known he was under surveillance, had he fed Serif a whole bunch of false leads? If so, nothing she'd reported back to Washington could be trusted.

Bolan mentally filed that fact and determined he'd have to exercise a double measure of caution.

After Amocacci finished having a discussion with the desk clerk, he turned and headed for the elevator. Bolan stood and started to walk toward him, but he didn't get on. He waited out of sight for the doors to close and then watched as the ticker counted up to the fifth floor. It paused there for a moment and then began to descend again, but oddly instead of stopping at ground level it bypassed and continued to the first and only underground level.

Bolan had studied the layout of the hotel when first choosing it as his mark, and he knew the basement included laundry and kitchen facilities and a staff access to underground parking for deliveries and employees. Bolan waited at the elevator bank for another minute or so and then when a young couple arrived and pushed the button for the elevator, he turned and went in search of the stairs.

He found the stairwell a minute later and immediately headed toward the basement level. Amocacci's attempt to fool him had been sloppy, at best. Amocacci had probably planned for Bolan to take the stairs or another elevator to the fifth floor and not wait to see if the elevator returned to the ground level. It was a pretty good bet there were some goons waiting on the fifth floor, either in the stairwell or hallway near the elevators, or both. They'd have a really long wait.

The Executioner pushed open the metal door after peering through a small, wire-meshed glass window. The door opened onto a long, narrow corridor that terminated at another door identical to the first. Something pricked the hairs on Bolan's neck and he liberated his Beretta 93-R from shoulder leather, keeping his back to the wall as he proceeded up the narrow corridor. He was thankful for the sparse, recessed lighting fixtures because the close space would have been like shooting fish in a barrel for even the worst shot.

Bolan reached the far door unscathed. He peered through the window and saw that it opened onto the parking garage. From that vantage point he could make out the doors off to the right that led to probably other service areas such as the kitchen and laundry. He also spotted a service elevator and its position suggested it had been the one ridden by Amocacci.

The Executioner verified nobody was visible and started to open the door when he heard movement behind him and the freeing of the door latch. He turned and crouched in time to avoid the volley of autofire unloaded by two men toting machine pistols.

Bolan leveled the Beretta in a two-handed grip and squeezed the trigger. He'd set the weapon for 3-round bursts. The first two rounds caught one of the enemy assailants in the gut and tore through organs and tender flesh. The third punched through his chest and drove him into the back wall.

The other man went to his belly and tried to reacquire a sight picture on Bolan, but the Executioner beat him to the punch. Bolan took aim and snapped off another three rounds. The man's head exploded as the 9 mm hardball slugs caved in his head and smashed through brain tissue, erupting in a bloody spray that painted the area around him in red splotches.

The echo of gunfire died and Bolan rose and went back to the door. He pushed through and emerged onto the parking garage. The area was more open and gave him a larger span to cover, but at least he had running room and it reduced the risk of being caught in narrow confines should his enemy attempt to pin him down with a cross fire. Bolan crossed the expanse in no time and reached a set of heavy, double doors. He tried a handle, found it unlocked, and then checked his flank before proceeding through the opening.

Bolan eased the door closed behind him and let his eyes adjust to the gloom. He'd thought this would take him into the kitchen, but instead he found himself in what looked like the boiler room. It was hot and loud, and surrounded by plenty of metal and concrete. There was no better place to find cover from gunfire, although the increased risk of being hit by ricochets was a given.

Bolan ventured farther into the boiler room and soon found a set of concrete steps that seemed to lead even deeper into the bowels of the hotel. Bolan descended, anyway, thumbing the Beretta's selector switch to single-shot mode and proceeding with the pistol extended to arm's length at eye level. There was a light at the bottom of the steps, and just beyond that, a man stood with his back to the stairs, leaning against the wall with his weapon slung casually over his shoulder.

The Executioner holstered his pistol, cat-footed his way to the guard and pounced, twisting the weapon in such a way that the sling pinned the man's arm to his side. He then snaked his left forearm around the guy's neck and clamped the muscles against the guard's throat. He wrapped the hand of the choking arm behind the buttstock of the rifle, which acted as a counter brace and made the chokehold stronger than it would have been without support.

Within thirty seconds the guard lost consciousness and Bolan eased his limp body to the ground.

The corridor the sentry had been guarding terminated at a dead end. Bolan continued along the concrete wall that dripped with dampness, turning to look behind him to ensure another ambush didn't ensue while also watching the area ahead. Two doors stood in the wall to his right, the opposite being either an exterior supporting or stem wall, perhaps part of the foundation. The first room he found was empty. The second room he encountered was quite another story. Lying in a reddish bath of light, crunched together on a bunk with her back to him, was a young woman with long dark hair.

Through the small open slot of the window Bolan called, "Alana Serif?"

The woman came awake with a start, flipped her entire body on the bunk and peered at him with dark, intense eyes that seemed afire in the red glow of the single dim light high on the cell wall.

"Who are you?" she asked.

"My name is Colonel Brandon Stone. I'm with the DIA."

"Please tell me you're here to rescue me."

"I wasn't," Bolan said. As he saw her face begin to fall he added, "But I am now. Just hang tight while I figure out how to get you out of here."

"Did you neutralize the guard?"

"Yeah."

"Check his pockets—he's the one with the keys."

Bolan nodded and went immediately to the fallen guard. He rifled through the pants' pockets first, then checked the breast pockets and finally found a large key. Bolan rushed back to the door of the makeshift cell, opened it and stepped inside. He went to the foot of her bunk and spied the restraint. He withdrew a pocketknife and quickly cut through the leather, since he didn't have the key to the small lock holding the restraint in place.

"So—" Bolan began, pocketing the knife and turning toward her.

The Executioner hadn't been ready for the woman to react in the way she did. Her agile form came off the bunk in a blinding motion and she charged at him like an angry badger. He stepped back, his combat-honed reflexes the only thing that saved him from the nails she tried to rake across his eyes. Bolan swatted her hand aside, contacting the nerve just above the wrist, which would cause her entire arm to go numb. He then turned inward as he sidestepped, wrapped his arm around her waist and executed a hip toss that took her off her feet. At the last minute he grabbed her body so that she didn't strike the concrete floor with the full force.

The impact still seemed tough enough to knock the wind out of her, and she wheezed a few times as her phrenic nerves struggled to recover. Bolan pinned her to the floor easily with his superior weight and strength, one knee on a pressure point between her hip and pelvis while pinning her shoulder with a hand.

"Mind telling me what you're trying to do?" Bolan said through clenched teeth.

She struggled, trying to escape, but realized the futility of it. Her breath still came in short spurts but she finally managed enough wind to reply, "I thought maybe you were trying to play me, get me to think you were an ally and this was a real escape."

"Well, I *am* your ally and this *is* a real escape," Bolan said. "Or at least it will be if you can trust me long enough for us to both get out of here alive. Now, are you going to be good or do I knock you cold and carry you out of here?"

She raised her hands and nodded slowly.

Bolan climbed to his feet and then lent a hand, pulling her up after him. She stood looking at him a moment and then forced a smile. "Sorry. But these days it's tough to trust anybody."

"Yeah, tell me about it," the Executioner replied. "You *are* Alara Serif?"

She nodded. "I guess someone in DC *was* reading my reports."

"You drew some attention, to put it mildly," Bolan said.

"I'm hoping it isn't going to take getting kidnapped every time to get someone to pay attention to me," she said, dusting the dirt from her hands.

"You'll be glad to know you got a whole lot of people paying attention to you," Bolan said.

Something clanged somewhere in the distance,

maybe the door of a delivery truck or a car driving over a drainage gate. "But we don't have time to get into that now. We need to get you out of here."

"Lead the way," Serif replied.

THEY MANAGED TO escape the hotel without attracting attention.

Maxwell wanted to speed them directly to the consulate, but Bolan counseled him against it. The Executioner figured it was better to get Serif as far away from danger as possible. Neither a hotel nor the consulate would do, and they couldn't risk going to Serif's apartment. Instead he had Maxwell take them to the other side of town where they checked into a tiny hotel room where Bolan and Jack Grimaldi had set up a sort of makeshift headquarters.

"Well, what would you like me to tell Colonel Bindler, sir?" Maxwell asked.

Bolan lent him a warning smile. "Tell him you were following my orders. My op, my decision. And if he wonders why you won't tell him where you dropped us, tell him those were my orders, too."

"Aye, aye, sir."

When they had gone, Bolan took Serif to their tiny little room on the second floor of the run-down building and introduced her to Jack Grimaldi. The Stony Man pilot's gregarious nature and devilish charm were an instant hit with the woman.

"They're not five-star accommodations," Grimaldi said when he noticed her inspecting the lounge area immediately off the two bedrooms. "But it's clean and cozy, and nobody who's anybody will bother us here."

Serif nodded as she looked up at the cracked ceiling

with major water spots and the cobwebs in the corners, and said, "Charming."

"I've stayed in worse for more money," Grimaldi quipped with a shrug.

"You want coffee?" Bolan asked, going to the burner plate where a plain metal percolator, the kind used for camping, sat with just the hint of steam coming off it.

"It's fresh," Grimaldi added.

"No, thanks. I'm a tea person."

"Sorry, no tea." Bolan poured himself a cup and then they sat in the wicker chairs that surrounded a table that barely came to knee height on Serif. "So tell me everything you know about Amocacci. You mentioned you spoke to him personally?"

Serif nodded. "He claims the entire operation, the Council of Luminárii, and all of the data I've collected in the past eight months was completely falsified. He says he knew I had him under observation months ago and that he used his connections to feed that information to me."

"And how did he explain that?" Bolan asked.

She shook her head. "He went on and on about how he could quote some of the content of my reports chapter and verse, and that was because he was the one who'd staged the whole thing. And he kept bragging about the associates he had on the inside of the DIA, or maybe someone high up working inside the U.S. Consulate."

"Anything else you can think of?"

"Well…" Serif paused a moment and blew a strand of dark hair off her forehead. "Nothing that stands out. He did seem to have an awful lot of negative things to say regarding the intelligence community at large."

That piqued even Grimaldi's curiosity and he'd only been half listening. "In what way?"

"I don't know exactly." Serif looked Bolan in the eyes. "To tell the truth, Colonel Stone, he sounded a bit like a crazy man. He definitely has some ax to grind with U.S. military intelligence, although I couldn't tell you why. And he did indicate he had some associates and they were planning something big. Something *really* big."

"The fact of the matter is that Amocacci probably is a whack job," Bolan said. "But that doesn't mean he's not as smart as a fox. As I suspected he would, he spotted me almost immediately on entering that hotel. And he had some definite connections in there. Beside the guard in that old storage and freezer area where you were kept prisoner, he somehow manages to run a legitimate business concern in Turkey. And his personal record is as clean as a whistle."

"That comes from his association with the Fellini family. Lady Allegra and her entire entourage are highly respected throughout Europe and the better part of Southeast Asia. And Amocacci's business dealings, while best not looked at too closely, bring the Turkish government a lot of money. As long as Amocacci continues paying his dues, they'll look the other way. That much I'm certain is true based on my analysis."

Bolan shook his head. "I'm not interested in going after any of his business concerns, or even severing his ties with Turkish officials. In fact, I'm hoping to exploit that as a way to get inside his organization."

"To what end?"

"So I can cut the heart out of it," Bolan said.

"You're not really DIA, are you?"

"Was there any doubt?" Bolan grinned. "I won't insult your intelligence by trying to convince you I'm a real military officer."

"Oh, you're definitely ex-military," Serif said with a smile of her own. "You got all the signs, anyway. I'm more curious to know, however, why you think exploiting his business concerns will bring you closer to cracking this thing wide-open."

"Something you may not have learned in all your training and schooling is that any organization must do its fair share of dealing with the less savory elements of the criminal underworld. In order for them to operate securely, they need to work cooperatively with everyone from terrorists to dope dealers to organized crime. They don't have the luxury of operating autonomously."

"Sarge is right," Grimaldi said. "Even the most powerful governments in the world can't do what they do without at least showing a little deference to the bad guys."

"Sarge?" Serif inquired. She looked at Bolan and smiled. "I thought you were a colonel."

Bolan ignored her. "What Jack's getting at is that the Council of Luminárii isn't the angelic and benevolent group it would like everyone to think it is. Just hours after your conversation with Amocacci, an assassin executed a man named Quon Ma. A former military officer and now high-ranking intelligence officer with Chinese MSS."

Serif nodded. "Ma was one of the other individuals I identified as being a possible member of the Council."

"If I had to take an educated guess, I'd say you're right. There's no way this Council, if it operates as you say it does, would risk contracting with an outside group to kill one of its own. After all, they're not nearly as strong as individuals."

Serif nodded in agreement. "It wouldn't do for them to work at cross-purposes with one another when they could accomplish much more together."

"Exactly. And it's *that* fact I'm going to use to take Amocacci off balance and keep him that way until I can control the situation my way."

"If you can find him."

"That's where you come in," Bolan replied.

"Okay, I can help you. But you have to take me along."

"No," Bolan said, shaking his head. "I have a responsibility to make sure you're delivered safely back to U.S. territory. That means the consulate. But I need to know where Amocacci is before I attempt that. I need to get his attention focused on something new. A fresh face. Once I get him to come around to my side, then we can move you. For now, you'll stay here with Jack."

Grimaldi smiled. "I even got a deck of cards."

"No disrespect, Stone—Lord knows I owe you a huge debt of gratitude for saving my life—but I don't answer to you. I take my orders only from Colonel Bindler."

"And I outrank Bindler on this particular operation," Bolan said. "So now you'll take orders from me for the duration of this operation."

"I *deserve* to be in on this when you take Amocacci down," Serif argued. "And that's the only way you'll get my cooperation. You want information on Amocacci's whereabouts, my tagging along is part of the deal."

"Look, Alara. Amocacci's still going to be sniffing around looking for you, and I can't risk him knowing we're associated or the deal will be blown before it's made. Just do as I'm telling you and if the opportunity presents itself, I'll let you in on a piece of the action. Deal?"

Serif thought it over a long moment and then stuck out her hand. "Deal. But I'm telling you now, Colonel. If you go back on the deal, there isn't a place on Earth where you can hide that I won't find you and make you pay for it."

"I don't doubt it," Bolan replied.

CHAPTER SIXTEEN

Mack Bolan located the building in downtown Istanbul where Amocacci maintained a small office on the sixth floor.

Getting into the building and up to Amocacci's office was essentially child's play. The Italian looked quite surprised, in fact, when Bolan's imposing form strolled through the front door of the office. The secretary tried to stop him, but Bolan continued right by her and walked into Amocacci's office as if he owned the place.

"Sir, he just—!"

Amocacci raised a hand and calmly replied, "I understand, Sari. Not your fault. Don't worry about it, he's an old associate. Just close the door behind you and hold my calls."

Sari threw Bolan a ferocious look before leaving to attend to Amocacci's instructions.

The man rose and waved Bolan toward one of the leather armchairs in front of his desk. As the soldier started to sit, he noticed the sunlight coming through the slat of the partially open blinds glint off the snub-nosed pistol the man now leveled at Bolan's midsection. The Executioner took note of the gun, looked Amocacci in the eyes and smiled before slowly taking his seat.

"Easy with that," Bolan said. "I wouldn't want to get blood on these nice carpets."

"Carpets can be cleaned, Mr....?"

"I'll be happy to explain if you put down the pistol," Bolan replied.

"Why should I do that? I could say you were an intruder. The police wouldn't blame me in the least."

"They might after you told your secretary that I was an old associate," Bolan said. "Plus, I'm unarmed. I don't think you'll kill me anyway."

"And why is that?"

"Because you're entirely too curious as to why I'm here."

Amocacci sighed and took his seat. He laid the pistol on the desk in front of him. "I saw you at the hotel."

"Yes, I guess I wasn't as careful as I'd hoped."

"It's interesting," Amocacci continued, obviously ignoring Bolan's almost flamboyant attempt to be charming, "that just shortly after I saw you in the hotel, two of my men were killed and something was stolen from me."

"It wasn't me," Bolan said quickly. "But I know who it was."

"And that is?"

"U.S. government agents. From the U.S. Consulate in Istanbul. They were sent by their commanding officer, who really isn't as much a CO as he is the head of a vast intelligence network."

"You seem quite well informed," Amocacci said. "But you still haven't told me your name or the reason for your interest in me and my business."

"It's quite simple, really." Bolan made a show of studying the palms of his hands, letting the suspense play out a little longer. "My name is Matt Cooper. I'm an intelligence cryptanalyst for the National Security Agency. I was sent in to uncover a mole working within military intelligence channels out of a base in Colorado. Our attempts to find our mole went wrong during a subsequent operation in Central America."

Bolan had been surreptitiously watching for any reaction. He didn't get anything until mention of that last little bit. Amocacci had a tell: an almost imperceptible twitch in his left eyebrow. Bolan decided to play out a little more rope to see where it took him.

"It was when I connected with the agent there while being held prisoner I realized what was really going on. We'd gotten some vague reports of some kind of freelance group—an international conglomerate of high-ranking intelligence assets that had banded together. Only trouble is, we didn't know for what purpose. But what I did learn was that there was a significant amount of cash available for anyone within U.S. intelligence circles who might be willing to stand up." Bolan splayed his hands and said, "Well, I'm your guy!"

"I don't have the faintest idea what you're talking about," Amocacci said as he leaned back in his chair.

"Really? Really, that's the best you can do? The old 'I don't know anything' routine?" Bolan snorted with derision. "Come on, Mr. Amocacci! I know what you're into, and I know who you're dealing with. Hell, half the spooks I know have heard the rumblings of this super-secret group of vigilantes, or whatever it is you claim to be. And frankly, I don't really care about any of that. I'm just interested in the cash."

"And what makes you think there's any money to be had from me?"

"Are you denying it?"

Amocacci said nothing for a long time. At one point, Bolan thought maybe Amocacci would retrieve his pistol and shoot Bolan. He hoped the guy didn't try it because he had been lying about not being armed. He wasn't stupid enough to go into the situation utterly defenseless, and if Amocacci made a play with the pistol, the Executioner would have to respond in kind. There was a fairly good chance Amocacci possessed enough skills as a marksman that he could take Bolan with the first shot, but he'd be harder pressed to hit a moving target if he was at all out of practice. Bolan, on the other hand, was well practiced in such close-quarter encounters and he just didn't miss.

Amocacci finally sighed. "I think you should leave now."

"So you're turning down my offer," Bolan replied.

"You didn't make an offer."

"You didn't give me a chance."

"I'm just not who you think I am. I'm not involved with so mundane a matter as you might think. In fact, you don't know anything about me, Cooper."

"And you really don't know anything about me," Bolan countered. "Which is exactly what would make this such a mutually beneficial arrangement."

"In what way?"

"Well, what would you say if I could help you with this most recent problem?" Bolan said.

"And to what problem are you referring?"

Bolan didn't hesitate. "The assassination of one of your own. A certain Chinese VIP?"

Amocacci's already somewhat impassive expression went suddenly cold and stony. Bolan thought he'd made an error at first, perhaps misjudging Amocacci's intelligence and savvy. The guy had been playing the intelligence game long enough to know it was filled with moves and countermoves.

"I don't know what you're talking about."

Bolan chuckled. "Really. That's funny because my sources tell me you know a *lot* about it. How are we going to become allies if we're not willing to trust each other?"

"You sound awfully naive. There are no allies in this business—no true friendships upon which one can rely. In fact, there's no room for friendship at all. It's merely a game. Governments and other entities maneuver us around the board like chess pieces. We're all pawns, you see, forced to play in one mindless game after another. We are sacrificed, unable to determine our own destinies. This is what the intelligence communities of today are all about."

"You'll forgive my candor," Bolan interjected, "but I don't really give a crap about your cause. I'm interested in making some money, and in return I can help you."

"Help us do what?"

It was the first time Amocacci had publicly acknowledged that "he" was actually a "we," and Bolan could now tell he'd grabbed the man's interest. It was time to tighten the noose.

"After seeing your handiwork in Guatemala and having a little chat with your man, I got to thinking that you can't do this alone. Despite your significant resources, you have one thing you can bleed more than any other. Cold, hard cash. On the other side of the coin, you need assassins, informants, weapons and other such sundries to barter with. I can provide those things because of all the various avenues my former employer has its fingers in."

"Your *former* employer?"

"Weren't you listening?" Bolan asked. "I *worked* for the NSA. But since I didn't go straight back there, and instead came to Istanbul to make contact with your little enterprise, I'm on the black list. A fugitive. I'm unwanted, and to cut their losses the only reason they'd look for me now is to cut off my head."

"You're forgetting something, Mr. Cooper," Amocacci said. "I've been doing this for a very long time. I know you were part of the military operation to take down the foreign agent operating within the DIA. Who do you think it was who set you up?"

Bolan produced a humorless smile. He now knew he had Amocacci against the ropes—the guy had just admitted that it was he who had played the USAF special ops team out of Tyndall for a sucker. But he couldn't let Amocacci know he knew. He would have to put the blame where it originally belonged.

"Not you, if that's what you're suggesting. A guy named Randy Shoup put the screws to me. He sent me right into a trap. If it hadn't been for my own friends, assets that you say don't really exist in our business, I'd be dead right now along with the rest of them."

"So why come here?" Amocacci asked. "If you think I or any of my associates had anything to do with the ambush, wouldn't your arrival here be nothing short of walking straight into a pit of vipers?"

"Your analogy is certainly colorful," Bolan replied. "You obviously have a flair for the dramatic. But the fact is, I'm a businessman. I have no more love for the intelligence communities than you do. Especially not military intelligence."

"And why is that?"

"They're ineffective," Bolan said with a shrug. "And I've stuck my neck out so many times for the NSA while all they've done is nothing but deny my existence."

"You're breaking my heart. And the plain fact of the matter is that of all the intelligence assets or agents in the world, I would trust someone from the United States the *least*."

"Except that hasn't stopped you from trying to recruit somebody on the inside," Bolan said. "Has it?"

When Amocacci remained silent, Bolan pressed on.

"I can see I've struck the nail on the head. Good, that will make this next part even easier. You see, I realized you had a problem when your guy in Guatemala tried to recruit me."

"Recruit you?"

"Yeah. You didn't know that?"

"I don't believe you."

Bolan shrugged. "Suit yourself, friend. But that doesn't make it any less true. Oh, they'd planned to kill me at first. That is until they realized that the CO of that team had attempted to dupe me, as well. I was sent as a DIA officer to find out where they had the mole in their organization. A snoop being sent to snoop the snoops. Only problem was, the guy they sent me to work with apparently turned out to be the same guy they were sending me to investigate. He got wise to me early."

"How?"

"That's the part I don't know," Bolan said matter-of-factly. "But my guess is he was working for you. Or at least one of your people. And you might as well not deny it because you just basically confirmed it."

Amocacci nodded slowly. "You have my interest so far. Go on."

"Look, it's no sweat off my back if you've got a hard-on for U.S. military intelligence. They just tried to kill me and I got no support from my own people when I told them that. So if that's their attitude, so be it. I can throw in my lot with you. I figure my chances aren't that great either way, so why not at least try to make some money and retire to some nice, cozy, out-of-the-way island country where there's no extradition treaty."

"You still haven't told me how you can benefit me."

"Besides the massive intelligence portfolio I can build for you on U.S. military operations, I'm also quite connected with many less reputable enterprises. I can get you just about anything on the black market. That means I can not only supply you with information critical to striking at high-value targets, I can also arrange your equipment and other needs for said missions."

"In return for?"

Bolan rubbed his hands together. "Some of that cold, hard cash I mentioned before."

"I already have enough resources in that area. Sorry."

"Oh, yes. The resources that tried to recruit me for a job."

"We've covered that ground already, Mr. Cooper, and as I mentioned before, I don't believe you. And beside the fact, you've still not given me one reason to trust you."

"What exactly do you think I was doing at the hotel last night?"

"I'm not sure."

"I was there to warn you," Bolan said. "Not only were you followed, but someone had the hotel under surveillance."

"Someone? Come now. I could tell you that much." At that point, Amocacci rose and strolled to a small side bar. He poured himself a drink but didn't offer Bolan one.

The Executioner made a show of pretending to ignore the slight. "Most likely agents from the U.S. government. There's a faction operating out of the U.S. Consulate. I think it might have been one of their teams that took whatever it was you say belonged to you."

"This is all very intriguing," Amocacci said, sitting with his drink. "But even if I were to believe what you're telling me, I wouldn't be able to take action until I'd consulted with my colleagues."

Bolan nodded and rose, fishing into his pocket. He produced a card with a single number emblazoned in plain black ink and tossed it onto Amocacci's desk. "I'll tell you what. You make some inquiries and if you decide you'd like to make a deal, you call me at that number."

"That won't be necessary, I assure you. I have no desire to do business with you, Mr. Cooper. Ever."

"Fine," Bolan replied nonchalantly. "Keep it, anyway. Never know when you might change your mind. And you might not want to wait too long."

As Bolan turned and headed for the door Amocacci asked, "Why?"

"Because word has it you're next on the hit list," Bolan said before he walked out and closed the door behind him.

THE EXECUTIONER WAITED until he was on the street and had gone about a block before he whipped out his cell phone and dialed a secure number. The connection took him through multiple satellite relays and a variety of encryption algorithms before connecting him with the hotline at Stony Man Farm.

"Price, here."

"Do you ever sleep?"

She laughed. "Not much, these days. I don't really do enough to relax."

"I can think of some ways to fix that problem."

"Stop it," Price replied good-naturedly. "Less empty promises and more facts."

"Fine. I think I have Amocacci dangling from the line but I don't know if I'll be able to keep him there."

"So you don't think he'll take you up on your offer?"

"He tried to pretend he wasn't interested, but I have the feeling he'll look into it very thoroughly. Or at least he'll call his contact."

"Well, we haven't had any luck yet identifying the man you spoke with in Guatemala," Price replied. "I don't know that we will. But it certainly isn't because you gave us a poor description."

"It was a long shot," Bolan said. "If I had managed to get a photograph of him you'd probably have a name to put to the face by now. What about travels out of Guatemala?"

"Nothing of significance, but that comes as no surprise. Travel in and out of that country is so poorly regulated it would be hard to find anything that wouldn't seem like we were grasping at straws. We certainly didn't see many Americans in and out of there during the window you gave us."

"Maybe he went out privately."

"You're sure he was American?"

"I can't be completely sure," Bolan said. "His accent was a little difficult to place. It had a slight East Coast pinch to it, but I couldn't swear he was from the area."

"Canadian, perhaps?"

"Maybe."

"So what's your plan?"

"I'm not sure yet. I thought Amocacci would bite," Bolan replied. "I wasn't really expecting him to take what I told him at face value. He may still take the bait, but I don't know if we have the time to wait. If it takes too long, I'll have to take a more direct approach."

"Walking into the guy's office was *pretty* direct, Striker."

"Yeah, but it still offered him some wiggle room. By direct, I mean forceful."

"I get you." Price sighed. "Meanwhile, I'll keep looking at Serif's intelligence. Maybe there's something I overlooked that will help you."

"That would be good. You can bet if I need something, I'll need it in a hurry."

"Understood. Take care."

"You, too."

Bolan disconnected in time to see a glint of light on metal in his peripheral vision. He turned and spotted a vehicle on an approach vector that couldn't have been classified as anything less than offensive in nature. And the Executioner's sixth sense was betting the occupants had him in mind as their target.

He was right.

The vehicle caromed off a parked car and squealed to a halt. The driver stayed put while the three passengers bailed. They produced submachine guns and wore dark clothing that resembled the black swathing of a mummy. They had beards and dark skin. Bolan marked them as locals, without question.

Bolan had the Beretta 93-R in play before the trio of gunners had even fully cleared their vehicle. He snap-aimed and took the guy in the rear driver's-side seat with a single shot that punched a third eye through his forehead and scrambled his brains. The man's head snapped back, the impact slamming him against the vehicle before his body collapsed to the pavement.

The front-seat passenger rested his arms over the hood and triggered a sustained burst. Bolan dived for cover behind a fruit vendor's stand, and the rounds trailed just a millisecond behind him. Ripened fruit erupted under the impact as the bullets exercised an explosive force on melons, grapefruits, bananas and other produce. The air came alive with the hot zing of bullets and a sizzling miasma of cooked fruit salad. Bolan shoulder-rolled and came up on the far side of the stand, his pistol tracking on the gunner. The man spotted him a moment too late and Bolan put two rounds through him, the first cutting a diagonal pattern across the neck and the other cracking his skull where it entered the left temple.

The last man managed to get off a partial shot before he lost the cover of his vehicle. The driver had apparently foreseen the futility of their efforts, surmising the battle would not end well for them, and tromped the accelerator and attempted to get away. The sudden lurch of the vehicle from its spot left the survivor without cover, and Bolan took immediate advantage of that, triggering a double-tap that perforated the man's chest wall. One of the bullets cut through the heart and ended the gunman's life.

Unfortunately for the driver, he'd been unaware that Bolan had some backup. The late-model SUV seemed to come from out of nowhere and accelerated into the path of the enemy vehicle. Bolan could see the grin on Grimaldi's face as the pilot swung the nose of the SUV away at the last second and hammered the side of the sedan with the rear quarter panel.

Bolan saw the driver moving inside frantically and then come up with a pistol in his hand, which he pointed out the passenger-side window at Grimaldi. Bolan raised the Beretta even as he flicked the selector to 3-round burst mode and triggered a hasty volley. At the same moment Grimaldi produced an MP5K and triggered it. The driver's head exploded and painted the windows immediately to his left and front with a gory spray from the dozen or so rounds that struck his skull.

As the echo from the reports died in the crisp morning air of downtown Istanbul, they were replaced by the roars from two more vehicles. And a double complement of new threats emerged from their interior.

CHAPTER SEVENTEEN

As soon as Grimaldi spotted the new arrivals, he went EVA through the passenger-side door. He toted the MP5K along with additional hardware more suited to their current needs, which included an M-4 for Bolan. Over his shoulder he'd also slung a military-grade utility belt with the holstered .44 Magnum Desert Eagle.

A flurry of hot lead burned the air just over their heads while a second grouping slammed into cars and other stationary objects the pair used for cover. Grimaldi tossed the belt on his shoulder underhand, which Bolan caught, slung around his waist and clicked securely in one fluid motion. He then clapped his hands to signal readiness and Grimaldi delivered the M-4 with a light, underhand toss.

The two four-man groups of gunners were now breaking off, angling in different directions to try to flank Bolan and Grimaldi's position. Unfortunately for the enemy, the two Americans were well protected and their location actually gave them the advantage. As he prepared to engage them, Bolan wondered who wanted them dead so desperately as to send this sizeable group of killers. And how the hell had they even pinpointed his location? Nobody except Grimaldi and Serif had known about his visit to Amocacci, and Serif hadn't been out of his or Grimaldi's sight. That meant Amocacci had somehow managed to pull a team together in a very short time—a scenario of which Bolan was highly skeptical—or someone on the inside of this affair had been tracking their movements from the beginning.

Bolan would have to find out, but right now the Executioner had bigger fish to fry.

Two gunners managed to break from the rest of the group and risked crossing the street to make for the entrance of a hotel. Bolan knew they were probably going to attempt to get to an upper floor and take him and Grimaldi from above. He hollered at his friend. When Grimaldi looked in his direction, he gestured toward the runners. The Stony Man pilot nodded and burst from cover to pursue.

Bolan swore between clenched teeth; he had hoped that Grimaldi would have concentrated on taking them out rather than risk exposing his position. By going after them, he'd broken up the team and put himself at some risk. Bolan turned his M-4 toward the remaining six combatants and opened with short, controlled bursts designed to take out some and keep others at bay, all for the purpose of covering Grimaldi's movements.

Bolan spotted one of the gunners draw a bead on the pilot. The Executioner held his M-4 steady and triggered a 3-round burst that hit his mark dead-on. One round punched through the guy's jaw, cracking bone and ripping out flesh as it passed, while another round created enough pressure inside the skull to blow out the better part of it. The third may have ricocheted and perhaps also made contact, but Bolan couldn't be sure.

The soldier suppressed his sense of frustration—he didn't like having to engage the enemy where so many innocents might get in the way or, worse yet, wouldn't be able to get out of the way in time. But there wasn't anywhere to take this fight that he didn't risk civilians getting hurt, and at least here in the open they could see what was happening and avoid it at all costs. Bolan swung the muzzle of his M-4 and took out another pair of gunmen. The 5.56 mm slugs were unforgiving against them, smashing through flesh and tearing out organs or cracking bones. Within a moment Bolan had reduced the odds by half.

This entire situation had begun to puzzle him. The gunners seemed barely competent, really, almost as if they were being sacrificed. They'd appeared to ambush him without any real plan, as if they'd thought they could attain victory by sheer force in numbers. They were poor marksmen and operated as if utterly unaccustomed to combat. They didn't cover one another, failed to operate in any sort of team fashion, and had no operational methodology in their techniques whatsoever. It was almost as if Bolan had been pitted against first-year cadets with little to no training.

Bolan risked a glance in Grimaldi's direction, but the Stony Man pilot was no longer in sight. Obviously the fight had been taken into the building. That would make things easier or harder depending on what Grimaldi encountered.

Bolan dispensed the rest of the M-4's magazine in a sweeping, sustained burst and then dropped the magazine and slammed home a fresh one. He wished he had a grenade to bring the battle to a swift end so he could help Grimaldi, but no such luck. Then he remembered there was a bag in the SUV that contained plenty of ordnance they'd managed to smuggle in thanks to Stony Man getting forged credentials to authorities that marked the plane as a diplomatic courier to the consulate. This had prevented customs from searching or inspecting their aircraft upon its arrival.

Bolan triggered another sustained burst on the run as he moved from cover and crouched, racing along the backs of the abandoned vendor stalls until he reached the rear hatch of the SUV. He tried the handle but it was locked. Bolan smashed the rear window with the butt of the M-4, reached inside and patted the floor blindly until his fingertips brushed the canvas bag. He dug a little deeper, got it open and put his hand inside. He was rewarded with the sensation of a cool, round object.

Bolan yanked the M-67 HE grenade from the satchel, primed the bomb and then lobbed it in the direction of his enemies. Amid the intermittent bursts of fire they directed his way, their eyes followed the object as it bounced off the hood of one of their vehicles and landed amid them. The trio of gunmen struggled to get rid of the bomb and finally opted to kick it under the vehicle and run. Bolan ducked behind the relative safety of the SUV just as the grenade exploded under their vehicle. The heat and shrapnel splintered the gas tank and the flames immediately ignited the fumes liberated by the shock of the blast.

A wall of flame erupted through the floorboards and instantly consumed the surface material of the interior, charbroiling the seats and one of the gunners who had somehow managed to get trapped between that vehicle and the other one belonging to his teammates. The remaining attackers managed to get far away enough to avoid destruction, but they moved right into the opening and Bolan's waiting sights. He took them down with a classic figure eight spray of bullets.

Bolan reached into the SUV, snatched the bag of valuable munitions, then turned and rushed across the street. He pushed through the front doors of the hotel as the wail of police sirens became audible. The cops would be on the scene in a minute or less and Bolan didn't want to be anywhere near there when they arrived. As far as the SUV, it had been a rental under an assumed name so they wouldn't be able to trace it back to him or Grimaldi.

The Executioner looked intently in every direction, searching for possible clues as to Grimaldi's pursuit path. Finally he looked toward the clerks and shouted an inquiry in halting Turkish. The two women at the desk looked absolutely pale with fright and pointed toward a hall at the far end of the lobby simultaneously. Bolan nodded and rushed off to search for his friend.

THINGS HADN'T GONE at all how Jack Grimaldi originally envisioned. He hadn't expected the Executioner to run into trouble so soon after making contact with Amocacci. And while he was always ready for action, he didn't necessarily go out of his way to look for it.

But such was the life of a field team member in the world of Stony Man and Grimaldi was more than equal to the task. In fact, he'd worked under the tutelage of one of the most proficient and consummate soldiers ever produced by America. It gave him an edge, but like any good student in the art of war, he'd learned not to underestimate his enemy.

That fact saved his life when the two gunners he'd chased into the hotel turned suddenly once they were inside the lobby and leveled their SMGs in his direction.

Grimaldi dived and rolled out of the line of fire as

bullets smashed into the doors behind him and heated the air around him. Grimaldi continued rolling until he found concealment behind the door frame of the inner doors leading from the vestibule into the lobby. The Stony Man pilot brought his weapon to bear as he scrambled to one knee. He peered around the corner and prepared to squeeze off a couple of shots, but his enemies had already broken off their attack and were retreating toward a hallway at the far end of the lobby.

Grimaldi gave chase once more, his dogged pursuit winding him. He kept in good physical condition, but the sudden rush of adrenaline that accompanied any combat situation gave him the extra endurance needed to not only sustain through the most difficult of situations but also added an edge to his reflexes. It was the basic flight or fight response, but Grimaldi knew how to channel that to his advantage.

"First one to flinch loses," Carl Lyons, the fearless leader of Able Team had once told him. Grimaldi could remember asking him, "So what's your point?"

"Don't flinch."

It seemed liked an arrogant and pompous answer at the time, but when Grimaldi reflected on it he'd come to realize how profound and correct it really was. It had certainly given him a new respect for Lyons, whose "Ironman" nickname had been well earned.

Grimaldi's legs ached, but he poured on the speed and skidded to a halt at the last second when he saw his quarry duck into a doorway that he assumed led into a conference room.

He slowed his pace and brought the muzzle of his weapon level to chest height. If his enemies were up to some sort of deception, he'd at least have a better chance of hitting them center mass. Thoughts of Bolan entered his mind right then, and he chastised himself for leaving his friend to deal with the other group. They had him outnumbered six-to-one, although that was hardly a fair fight for the enemy.

Grimaldi shoved distracting thoughts from his mind and slowed, almost creeping. He stepped so lightly, in fact, that he barely made any noise on his approach. He eased up to the door through which the pair of gunmen had disappeared. Had he been thinking ahead, Grimaldi thought, he would have grabbed the grenades in the back of the SUV. One might have come in handy right at that point to help him with clearing the room.

If these two men had, in fact, entered a conference room, chances were good they had only one way out, unless there was another door at the rear that led into a hall or kitchen service area. Of some type. That wasn't uncommon in a lot of hotels, but that didn't mean this one was of the same modern design.

Grimaldi was about to open the door when he heard footfalls to his right. He whipped his head in the direction, weapon held at the ready, when he saw the unmistakable approach of the Executioner. The man moved with a grace and practiced ease Grimaldi and many others could only hope to emulate. Bolan had been in combat many times, with more of his waking hours spent engaged in violent confrontations than not, and yet every step was purposeful, every movement calculated to be as efficient and conservative of energy as possible.

"Need some help?" Bolan asked as he came near.

"Yeah. I'm not ashamed to admit I'm *very* glad to see you."

"Did they go in there?" Bolan gestured to the door.

Grimaldi nodded. "Yeah. Both of them. They nearly got me back there at the lobby, but I didn't see them."

"We should leave them be," the Executioner stated.

"What? Why? We can't afford to let them get away, Sarge."

"I understand," Bolan replied easily. "But we also can't afford any encounters with the police. And they're crawling all over my handiwork back there. Won't be long before I'm sure witnesses will point them in this direction. It's time to move out."

Grimaldi didn't like it, but he knew Bolan was right. Moreover, this was the warrior's mission. He called the shots. Grimaldi knew the plan, and he didn't really mind subjecting himself to Bolan's authority. The guy knew what he was doing; that was an indisputable fact, and Grimaldi trusted his judgment implicitly.

"Okay, Sarge, your show. Let's get out of here."

Bolan nodded and pointed toward some rear doors. "I'm guessing that would be an inconspicuous exit."

"Lead the way, my friend," Grimaldi said.

GASTONE AMOCACCI SAT for a long time in solitude and pondered his visitor's words. He found it difficult to believe that Savitch's people could have screwed up the assassination so completely as to allow someone like this Matt Cooper to not only learn of it but also to escape alive with the information. This could prove to create a serious compromise, not only of security in the Council of Luminárii but also of his own personal safety.

It was no secret that any organization bent on doing the things the Council did *had* to deal with types represented by men like Cooper. But that didn't mean they had to trust everyone who came along with a story. Thus far, the Council had left Amocacci to deal with most of the details such as this, and things had gone pretty well. Until now.

Amocacci dialed the number he'd long since memorized and his contact answered on the first ring. "Where are you?"

"Good morning to you, too."

"It hasn't begun that way," Amocacci snapped. "I just received a very interesting visit from someone calling himself Matt Cooper. Does the name mean anything to you?"

He responded a little too quickly for Amocacci's tastes and the former Interpol officer knew immediately it was a lie. "Doesn't ring any bells."

"Well, that's interesting, because he seems to know all about *you*."

"Is that right?"

"He claims you tried to recruit him in Guatemala. I thought we'd agreed there would be *no* outsiders."

"If you're referring to the guy that we took prisoner, the name he gave me was Colonel Brandon Stone."

"That's his cover name. Apparently he's operating as a DIA officer and when he got on to Shoup he also got on to your operation. He seemed to also know that we set him up to start with. He even knew about the Council. He told me you had quite an extensive conversation, and he revealed that he worked for the NSA. He also claims to have told you this. So one of you must be lying."

"It sounds as if you're accusing me of something."

"I made no accusations."

"No? Because I've been accused of things before and

that sounded very much like an accusation. If there are certain things I don't choose to tell you up front, my friend, it's because either it's none of your business or the knowledge might compromise you in some way."

"That sounds very ambiguous, as if you were trying to use it as an excuse to hide the truth from me," Amocacci stated.

"Does it? Interesting that you say so because one of the things that you've made very clear to me time and again is that you expect neither your identity nor affiliation with the Council to ever come into my conversations with other associates. I have honored that request."

"Get to the point and quit all of the double-speak."

"The point is that you're treading dangerously close to things you don't understand. Think about it a moment. If I'd never spoken to anyone of my affiliation with you, and I think I've proved my loyalty as a business associate, how do you suppose Stone or Cooper or what's-his-name knew about you?"

Amocacci thought hard. It hadn't occurred to him that maybe Cooper *had* played him, when he considered the guy claimed his knowledge came from talking with Amocacci's contact. None of this was going the way Amocacci had originally envisioned it.

"You make a good point."

"I thought you might think so."

"But that *still* doesn't explain how Cooper knew about the business with our Chinese friend," Amocacci said.

"He did? Why the hell didn't you say that from the start?"

"Because I cannot read your mind. And because, as you just alluded, he is getting his information somewhere else. In fact, the bastard had the audacity to walk straight into my office first thing this morning."

"What was his reason?"

"Well, his stated purpose was to offer services."

"What kind of services?"

"Much of it sounded like the same services *you* already provide."

"That's very interesting, indeed. I can tell you I'm both humbled and complimented."

"I thought that would make you furious."

That caused the man to laugh with considerable amusement; the first time Amocacci could recall ever hearing him do so in that fashion. "There's nothing wrong with a little healthy competition. In my line of work, it helps me keep a bit of an edge. And it provides a great reference point when my services far and away exceed those of most others."

"Never mind the sales pitch!" Amocacci said, utterly furious now. "I want to know what you plan to do about it."

"Me? What would you *like* me to do about it? In fact, I'm not sure what I *can* do about it. Until I know his identity or can determine who might have sent him, it would be difficult for me to eliminate your problem. If I had to guess, though, I would say he's probably working for a special branch of the U.S. government. Maybe a special operations group of some type."

"That might be where I could help you."

"In what way?"

"I first spotted him at the hotel I frequent. Not long after I spotted him, someone snatched Serif right out from under my nose. I accused him, but he denied it."

"Did he give any other explanation?"

"He said that I'd been under observation by someone at the consulate for some time," Amocacci replied. "He claims he'd come to the hotel to warn me."

"But he didn't."

"No. I didn't know who he was, but I spotted him as a tail right off. I didn't know what he wanted, so I set it up for him to follow me."

"But he didn't." ·

"No." Amocacci paused and then said, "I think maybe he saw that I'd spotted him and decided not to stick around. Maybe he was smart enough to know I was setting a trap for him."

"Or maybe he wanted you to see him."

"That's another possibility I hadn't considered."

"It seems entirely too coincidental that he would be there at the same time as this mysterious group he claims was tailing you. And that you lost your prize just shortly after encountering him. I think it's also interesting that he knew where your office was located."

"He obviously looked up my public profile. It's not like I work in secret."

"I'm aware of your cover. But he obviously knows a lot more than he's let on to you."

"That wouldn't be entirely unusual for a man in his position. If he is who he claims to be, then it would be natural for him to be less than forthcoming about all he knows."

"Did you get any sense for his motivations?"

"He's basically looking for work. Money. He mentioned cash a couple of times. I think, if he is a member of the NSA, that he's on the outs with them. Maybe whatever happened there in Guatemala caused him to change his priorities. There's very little question that

Shoup betrayed him, set him up to take the trap we'd set for them."

"I told you that wasn't a good idea."

"It's done now," Amocacci said. "You should move on."

"I will check into this man and let you know what I find out. You should let me know immediately if he contacts you again."

"I will."

"And we did receive the funds. I thank you very much."

"Just figure out what's going on here, and there will be more where that came from."

"Consider it done," the man replied.

Amocacci hung up without saying goodbye. He didn't like the situation at present—it didn't feel as if he was in control. Up to this point he'd been holding all the cards. Now there were other players in the game manipulating the situation. Well, Amocacci wouldn't play that game. It was those games that had caused him such turmoil to begin with. The moves and countermoves on the intelligence playing board had cost him dearly with the loss of his family. Each man on the Council had his own motives for participating, but for Amocacci it was personal. He would make the U.S. intelligence pay. He'd already proved they could do it with the operations in Europe and the Middle East.

And soon, very soon, he would show them his resolve by making a play in the U.S.

CHAPTER EIGHTEEN

"Attacked?" Alara Serif said in utter disbelief. "Completely crazy!"

Grimaldi grinned. "That was pretty much our assessment, as well."

"Who do you think's behind it?"

It was the Executioner who fielded that one. "Hard to tell. But whoever it is doesn't change the fact it happened, which means somewhere along the way we've been compromised."

"And worse, this is the second time it's happened," Grimaldi added.

"That's what bothers me most," Bolan replied with a frown. "Up to this point, I've had to *react* to situations regardless of how well I plan. Someone has managed to stay a step ahead of us this time. Someone with a lot of clout and who is privy to a lot of classified information."

"You mean someone inside the intelligence community," Serif said.

Bolan nodded. "There's no other explanation, Alara. There are a lot of fingers in the pie here. It's like I said before. If Amocacci and Ma are card-carrying members of the Council, then there are probably others. Most likely former intelligence agents who have an ax to grind with the U.S., or possibly even intelligence agents with some sort of current status, like Ma."

"But if that's true," Serif said, "then who assassinated Quon Ma?"

"I don't think Ma's dead," Bolan replied.

Grimaldi pinned his friend with a querulous expression. "Huh?"

"I checked with the Farm just a little bit ago," Bolan explained. "They told me there have been no rumblings about the assassination. Kirklareli should have been flooded with MSS investigators right now. Instead the place is totally quiet. Too quiet. In fact, not even any of Ma's internal security has been seen making inquiries."

"You think they got the wrong guy," Serif said. It wasn't a question.

"I'd bet money on it," Bolan said. "And since it would appear Amocacci's not taking the bait I set for him, I'd lay odds he's the one who ordered the hit."

"But to what end?" Serif asked. "There's every reason to think that this group operates in a very symbiotic fashion, just as I concluded in my analysis. To kill one of their own would be harming the organization, not helping it."

"Maybe so," Bolan said. "But I'm betting the guy I encountered in Guatemala knows a lot more about all of this than he let on. In fact, I'm guessing Amocacci is working with this man. And I'd also bet he doesn't know his identity any more than we do."

"What makes you think so?" Serif asked.

"Because we work with people who use some of the most advanced technology available," Grimaldi pointed out. "We gave them a first-rate description, and not even the facial recognition software has been able to pull a face or name out of the crowd."

"Really?" Serif tapped her finger against her lips. "I

might be able to help you with that. Part of my training with DIA involved a project where we built a new facial recognition program. In fact, it was widely adopted by all sorts of intelligence groups—it's possible you're using the program I helped build."

"Even if that's true, we have some pretty top-shelf technical people working for us," Grimaldi said. "They're capabilities are quite significant."

"I don't doubt it," Serif said. "But my point was that I learned a few things about that science, flaws that might well create problems your people can't foresee."

Her statement immediately engaged the Executioner's interest. "Such as?"

"Well, for one, facial recognition software doesn't look at probability markers—it can only assess specific and known markers."

"You're talking about people who've had cosmetic surgery," Bolan interjected.

Serif's face brightened and she did nothing to hide her surprise at Bolan's insight. "Precisely! And there are other factors, too, such as aging and genetic predisposition. Even medical considerations."

"You mean like when somebody is disfigured?" Grimaldi asked.

"That wasn't what I meant, but that certainly is another factor. Consider also that medical conditions can change facial structure significantly. For example, problems with the liver can change color and tone, and due to imperfections in capture technology, a person with something such as liver disease can appear much differently in a picture than in person.

"Then there's rapid weight loss or gain, such as might occur with cancer patients or eating disorders."

"Like bulimia and anorexia," Bolan said.

"Right. And there are many others I can list. All these things can make a significant difference in facial recognition software. Cosmetic surgery is usually the biggie, especially when talking about someone within the intelligence community."

"What makes you think this guy is from that area?" Grimaldi inquired.

Serif shrugged. "It only makes sense, really. You're talking about someone who has significant resources, someone who can arrange assassinations and potentially travel from one continent to the next on short notice. You also would think that only someone inside the intelligence community could manipulate Amocacci."

Serif pointed at Bolan. "You yourself tried to use that angle as a way to bait and manipulate Amocacci. Is it all that unreasonable, then, to assume that he might throw in his lot with a similar mark?"

Bolan nodded. "What you're saying makes a lot of sense. If I could put you in touch with our people, could you help them with modifying their facial recognition procedures?"

"I'd be happy to, Colonel Stone."

She smiled. Bolan smiled. Grimaldi looked between them and then stood and checked his watch. "Well, if you don't mind, I think I'd best make myself scarce."

Bolan looked suddenly at his friend. "Why?"

"First, I need to acquire a new set of wheels before all the rental places close. Second, it's probably a good idea for me to go back to the plane and get some more equipment."

Bolan had thought Grimaldi had some sense that he and Serif wanted to be alone. But what the pilot said made absolute sense. "Yeah, good idea. We're going to need a new ride for the soft probe tonight."

Serif raised one dark, graceful brow. "Soft probe?"

"Later," Bolan said.

He gave Grimaldi his full attention. "See if you can get us something fast, Jack. Fast as possible, in fact."

Grimaldi smiled. "Expecting to possibly have to make a quick getaway?"

"I'd prefer to be prepared for it. I mean, the SUV was a good thought, but this time I don't want to be caught off guard. Police patrols are likely to be on heightened alert for a while, not to mention we were out there long enough they probably got some decent descriptions. Maybe somebody's cell phone picture. I'd like to be able to outrun the police as well as any potential enemies."

Grimaldi nodded. "Roger that. I'll be back within the hour."

The pilot nodded at Serif, then split.

Bolan sat on the couch in front of the laptop and withdrew a device from his pocket. He plugged the secure satellite scrambler to the laptop and made a connection via its non-broadcasted mobile hotspot identifier. Within a couple of minutes, Aaron Kurtzman's haggard face appeared.

"I woke you up," Bolan said. "Sorry."

"It's okay," Kurtzman said. "I've given up on sleep a century ago. What's up, Striker?"

"I have someone here who wants to talk to you. I think you'll want to hear what she has to say."

Stony Man Farm, Virginia

WITHIN AN HOUR of speaking to Serif and plugging in the additional parameters and co-factoring algorithms she provided, Kurtzman was convinced they'd hit on a solid lead. He immediately placed a call to Price and Brognola, who were burning the midnight oil in the War Room and asked them to come to the Annex.

Within twenty minutes the two were seated at a table in the Computer Room as Kurtzman manned the master console. He displayed the picture of a young man with a lean face and beady eyes. "Ladies and gentlemen, I give you Mr. Derek Savitch, Esquire."

"Come again?" Price said.

"This is Striker's man down in Guatemala."

Price frowned at the picture. "When was this taken?"

"Less than fifteen months ago."

"I don't know, Bear," Brognola said. "Other than the similarity in the eye color I don't see it at all."

"Agreed," Price added. "And how could there have been such a distinctive change in the face we're seeing here and the one described to us?"

"Simple. Hashimoto's Thyroiditis."

"Explain," Brognola said.

"It's an autoimmune disorder marked by an attack of the thyroid gland. The body thinks it's cancerous and so goes after the thyroid, causing significant drops in hormone levels. It's normally more common in women than men, but once I knew we had our man and plugged in his information, I discovered in his medical records that he was not only diagnosed with non-Hodgkin lymphoma but celiac disease. This is what actually precipitated his condition."

"So this caused the sudden weight gain," Price said.

"And in turn explains why our facial recognition software wasn't able to pick him out," Kurtzman said with an emphatic nod. "I did some additional digging and discovered that in the four separate office visits he had to specialists in the twelve months following his diagnoses, Savitch gained ninety pounds."

Brognola let out a low whistle. "That *is* significant."

"Now you said something about 'esquire,'" Price said. "Tell us about that."

"He's a Canadian citizen and attorney." Kurtzman tapped a key and a copy of the highlights from Savitch's full dossier appeared. "You'll see on line four his most recent appointment."

"'Security Intelligence Review Committee'?" Price read out loud.

Kurtzman nodded. "Exactly. They're an independent agency of the Canadian government responsible for overseeing the Canadian Security Intelligence Service. You could pretty much equate them to our own CIOC."

"So he would have access to significant intelligence information," Price said. "And I daresay a lot of the community scuttlebutt, too."

"But the SIRC doesn't really play any direct role in CSIS operations. Their primary duty is to ensure that they don't abuse their powers to violate the rights of Canada's citizens," Brognola said.

"I remind you they've been the center of some significant controversy as of late," Kurtzman said. "There was the resignation of SIRC's chair in 2014 over a conflict of interest. And a few years back there was that business with a guy who was nabbed by the Feds who charged him with a number of criminal counts that, among others, included government fraud and money laundering."

"I remember reading something about that," Price said. "Didn't they nab him in Panama?"

Kurtzman nodded. "Yeah."

"So it would appear that the affiliations of Canadian intelligence members and their associations with Central America continue," Brognola deadpanned.

"No more than right here in the U.S.," Price reminded the Stony Man chief. She returned her attention to Kurtzman. "So let's assume you're correct. What would motivate Savitch to work with a group like the Council of Luminárii?"

"Well, we obviously don't have anything other than Striker's testimony to tie him to either Amocacci or Quon Ma," Kurtzman said. "Not that I wouldn't trust the big guy's assertions. My guess would be that regardless of Savitch's ties, he's probably being motivated by money. He's had major medical expenses and, most recently, he's in the wind. In fact, his housekeeper reported him missing more than a month ago and local authorities haven't had a single lead in the case."

"I'd say his being in Guatemala at the time the special ops team out of Tyndall was compromised is evidence enough he's heavily involved with the Council," Brognola said. "The only question now is where he's gone and how do we find him?"

"Well, now that we have an identity to match with a face, we shouldn't have much trouble locating him," Kurtzman said. "And once we *do* locate him, I think it would be really good to turn every law-enforcement agency on to his description and issue a Be on the Lookout order."

"What do you want to bet he's either on his way to Istanbul or already there?" Price offered, looking at Brognola.

He nodded. "It's worth checking out. Get on it. And

let's get this information to Striker as soon as possible. He's got boots on the ground and he may be able to use this information to run the guy down."

"Right," Kurtzman said. "And it will give him a potential bargaining chip with Amocacci."

"I'll use this information to pursue my own contacts," Price said. "Maybe I can come up with more intelligence to help us out."

"Sounds like a plan," Brognola said. "Let's get cracking. I don't think we have much more time before Amocacci and his friends in the Council decide to unleash whatever little plan they have for the U.S. And, frankly, I'd prefer not to read about it in the morning's headlines."

BOLAN RETRIEVED HIS vibrating cell phone.

"Striker, here."

"We got your man," Price said.

"Talk to me."

Bolan listened for the next few minutes as Price laid it out for him. Finally she said, "I also reached out to some of my contacts. Seems that Savitch may be doing business with the British. SIS internal affairs in Britain have monitored some unusual scrambled communications between Savitch and one of their own agents. But they wouldn't be more forthcoming than that."

"Then it's possible there's a British agent on the Council, too."

"Yes, that was my thinking."

"That's good news, lady."

"'Lady'?" Price fell silent for a moment and then said, "You're not alone."

"No."

"Okay, I understand. Just watch yourself. There's a lot of double-cross and triple-cross going on here. I want you to be careful."

"I always am," Bolan said.

"I know, and I don't have to say it. And I don't mean to sound like I'm mothering you," Price said. "Sorry. It's habit—I always do it with the boys."

By that remark Bolan knew she meant Able Team and Phoenix Force. In a good many respects, she was much like a mother for that motley crew. A role forced more on her by situation than out of any real desire to play true to it on Price's part. Sure, they were eight of the toughest and most skilled soldiers in the world, but they had a tendency to act like a bunch of adolescent hooligans to such a degree Price often found herself continuously moderating the behavior of one or another. It was only natural such a task would roll naturally from her where it concerned Bolan, too, regardless of the nature of their personal relationship.

"I hear you," Bolan said.

"Take care, Striker."

"Will do. Out."

Bolan disconnected the call and turned to see Serif studying him intently.

"Well?"

"They found a match," Bolan said. "Thanks to you. Ever heard of a man named Derek Savitch?"

"No, I haven't."

"Never came across the name in your surveillance?"

"I already told you no." She cocked her head. "You sound as if you don't believe me."

"It's not that, Alara," Bolan said easily. "I was just trying to jog your memory. You've been through an awful lot lately, and that kind of stress can cause you to forget things."

"I understand…I guess."

"Don't take it personally. Really. I would have asked the same question of anybody else."

"That's what bothers me," Serif said, staring into his eyes. "But I'm a big girl, I get it. So you never explained this soft probe thing you were talking about before."

"My people came up with a couple of additional leads," Bolan replied. "One of them is an export warehouse Amocacci operates. I'm going to check it out, see what I can sniff out."

"What are you hoping to find?"

"Maybe something that will give me a clue as to the whereabouts of these other Council members. They must have a meeting place of some kind."

"I've always thought maybe it was his house."

"Where? Here in the city?"

Serif shook her head. "No, it's somewhere west and south of Istanbul. I don't even know where, exactly. Every weekend he takes a chopper to Malko Tarnovo. At first I thought he lived in the city, but records show he purchased property somewhere in the foothills of the Strandzha. I've always believed he owns a residence and that he shares it with the Lady Fellini. I've just never been able to get the resources to pursue it that far, since most of my surveillance was unauthorized."

Bolan shook his head as he donned his utility belt from which dangled the holstered Desert Eagle. "Well, maybe they'll start listening to you more now that so much of your information has panned out."

"Really?" Serif looked suddenly proud.

"You bet," the Executioner replied. "Now get your jacket."

"I'm coming with you?"

"I promised you could," Bolan said. "Besides, I'd rather keep my eye on you. You have a propensity for getting into trouble."

CHAPTER NINETEEN

Sofia, Bulgaria

Hurley Willham wouldn't have remained in Bulgaria by choice. He hated the country, despite the fact it had become one of the largest producers of wind-driven energy in the world. Word had been spreading for a while that Bulgaria was a good target for exploiting nuclear energy, but like most countries of the region, there were worldwide concerns about how this could be turned toward the production of nuclear weapons.

Despite the sociopolitical climate in the country, and the growing unrest in surrounding nations, Bulgaria remained a key European center of energy production. It also had a lot of money going through its financial sector in Sofia, and that played right into Willham's wheelhouse. It was the key reason he'd chosen to remain as the SIS case officer for Her Majesty's secret service. He was a decorated officer with a stellar reputation of foreign service, and that lifestyle had afforded him an ability to make a bucket-load of cash.

It amazed Willham how many of his foreign colleagues participated in some sort of graft. Willham could recall the history of many large police forces in the United States at one point, where political and economic corruption was so large that anyone who didn't participate found themselves an outcast and in the minority. Of course, that kind of environment also landed even those who were supposed to suppress the corruption in a swirling pool of hypocrisy.

Willham, however, couldn't have cared less about those problems. He'd easily been able to operate under the radar, and it was only happenstance that had forced him to work with men like Derek Savitch. Although he'd learned Savitch had his uses. Already they had done a deed that eliminated the competition and earned him a healthy sum of cash, only half of which he'd been forced to share with Savitch.

But there was the issue of the proverbial exaggeration of Quon Ma's demise. Word among certain circles had it that Ma wasn't dead; a scenario that seemed to be supported by the fact Turkey wasn't crawling with agents from the Ministry of State Security. If Savitch's assassin *had* botched the job, it was going to make the rest of Willham's plans that much harder to achieve. He would have to assign someone else to the deed, and he would now have no choice but to arrange for the elimination of Gastone Amocacci, too. They couldn't afford to keep the Italian alive if the job on Ma had been botched, and the man who now sat in front of Willham in his undeclared luxury residence in the Spa resort of the Kostenets was busy hammering that point home.

"I'm telling you, Comrade Willham," Mikhail Ryzkhov said. "If your informants are correct about Ma still being alive, Amocacci must be terminated at any costs."

"I agree," Lev Penzak added. The Mossad agent had been standing at the mini bar and staring out the tall window that looked on the lake. The sun was just setting behind the hills and the amber light glimmered with a beautiful glow on the water.

Penzak turned toward Willham and said, "I have to admit your taste in location is impeccable."

Willham nodded at Penzak. "I appreciate your remarks. I take it as a compliment."

"As you should," Penzak said, taking a seat next to Ryzkhov. "It was meant that way. But it goes without saying that the good comrade general is correct. Gastone's dealings with your contact show he's not above killing any of us if he thinks we're standing in the way of the best interests of the Council."

"Some would call that kind of loyalty admirable, gentlemen," Willham said. "And after all, isn't our very conversation now much the same thing as Gastone's been doing? How right is it that we would condemn him for something in which we ourselves are complicit?"

"That's hardly the point," Penzak said. "We didn't start this. If there had been an actual leak within the organization, Gastone should have come to us immediately about it. Instead he assumed that one of us was responsible and took matters into his own hands."

"But we all know that Quon Ma *was* responsible for the bloody leak," Willham said with splayed hands.

Ryzkhov shook his head. "That's hardly the point. We all knew about it and we could have all dealt with it as one. Gastone made the decision on his own, which would imply he thought it was his right to do so despite any agreement to the contrary. If you ask me, we've given him too much of a free hand up to this point, and he's taken advantage of that."

"But he's done most everything else with the blessing of the Council," Willham said. "I just think we're being a bit hypocritical. Especially since we're going solely off information we received second-hand when it comes to Ma's treachery. Have we even bothered to convene and ask him pointedly if he did betray us and leak information about our operations in the U.S.?"

"We didn't have to," Penzak said. "It was a mere process of elimination. Mikhail and I didn't even know about the station in Colorado until after we were informed it had been discovered by the agent out of Washington. That left only you, Gastone and Ma. You have since proved beyond any reasonable doubt that you weren't the source of the leak, since you came to us with incontrovertible evidence Gastone ordered the hit on Quon Ma. And since it would not make sense for Gastone to risk arranging Ma's assassination unless he knew with certainty that the leak had originated with Quon Ma or one of his people, Ma *had* to be the guilty party."

Willham couldn't argue with that logic, although he knew the truth. He'd been the one to arrange all of it. He'd offered the information to Amocacci about putting Savitch in place as a sort of failsafe. Willham had been the first one to take up Amocacci's offer in forming the Council, and he'd acted as Amocacci's strongest supporter through every phase of their projects. Hence, he'd be the last one in the world Amocacci would suspect of any such treachery, particularly since the Italian had no idea about Willham's long-standing relationship with Savitch. In fact, Amocacci didn't even know Savitch's identity, and Willham had pretended he didn't know, either. At least, Willham hadn't offered the information and so couldn't be responsible for any assumptions on Amocacci's part.

"It doesn't sound as if we're left with much of a choice at this point," Willham said. "If Quon Ma's still alive, then I think it's better that we attempt to locate him rather than implement an alternate protocol."

"What are you suggesting?" Penzak asked.

"I'm suggesting that maybe we shouldn't stick our bloody necks out on this one for Gastone. Maybe we should ally ourselves with Ma, send whatever aid and resources we can to Kirklareli. Show that we're going to rally around him and do whatever it takes to find out who attempted the assassination. If he sees this, he'll likely take it to mean that we had nothing to do with it and he'll show himself. This way, we'll be able to keep an eye on him and truly verify that he's the source of the leak."

"And if it proves that he didn't betray us?" Ryzkhov interjected.

"Then we'll know that the treachery is Gastone's, and we'll deal with him in an appropriate fashion." Willham did his best to look subjective and nonthreatening. "My friends, we agreed long ago that the Council of Luminárii could only be effective if we operated with honesty and equality. We should hold fast to that because it's all we have."

"Save the philosophy for those who can make use of it, my friend," Ryzkhov said. "In our world today there is no fantasy. We face a harsh and uncaring existence, and if we aren't diligent we will face it at the hands of someone else. I don't know about you, but I would prefer to control my own destiny rather than turn it over to those who care only for themselves. Otherwise, there is no more point to our continued association and we should disband."

Penzak and Willham watched with surprise as Ryzkhov rose and headed for the door. When he was near it, he turned and said, "I will leave this in your hands. Call it…call it a show of good faith. I hope that it turns out to be to the advantage of the Council. For all our sakes."

With that, the Russian GRU agent left.

Penzak and Willham sat in stunned silence for a time before Penzak spoke up. "I think there's a significant amount of external pressure being placed on Mikhail. I know that I've been doing all I can to stave off suspicions from my own government. I imagine you face very similar issues."

"I would love to say that's something I can appreciate, Lev, but it's not," Willham said. "Honestly, I think my government has all but forgotten about me down here. I file my regular monthly reports and life just goes by in London. I receive no orders, no real directives to speak of. You see, Her Majesty doesn't consider the financial heart of Bulgaria to be of any consequence to British interests. And why would they? The country has only been a member of NATO since 2004. It has no strategic military or political value, at least not to my country, and it is not an exporter of any goods we couldn't live without. Its geographical location is the most important aspect of its existence, and the sole reason my government keeps a presence here."

"What's your point?" Penzak asked with obvious boredom.

"My point is that whether the Council succeeds or fails in foiling American military intelligence efforts, or the grand plan for our strike in the heart of U.S. territory, our position in this region remains the same. Our actions are not likely to have long-standing effects, which means our operation comes down to satisfying the personal whim and vendetta of a man who has not proved himself to be very trustworthy. It's for those reasons I think we should seek some personal gain out of this."

"Weakening U.S. military intelligence infrastructure will pay huge dividends to my own country and the Mossad. America has done nothing but repeatedly declare its unwillingness to continue to support Israel in her own objectives, and they have done so in a very public way. If they are weakened, particularly in the Middle East, it may cause them to change their attitude toward us. There was a time they consulted regularly with our agents, and showed us full cooperation. It's my hope that our efforts will restore that relationship. Despite its faults, the United States of America is a powerful ally."

"Oh, bloody bollocks!" Willham said with a dismissive wave. "America hasn't showed herself to be a strong or powerful ally to anyone. They've sold their entire financial future to the Chinese and diminished the capacity of my government, a government that at one time was their greatest ally. So since they no longer take their relationship with us to be serious, I no longer see any reason to think they should care what happens between us. And if there's any value to be had from this, it's going to be in the profit."

"Materialism," Penzak said. "It is the greatest weakness of an empire."

Willham snorted. "Empire—what empire?"

"If you don't know, then I pity you," Penzak said, rising. "I really do."

"Well, it would appear that Mikhail has left it to you and me to decide what to do about this situation."

"If you want to know my opinion, I think it's high time we give Gastone a taste of his own medicine."

"What are you suggesting?"

"I'm not *suggesting* anything," Penzak said. "I think you need to send him a very clear and direct message."

"I already tried that once, with the people *you* suggested," Willham said. "It didn't turn out too well, if you'll recall."

"I had nothing to do with that," Penzak stated, pointing an accusing finger at Willham. "I told you to hit his interests *directly*. Instead you chose to go after the American."

"He was attempting to deceive Gastone," Willham said. "We can't bloody well let that happen. Period!"

"The Americans are inconsequential in this," Penzak said. "They will undoubtedly begin to look harder at Gastone, and they will most likely be looking for Savitch. You should have had Stone eliminated immediately as discussed. But because you didn't, the man's now walking the streets of Istanbul and the woman analyst has been freed. It's turning into one big mess, a mess *you* started. So fix it. Once you do, you'll have earned my trust once more and I will assist your future efforts including putting my full support behind you publicly to the Council. But not until you get this mess straightened out."

Penzak nodded with a grunt to affirm his words, then turned and left through the same door Ryzkhov had used.

Willham sat back in his chair and folded his arms, contemplating Penzak's words. It would definitely not do to have either of these men lose confidence in him. Success ultimately depended on keeping the Council intact until the end, when he had all the pieces in place. Then he could divide and conquer, and his victory would be ultimate. There would be nothing to stop him if he could achieve this one final victory. To do that, he needed every single one of them alive until he could maneuver them into their proper place.

He would have to start with extending an olive branch to Quon Ma. He thought he knew how to do that. They had a mutual acquaintance, a woman of some beauty and who was renowned for her ability to facilitate communications between Chinese agents and those representatives from other organizations. Yes, he could reach out to her to see if she could make contact. If Ma was alive, as his informants suggested, the possibility existed Ma would respond to the inquiry. That would also take Willham out of the list of potential suspects, assuming he crafted his message very carefully.

Yes, perhaps the entire thing was salvageable after all.

A WARM, LIGHT mist rolled through the air surrounding the docks. In the distance, the horns of ships and ferries traveling across the Bosporus reached the ears of the trio keeping vigil in the Citroën sports coupe, the fastest and latest model Grimaldi had managed to round up on such short notice. It wasn't exactly what Bolan had in mind when he'd requested it, but it would do. At least it would be more comfortable given Serif was with them.

Bolan raised a night-vision scope to his eye and scanned the front of the warehouse for at least the fifth time in the past hour. So far there hadn't been much activity that looked out of order for a business in exports.

Forklifts and pallet haulers moved among a variety of trucks parked at the docks, and another group handled the conveyer that led out to a ship on the dock.

"Awfully busy for this time of night," Grimaldi remarked.

"Not really," Serif said. "The Bosporus is one of the busiest waterways in the world. Operations run around the clock, so activity like this would be normal. In fact, this is probably the skeleton crew operating. During the day, it's hopping at least three times as much as you see right now."

"This is going to make a soft probe next to impossible," Grimaldi said, looking at Bolan.

The Executioner shook his head. "There are all kinds of ways to get inside. I'll just have to improvise."

"Dressed like Batman?" Serif said.

"I'll leave analysis to you," Bolan said with a grin. "And you can trust me with breaching a hard site."

Bolan went EVA before Serif could respond, crossing toward the warehouse at an angle. He nearly disappeared from view, becoming one with the night as if merging with the shadows. He was like an inky specter or dark vengeful wraith against the blackness of the night. And it was for this reason the occupants of the truck that entered the perimeter didn't see him as he lay prone in the high grass, and why the sentries didn't see him rise and leap onto the back of the truck.

As it neared the docks Bolan scaled the truck to the roof and kept low so he couldn't be seen. Even at a distance, the blacksuit made him nothing more than a shadow and nobody noticed—not much of a surprise given the harried activity going on all around him. The truck came to a halt and Bolan had to dig his hands into the roof to keep from being tossed off. The grinding of gears and lurch as the truck backed into one of the dock spaces made it evident the driver wasn't all that experienced.

Bolan had to admit to a sense of relief when the truck finally came to a halt.

The Executioner didn't wait for the driver or passenger to get out. Instead he crawled on hands and knees to the rear and immediately vaulted the lip to land undetected on the dock. He quickly located a standard access door, one of several spaced at regular intervals between sets of bay doors, and slipped inside.

He was thankful to discover the particular place he entered wasn't well lit, and near the door were metal stairs that led to the second floor. Bolan ascended them without anyone noticing and eventually reached an enclosed catwalk with massive windows that looked onto the main warehouse floor. He proceeded up the hall and eventually came to a T intersection. He peered down the corridor to his left and saw nothing but offices. A quick inspection toward the right appeared to contain much the same layout.

Bolan opted to go left and traversed the hallway until the end. If he didn't find what he sought in that location, he could start to work his way toward the exit. At least he wouldn't be pressed for time. He got to the last door on his right and noticed the stencil on the burnished wood: AMOCACCI, G., PRES. Could it really be *that* easy?

Bolan suddenly got a sinking feeling in the pit of his stomach but he didn't have time to react to that because his sixth sense suddenly rang warning bells. He cocked his head and immediately heard the sound of footfalls coming up the stairs. Had he actually been spotted and all they had done was let him walk right into a trap? If that was what had happened it would remove any doubt that someone was tracking them or watching them; somehow Bolan would have to deal with that.

The soldier tried the door handle to Amocacci's office and it turned smoothly. He pushed through and eased the door closed behind him, then crouched against the low wall just below the massive glass window that afforded a view into the office. Bolan waited, keeping his breath measured and steady. Eventually he saw the brilliant beam of a flashlight sweep across first the hall outside, glinting ever so briefly on the plate-glass window and then eventually fully shining into the room.

Bolan hunkered as low to the floor and close to the wall as his large frame would allow. The door swung open and the Executioner froze. He didn't move a muscle as a shadowy form stepped into the room—the newcomer had a flashlight and he swept it across the office against the back wall. A moment later the silhouette eased out of the office and secured the door behind it.

Bolan let out a long, low breath and let the tension of the moment fall from his shoulders. Probably a night watchman just on his normal rounds, which put Bolan's mind at ease. No point having to take the guy out, even if on a temporary basis. He probably wasn't the only guy on the security team for a place of this size. Any prolonged absence might bring others to investigate and that was something the Executioner definitely didn't need right now.

Bolan waited another minute before rising and heading straight to the file cabinets along one wall. He found them locked, which he was able to bypass with a red-lensed flashlight and lock-pick set. In less than a minute he had access to the files and was riffling through them. All standard fare: shipping manifests and purchase orders or receipts. File after file, organized by companies with which Amocacci did business, contained more or less the same documents. It all looked legit and that's probably because it was. Amocacci was probably too smart to keep any incriminating files.

He went through a couple different drawers in the course of five or ten minutes and found exactly what he'd thought he would. In fact, the files were almost *too* perfect. Every file was complete with meticulous detail and utterly organized. There wasn't one scrap of paper out of place and every document was the same.

Bolan replaced the last of the files. He'd seen enough. It was plainly obvious Amocacci wasn't using his business to front Council activities, although he was doing his best to make sure it *looked* as if he was. That was exactly what Bolan had expected based on what he'd told Serif. It was very similar to a game of bait-and-switch, although Amocacci was obviously getting some advice on how to play his hand. Everything he'd seemed to tell Serif about this being a way to lead her by the nose into "discovering" the Council of Luminárii was the complete vision of legitimacy, which was exactly why Bolan believed just the opposite case to be true.

Bolan stepped into the hallway and walked to the next office in line. The stencil on this door was in Turkish. Obviously a name, but in the Turkish script he couldn't read. Bolan didn't bother to go inside and search the files. He knew he'd find exactly the same thing: a meticulous record of their entire financial portfolio. Bolan continued up the corridor until he reached the hall that led to the stairs.

He was about almost there when he saw the dozen armed men break through the exterior doors and onto the warehouse floor.

CHAPTER TWENTY

These men weren't dressed in the black swathe mode of those who had attacked Bolan and Grimaldi. This group was composed of Asians and they wore black battle fatigues and toted full-profile assault rifles. Moreover, they moved like practiced commandos.

One of the men let out a high-pitched, sustained shout and then leveled his AR at the nearest group of workers and triggered his weapon. The unwary workforce had been caught completely off guard by the sudden appearance of the new arrivals and they scattered like frightened sheep, running in any direction that would take them away from the murderous assault. It didn't do them a whole lot of good.

The weapon chattered with the distinctive report of an AK-47 and it bucked in the Chinese gunner's hand as he swept the flashing muzzle in a wild pattern. Bolan watched as the other commandos followed suit and turned their weapons on select groups spread throughout the warehouse. The one place they didn't look was up at the glass walls through which Bolan overlooked them.

The Executioner's icy blue eyes drifted up and he noted the thick, metal cables that ran in parallel strands across the roof. They were greased, and a quick look at the far side of the warehouse revealed a fully integrated pulley system that was probably used to move large crates from one end of the massive warehouse to the other so they could be staged easily in appropriate sections.

Bolan whipped out his .44 Magnum Desert Eagle and triggered two bursts that shattered the window in front of him. After holstering the pistol, he reached to the military web belt and withdrew a grappler and high-tension climbing safety cable. In a single toss he managed to get the fifteen-hundred-pound tensile strength cable wrapped around the much thicker freight-hauling cable and then stepped over the jagged glass and into open air. He pushed off and the momentum carried him to a point where he was just above the heavily armed group of Asian terrorists.

Bolan withdrew an M-67 grenade. He primed the pin and then dropped the bomb, watching with interest as it plummeted to the floor below. It landed in the midst of the gunners. Most were so busy firing on unarmed civilians that only one actually noticed the bomb fall seemingly out of nowhere. The leader stopped firing, looked up with complete surprise, and then looked down just a moment before a look of shock spread across his face.

The grenade went up and even as the thunderous boom from the explosion reverberated through the factory—threatening to deafen half the occupants, including Bolan—the Executioner descended slowly via the cable as he swung the MP5 into target acquisition and opened with a full salvo on his enemies. Bolan had no idea who these killers were, but they had murdered at least a half-dozen innocent bystanders and the soldier couldn't stand by and watch that happen. His sense of justice simply wouldn't permit it.

Bolan wondered about the timeliness of these hard-men showing up with Kalashnikov AK-47 variants. In Kirklareli, someone supposedly kills an agent high up in the MSS and more than halfway across the country less than twenty-fours later, this crew shows up and begins to kill the workers in Amocacci's warehouse. That was *not* a coincidence.

By the time Bolan reached ground zero, three-quarters of the terrorists were either dead or dying. One pair tried to maneuver toward some sort of cover, but they never quite got there. Bolan cut them down with several short bursts that cut the legs from under one of his targets and perforated the chest of his partner. The last one managed to get off a single shot before his weapon jammed, although he made the shot count. The bullet winged Bolan and tore a furrow in his blacksuit, taking some skin from the top of his shoulder.

Bolan landed on his feet, rolled out of the impact and came to a stop on one knee. He leveled his MP5 and triggered a short burst from nearly point-blank range. The rounds drove the Chinese gunman backward, his useless weapon flying from numbed fingers as he jerked under the gut-shredding effect. Blood and flesh exploded from his bowels before he toppled to the rough material of the safety floor face-first.

The Executioner climbed wearily to his feet and raced for the door. The few unarmed civilians still in the immediate vicinity gave him a wide berth as he kicked one of the access doors open and sprinted through the doorway onto the dock. Bolan found a set of concrete steps, descended them and raced for the Citroën. Grimaldi apparently saw him coming because Bolan heard the engine come suddenly to life and then saw the headlights wink on and off twice to give him bearing.

Bolan made it in the nick of time and Grimaldi floored the accelerator and maneuvered out of the adjoining lot even as the flashing lights of the police squads winked into view. Fortunately they were out of view just as quickly as Grimaldi got clear of the dock and onto a main thoroughfare packed with enough cars that they could blend in and disappear quickly enough.

Nobody spoke for about a minute as Bolan and Grimaldi kept vigil on every mirror in the car. Finally the Executioner laid his head back and sighed deeply. He reached out to massage the pain in his shoulder. Based on the small amount of blood, he knew it had been a minor hit.

"You okay?" Serif asked with concern.

"I will be," Bolan said. When Grimaldi fired a look of concern in his direction, he added quickly, "Just a nick."

"What the hell happened?" Serif said.

"That was going to be my question," Grimaldi interjected. "We saw those guys come out of that truck, but we had no idea who they were. Not that we could have done anything about it."

"What truck?" Bolan asked. "You mean the one—"

"That you rode into the hot zone," Grimaldi finished. "Yeah, that would be the one."

Bolan shook his head with the irony of it. Here he'd been riding on the very vehicle that had brought the gunners into the factory and he hadn't even known it. "They were Asian, wearing combat gear and toting AK-style assault rifles. I'm betting they were Chinese."

"Quon Ma?" Serif asked.

"Possibly," Bolan replied.

"Looks like maybe you were spot-on about that guy and his involvement with the Council," Grimaldi remarked.

"I don't know about that," Bolan countered. "I'm not sure they were even his. I think they were meant to *look* that way. But whether he sent them is another story entirely."

"What makes you think they weren't sent by Ma?" Serif asked.

Bolan shook his head as he reached into a pouch on his belt and withdrew a wound pad. He slapped it on his shoulder before saying, "Well, think about it. First, they're showing up at Amocacci's warehouse. Why? What evidence does Ma have that it was Amocacci who ordered the hit? Second, they were killing innocent workers. How does that hurt Amocacci? The hit on Ma was up close and personal, so to speak. A guy like Ma wouldn't respond to that by killing bystanders—he's too much of a pro."

Serif blinked. "I hadn't really considered it that way before. But you're absolutely right. It wouldn't make sense for Ma to be involved at all."

"Right. But it *would* make sense if someone wanted Amocacci to think that it was Ma behind it."

Grimaldi nodded. "And they would have left plenty of witnesses to tell his people the guys were Asian."

"And let's assume Ma's actually dead," Bolan replied. "How would his people have learned so quickly who attempted the hit? We still don't have any answer as it relates to motive. There's no defensible reason for Amocacci to want Quon Ma dead, especially not if Ma plays a vital role in the success of the Council."

"This is getting crazier by the minute, Sarge," Grimaldi said.

"Actually this little incident has brought it all together for me. Someone's manipulating this entire group, and they're using Amocacci to do it."

"What makes you think so?" Serif asked.

"When I went to Amocacci and offered my services, he immediately turned me down. But what was more interesting was what he said to me just before I left. He said before he could take me up on my offer he'd have to discuss it with his colleagues."

"So?" Serif said with a laugh. "Maybe he was just putting you off."

Bolan shook his head emphatically. "Not likely. Because it was right after he'd denied working with anyone or knowing anything about the Council. Those aren't the words of a guy who's careful. That's why I decided to bait the hook by saying he was next on the hit list. I wanted him to think that whoever he was working with had betrayed him."

"So this attack will only help to reinforce your position," Grimaldi said.

Bolan nodded. "Right. And there's no doubt word will get back to him that I foiled the little plan to destroy his holdings and murder a bunch of his innocent workers. That ought to put me in real good with the guy. Especially when I show him I was wounded doing it."

"To say the least," Serif agreed.

"So, what next?" Grimaldi asked.

"Let's get back to the apartment so I can get this wound cleaned out. Then I'm going to see Amocacci while you take Alara back to the consulate."

"Where are you going to find him?" Serif asked. "He's probably gone into hiding."

"I'm going to knock right on his front door," the Executioner said.

Kirklareli, Turkey

JIAO PEI STEPPED from the rear of the cab and inspected her surroundings with just the barest hint of apprehension. This wasn't the best neighborhood in the city by any measure, and Pei wasn't accustomed to such surroundings—although she perfectly understood why Quon Ma would choose such a location in which to wait while the news died down of his alleged death.

As the British agent had explained to her, this was a peace offering, so Pei knew she had no reason to be concerned. It hadn't taken her long to reach out to her contacts in the highest echelon of the MSS to discover two truths: that Ma was very much alive and the location of his hiding place. It was then just a matter of getting word to him to let him know she would be coming. Better to be straightforward about it than to just show up and have his men kill her on spec.

This wasn't the first time Pei had served as a courier to one of her own countrymen. Normally she did this kind of work for lower-level agents and most of them she didn't know. But she was familiar with Ma, if only by reputation, and he had a notorious reputation for not trusting outsiders. Only Pei's own good reputation had probably been the reason he'd agreed to meet with her. That and the message she said she brought from a man she'd been told to identify only as "a friend with the Lion."

Pei didn't let on she knew the identity of the message sender but of course she did. Anyone who had been in the intelligence game long enough knew Hurley Willham quite well, if not personally then by his reputed connections. The guy was a weasel, of course—that's how Pei viewed him, anyway. But he paid well, and he supposedly knew how to show the proper deference to Pei's very stringent requirements, so she'd allowed him to use her services now and again. This was the first time he'd asked her to reach out to Quon Ma who, according to very reliable resources, had allegedly been reported dead less than twenty-four hours earlier.

As Pei descended the concrete steps outside the dilapidated building that led to basement level and was shown inside, men in black suits and bulges in their jackets fanned out to check the perimeter to ensure nobody had followed her. The same activity would doubtless hold true upon her departure.

Pei sat on the crimson settee and crossed her legs. She tugged the white gloves from her hands—the neutral signature and trademark of her particular business—before tucking them into the folds of the expensive silk blouse she wore. An odd, swirling pattern of shiny jade thread ran throughout the blouse, a pattern that looked random until one stood far enough back to realize it was actually a dragon's profile. The red gemstone she wore above her left breast actually served as the dragon's eye.

Quon Ma entered the living area less than a minute later. He wore dark gray slacks and a short-sleeved casual shirt with a polo-style collar. The MSS lead agent sat and stared Pei in the eye a long moment.

She met his gaze, refusing to lower her eyes as most any other woman would do in a show of subservience. It was after this long period of silence between them, one that was apparently making Ma's bodyguards very uncomfortable, that she rose and bowed formally to him. Ma followed suit and then they sat and he waved at a servant to bring tea.

"It's very agreeable to see you alive, Quon," Pei said.

"Thank you," Ma said. "And it's good to see you, as well. Actually, I was expecting you to contact me sooner or later."

"That's very interesting," she said. "Since I only learned that you were still alive a short time ago."

"The individuals you contacted within the ministry are all close allies," Ma replied. "It shouldn't surprise you in the least."

"And here I thought maybe I had a proprietary access unknown to the rest of the ministry," Pei said.

Ma shrugged. "I would say that for the most part you do. In fact, your ability to maintain both your anonymity and autonomy in such a business as yours is legendary. But you can probably forgive some old men an indiscretion or two under the present circumstances."

Pei seemed a little frosty. "Not likely forgivable. But I suppose I have no choice but to tolerate it."

"Quite." Ma paused as the servant brought in the tea. They waited while he performed the familiar ritual of pouring and then Ma resumed the discussion. "So on to your message. I found it…interesting."

"As did I," Pei replied. "The fact of the matter is I don't know whether you can trust Willham. His loyalty is up for *you* to decide. What he did tell me was that he knew you were alive, and he knew who had made the attempt on your life. He also said that he's willing to offer any assistance you might request if only you will trust him."

"Did he identify the person by name who ordered my death?"

She shook her head. "He was insistent that he would reveal that name *only* to you, and under only the most secure conditions."

"Did he give any reason?"

She shrugged. "He didn't say specifically, but from his reply when I asked, he seemed concerned about his own security."

"So he thinks he might also be a target."

Pei took a sip of tea before returning the cup to the saucer and nodding. "Yes."

Ma said nothing, instead choosing to ponder her statement. It didn't make much sense to him, that much seemed certain. Pei didn't really know what else to tell him. She could have made some assumptions based on her conversation with Willham, but that would have far and away exceeded her mandate. She delivered messages, and other than that she kept her nose out of the affairs of men like Quon Ma. It was how she'd stayed alive and how she'd profited. Her business was a very lucrative one, much more lucrative than most might have thought. Delivering cryptic messages between intelligence agents in the MSS was a valued enough skill, but when able to deliver them between entire agencies, whether allies or enemies, it was profitable by a hundredfold.

"There's very little reason I have to trust Willham," Ma said. "For all I know, he's the one who ordered my death."

"Again, it's not my place to determine the loyalty of

your associates to you, or yours to them. Frankly, I've found this entire situation most interesting."

"What do mean?"

"Let's not be coy with each other, Quon. We've been acquainted too long for that. I know you have many enemies, as do you, but it seems rather bold for someone to make such an attempt. The individual in question is either *very* angry with you, which wouldn't be unlikely if the hand of someone from another agency, or someone within the ministry wants you out of the way. As I see it, those are the only likely candidates in this given scenario."

"For someone who does not presume to judge loyalty, you seem quite opinionated on this subject," Ma replied.

"It's not opinion, it's only logic," Pei said. "Logic puzzles intrigue me. But that's not to say that I don't feel a certain amount of empathy for you."

"The Dragon Lady? Feeling empathy?"

"Now you're just attempting to be hurtful," Pei said with a knowing smile. "I *respect* you, Quon Ma—nothing more and nothing less. But I do not like the thought of those with whom I do business going around and killing each other at a whim. First, it cuts into my own profits. Second, it makes the survivors much less trustworthy, and I feel the urge to go somewhere else and start again. I really don't wish to do that as it's very difficult to find good clients and can be, given this line of work, even more difficult to *keep* them."

"Your point is well taken, madam," Ma replied.

"My point is merely that I wish no harm to come to you unless it is deserved. And I can't be sure, but I would guess that Willham may probably be trusted.

After all, he did pay my fee without question in order to reach out to you."

"How much?"

Pei shook her head. "I never discuss money. But *you* have used my services before, and you know my fee schedule. Let us merely say it was a considerable sum."

"What disturbs me most is that he reached out to you at all."

Pei cocked her head. "And why should it?"

"Because for all he knew I was *dead*," Ma said. "Why would he even think that I was alive?"

"I did ask him that, and his answer seemed quite valid. Would you like to know what he said?"

Ma set down his teacup, sat back on the couch and draped his arm over the back of it. "Of course."

"Well, he pointed out the fact that this city wasn't immediately crawling with a dozen agents from the ministry. He also noted that he'd not heard from any other of your associates regarding your death. In fact, the information came to him by some other mechanism, although he adamantly refused to tell me the source. This concerned him greatly on a number of levels, particularly that he'd not been contacted by the aforementioned associates. I frankly didn't understand much of it, since I wasn't aware you had many mutual friends."

"We have *no* friends in this business," Quon Ma interjected. "You know that. But I do now understand from what you've said how he might have drawn the conclusions he did. It would seem he is doing his best to show me his support."

Pei nodded and rose. "Then I believe my work is finished here and I should be on my way. It's a long journey back home."

"You're welcome to stay. I have additional accommodations, and you would be able to rest in private until feeling renewed enough to return home."

"No," Pei said, shaking her head. "I thank you for your generous offer, but I believe it would be best that I not stay here any longer than absolutely necessary for both your security and my own."

"I understand. Until we meet again."

They bowed to each other before Ma gestured for his men to show her out.

Pei went through the door and up the stairs quickly, checking the area around her one last time before heading to her vehicle. As the driver opened the door, her small head seemed to implode and her face caved in as if smashed by an unseen force. The gore sprayed the men around her, but they reacted with incredible speed. Even as her body toppled, one of the men grabbed her and shoved her into the back seat of the car. He then threw his body on top of hers.

The others drew their pistols and fanned out, crouched and looking wide-eyed in every direction like a herd of crazed jackals. There had been no warning, no report from the weapon, although it was clear someone had just assassinated Jiao Pei with a high-powered sniper rifle. They waited a long time before anyone moved.

Probably not so much out of concern that the sniper might decide to take out another target, as out of worry about the repercussions when they reported the incident to Quon Ma.

CHAPTER TWENTY-ONE

Istanbul, Turkey

If Gastone Amocacci had not seen it with his own eyes, he probably would not have believed it.

That didn't change the effect Bolan had when he walked right to the front door of Amocacci's residence in an upscale neighborhood. When the head servant answered, Bolan pushed his way past him and entered the sitting room where Amocacci sat reading. Bolan wore a blacksuit, weapons of war dangling from the belt and suspenders. He'd changed into a fresh one, the other no longer salvageable as a victim of a bullet and some blood.

Bolan wasn't interested in frightening Amocacci, although it would have appeared that way to the several staff members who observed this black-clad avenging angel. Bolan was much more interested in having the polar-opposite effect; an effect that would make Amocacci view Bolan as the hero and protector of all he valued. If the story had reached him yet about what had happened at the warehouse, he would surely not be surprised by such a visit.

The Executioner could tell immediately from the expression on Amocacci's face that he *had* heard of those recent activities. His suspicions were confirmed when

Amocacci set down the book he'd been reading, took off his glasses and looked Bolan in the eye. "I've been expecting you."

"Have you?"

Amocacci managed a smile, although Bolan could tell it was somewhat forced. "I don't suppose it would do much good to lie to you and say I hadn't."

"It wouldn't."

"Have a seat," Amocacci said, indicating an armchair near him.

There were now three staff members standing in the entryway to the sitting room. Amocacci tried to put on as normal a front as possible. "No need for alarm. Mr. Cooper is here as my guest. Please return to your duties."

The staff seemed hesitant at first, but with an unspoken exchange of looks from Amocacci they immediately departed for parts unknown, probably to make as much distance from the room as possible. Bolan supposed it might have been a secret signal and at any minute a dozen Turkish cops would show up, but he doubted it. For Amocacci to explain why an American armed to teeth would be showing up at his home, especially after what had happened at the warehouse earlier in the evening, would indeed attract much more intention than the Italian businessman could afford.

"I take it the cops have already been here," Bolan said.

"They have."

"How did you explain what happened down at your warehouse?"

"I was an intelligence agent with Interpol. You think I don't know the art of telling a good lie?"

"I'm waiting."

"For what."

"A real answer," Bolan replied.

"I said I didn't know."

"Which just happens to be the truth. Mostly. So you were able to make it quite convincing." Bolan chuckled. "I assume because of your affiliations in some of the highest seats of government, the locals weren't too eager to press you on it."

"Correct," Amocacci said with a smile. "Although I'm still very puzzled by the reason behind all of this."

"I warned you this morning you were next on the list," Bolan said.

"Mr. Cooper, let's be frank," Amocacci replied. "First, there's no reason for me to assume that the murders of some of my dock workers would do any harm to me personally."

"Maybe it was a way to discredit you."

"In the eyes of *whom*?"

"The other members of your little group—your Council of Light or whatever the hell you choose to call yourselves."

"I don't know what you mean."

"Come on, Amocacci!" Bolan snapped. "Stop playing games. You tell some people that you made the whole thing up, then you turn around and tell others it exists. Then you arrange the assassination of one of your team, and when you get your hand caught in the cookie jar you deny everything up to and including trying to deny your own rotten existence. No more pretending. You can't afford it. The only way out of this is to work with me."

"Is that right?"

"That's how I see it."

"And if I disagree?"

"It's nothing to me," Bolan said with a shrug. "I've told you that before. But stop and ask yourself for a minute why I happened to be at the warehouse when that hit went down. How did I know?"

"Perhaps you were there trying to dig up dirt on me."

"Like you'd leave anything incriminating there? Get real. I was there because I knew something like that was going to happen. And you're right to think that it's nothing but a ruse because it is. Those guys weren't working for Quon Ma any more than whoever you green-lighted to take out Ma doesn't know by now they failed miserably. And by the way, Quon Ma is quite alive and well."

"Only someone with connections to Alara Serif and the American government could know all of that."

"Not so," Bolan said. "Your contact has a big mouth—too big, you ask me."

"I have many associates, Cooper. Which one are we talking about now?"

"I just told you. The guy you had take out Ma, or *try* to take him out. The same guy who tried to take me out right after I visited your office this morning."

"I heard about that trouble," Amocacci said. "And I assumed it was you. But I promise you that I had *nothing* to do with it. I could not call on such resources so fast. There are some things even out of my reach and performing a miracle is one of them."

"I figured you'd say that."

"But you don't believe me."

Bolan sat back and purposefully kept his face impassive. "Actually, I do. I think your contact is the same guy who tried to recruit me in Guatemala. I also think he's the one who botched the hit on Quon Ma, and the one who sent that team to the warehouse."

"Let's suppose you're right," Amocacci said. "Why would he do that?"

"The same reason I would have," Bolan replied. "Money. The difference is, he's probably splitting it with one of your partners on the Council. Not Ma, obviously, which means you're working with others. Maybe rogues like yourself, or possibly even those with legitimate posts inside certain intelligence circles."

"And I suppose you're here to tell me that you can identify this individual."

"The guy inside your group who's pulling the strings?" Bolan let out a mock snort of derision. "Not likely. But I'm also positive I know who your contact is. And I don't think it would be difficult to trace him back to the real brains behind all of this if we work at it together."

"How do you propose to do that?"

"Call a meeting."

"A meeting?" Amocacci said, visibly stiffening at the suggestion.

Got him, Bolan thought. "Yeah. Gather your team all in one place and then you can do your big reveal."

"But you just said one of them is the traitor," Amocacci countered. "Wouldn't that be playing directly into the hands of that individual?"

"No," Bolan replied. "Because when I give you the identity of the individual who's behind all of this, and you out him, the traitor in your group is going to think they're blown, too."

That brought a scoffing laugh from Amocacci.

"Hardly! These men have been in the intelligence game too long."

"What men?" Bolan said with a wicked grin. "The Council? The men you say don't exist?"

Amocacci took on a hue perilous enough to detect even through his darker skin. "I think you're playing a dangerous game, Cooper. A *very* dangerous game indeed."

"Maybe so," Bolan said. "But it's no more dangerous than the one you've been playing with this guy."

"There's no way I could bring you in to see my associates, anyway. It violates the rules. You would be marked for termination within the day."

"Unless you vouch for me."

"I would have to do that *before* I brought you in."

"Fine, do it before then."

Amocacci cocked his head. "You told me you weren't interested in being a part of our organization. That you were only interested in the money."

"The two aren't mutually exclusive. Are they?" Bolan made a show of looking around the very nice home and waved toward the ceiling. "I mean, you seem to be doing just fine for yourself."

"I suppose."

Bolan rose. "Look, pal. I'm not going to waste any more time with you. You put the feelers out there for an American inside the intelligence community. I'm that American. I'm disenfranchised with the NSA and, like I told you before, I won't be welcomed back there at this point. Anyone who could connect me with the operation in Guatemala is dead. That means you got no risk of exposure from that angle."

"Agreed."

"So you have your little secret meeting or whatever it is that you do, and you submit my candidacy. I'll wait right here in Istanbul for three days."

"That's barely enough time to—"

"Three days," Bolan cut in. "After that, I have to become a ghost because I'm sure if I can't disappear into your little fold I'll be at risk of exposure. And we can't have that. As to a reason you should show me any loyalty, consider I risked my neck to keep those goons sent by your contact from starting an all-out war between you and the Chinese Ministry of State Security. And believe me when I say, you don't want any of that."

"Fine," Amocacci said. "But aren't you forgetting something?"

"What?"

"The identity of my contact," Amocacci replied. "You said you're pretty sure you know who he is."

"What…you mean you really *don't* know who he is?" Bolan said with his best imitation of a guffaw. "That's rich, Amocacci!"

"Who *is* it, goddamn you?"

Bolan's expression went flat and hard. "His name is Derek Savitch. He's a lawyer in Canada, some sort of mucky-muck on a committee that oversees Canada's Special Intelligence Service."

"How do I know you're telling me the truth?"

"Check it out." Bolan spelled the name and then walked out. As he left he added, "But you already know I'm telling the truth. I've done all I'm going to do to demonstrate my loyalty, Amocacci. From here out, it's on you."

"SO WHAT HAPPENED?" Grimaldi asked.

He was seated at the table in the U.S. Consulate along with Bolan, Serif, Colonel Bindler and Major Maxwell.

"Hook, line and sinker," Bolan said.

"Finally!" Serif declared with a clap of her hands.

"Okay, but just how sure are you that he'll be able to round up the rest of the Council members, Stone?" Bindler asked.

"He's been put into a corner and he knows it," Bolan said. "Now that I've given him Savitch's scent, that aspect of it becomes a secondary consideration. If Amocacci thinks he can use Savitch as the scapegoat, and I have no reason to think he can't, he may see this as an opportunity to glue the pieces back together."

"Then once they know that they were duped, they'll rally behind him," Maxwell said.

Bolan nodded. "Exactly. He'll be hailed as a hero once more and they'll go ahead with whatever major operation they had planned."

"Do you think he'll bring you into it?"

Bolan shook his head. "No. But he doesn't have to. In fact, I'm counting on the fact he won't. He'll figure I'm sitting on my hands in Istanbul, awaiting his reply with bated breath."

"When in fact what we'll be doing is tailing him straight to their base of operations," Serif interjected. "Which we're now pretty confident is in or near his home near the Yildiz Mountains."

"You located it?" Bolan asked.

It was Bindler who replied. "She did, once I authorized the surveillance. You see, Alara was always convinced that's where Amocacci met with the other members of the Council. But we could never allow her to pursue it in any official capacity. In fact, the few times I sent reports to the Pentagon I was ordered not to pursue the matter further. Apparently they didn't want to waste resources on it."

Maxwell shook his head. "Stupidest decision I've ever seen them make. One that almost cost the lives of some good men." He gestured at Serif. "And *this* woman."

"At ease on that shit, Major," Bindler snapped.

"Aye, sir."

Bindler continued. "It was completely amazing to me to learn, however, that as soon as this Hal Brognola got involved, all of a sudden I had whatever resources I needed. I even had representatives from the Pentagon shouting, 'Yes, sir, no, sir, three bags full.' Now how do you explain that?"

Bolan grinned. "That is quite interesting. But I don't think we should spend too much valuable time pondering the why. Do you, Colonel?"

"No, I don't suppose I do."

"So how did you resolve finding his location?" Grimaldi inquired.

Serif grinned and looked at Bindler, who nodded. She turned to a nearby computer keyboard and began to type while Maxwell picked up a remote and turned on an overhead projector. It wasn't exactly the high-tech setup at Stony Man Farm, but the U.S. Consulate to Turkey didn't have near the same budget as the most covert special operations group in the world.

"These are satellite images taken at Colonel Bindler's request," Serif said. "This topographical map overlay shows us the exact coordinates of his residence. Now, if you look carefully, you'll notice these heat signatures."

Bolan nodded. "Way too regular to be natural springs or geographical phenomena."

"Correct! And financial records confirm the residence there *was* purchased, along with the land grant of twenty-five acres surrounding it, by Amocacci and Lady Fellini under special authorization of the Turkish government."

"So when he leaves every weekend," Bolan said, "you think he was going to meet them."

Serif nodded. "I do believe so, yes. And while I don't have any substantial proof, if he calls a meeting of the Council and then departs immediately for Malko Tarlovo by his personal chopper..."

"We'll know *exactly* where he's headed," Grimaldi said.

"Yes!"

Bolan turned to Bindler. "You have a chopper here at the consulate."

It wasn't a question and Bindler nodded. "Yes. But it's strictly for the use of the consul or his chief of staff. And it's not equipped with any weapons."

"What kind is it?" Grimaldi asked.

"Huey YH-40," Maxwell replied. "One of the six that was originally prototyped and then given to various agencies. It was meant to be a replacement for the Iroquois but with the stretch cabin."

"I'm familiar," Grimaldi said. He turned to Bolan. "It could be easily modified if we had the right equipment."

"What about range?"

"If nothing else, it will definitely make the trip with fuel to spare. And since we'll be light, we can add extra fuel drums."

"Excuse me," Bindler said. "I don't mean to rain on

your parade, but there's no way the consul will agree to let you borrow his helicopter."

"Then we won't borrow it," Grimaldi said. "We'll just *take* it."

Serif's eyes went wide. "You can do that?"

Grimaldi merely nodded and replied with a grin, "The President will usually ask nicely first. Then if he gets any flack, he tends to become a bit tougher about it."

The three consulate staff members all looked suddenly and properly demure.

Bindler cleared his throat. "Okay, well, I guess that answers any questions about use of the helicopter. So what's your plan?"

Bolan scratched his chin and studied the map for a minute. "That's going to be pretty rugged territory. Even if we can get in close with the chopper, we have no idea what we'll be up against. Not to mention there's the question of possible security or other resistance."

"You think they'll have the place guarded?" Maxwell asked.

"I'd bet money on it," Bolan replied. "A house that size can't be easily defended by just man power. There's probably a full security system in place, to alert them if anyone comes around. That means we'll have to approach from the hillside and drop in via air assault mode. I don't think Amocacci or his people would expect that."

"Makes sense," Serif said. "I'm an experienced climber, so it won't be a problem."

Bindler looked at her with surprise. "You're going?"

"I am," Serif said immediately. She pointed to Bolan and said, "Colonel Stone promised I could accompany him when he brought down the Council of Luminárii. I've been following this group for a *very* long time and I deserve to be there as part of the team that brings it down."

Bolan thought about arguing the point, but he realized, given the resolve in her face, it would be futile. Besides, he'd given his word and he was a man who kept his word. Under the worst circumstances he might have gone back on it—he couldn't find any reason to do so this time. At least not one he could defend.

"It's true," Bolan said. "And frankly, I could probably use her help. She's much more familiar with Amocacci's operational background. And she also knows a lot more about the Council than any of us. Her strategic input may come in quite valuable."

"I don't know," Bindler said. "I don't think this is a good idea. But I've been told to cooperate with you, Colonel, and that's what I intend to do."

"I don't blame you, sir," Bolan said. "But we all have to follow orders and we're all on the same side. Goes without saying, then, your cooperation is appreciated. One officer to another."

Bindler nodded.

"Well, if that wraps up the details, I guess we should get cracking," Grimaldi said. He looked at Maxwell. "Major, would you mind giving me a hand with the chopper?"

"Not at all."

When the two were gone, Bindler made small talk with Serif and Bolan before dismissing himself to other duties, leaving Bolan and Serif alone.

"Thank you," she said.

"For what?"

"Keeping your word. You know…letting me tag along."

"There's one condition," Bolan said with a firm but level gaze.

"I know, I know…you're in charge."

"Smart lady," Bolan replied.

CHAPTER TWENTY-TWO

Kirklareli, Turkey

"And you believe Gastone?" the voice of Hurley Willham queried.

Quon Ma hesitated only a moment before replying. "I don't know if I believe him. I simply know that what he said is quite feasible. There could have been someone operating between us, manipulating the situation from the beginning."

"And why do you have any bloody reason to believe he's telling you the truth?"

"Because he gave me an actual *name*," Ma replied.

The long silence on the other end of the line both surprised and worried Quon Ma. He'd never trusted Hurley Willham. Worse yet, the guy had sent Jiao Pei to courier a message to him, with some miraculous guesswork involved that Ma was actually alive, and then she'd been wasted just hours after taking the assignment. Part of this didn't make a bit of sense to Ma, and he was very hard pressed to think that Willham would have had anything to do with her death. After all, her demise would not have benefited Willham in any way any more than Ma's death would have. Not to mention that his reaction had been proportionately shocked when Ma contacted him directly to advise of Pei's assassination.

Ma decided to test Willham. "Have you spoken with the others?"

"No—why?"

"I just wondered if either of them was as concerned as you seem to be."

"I had no reason to talk to them," Willham said quickly. "My assumption was that since Gastone was calling the meeting he would contact each of us, as per protocol."

"But of course he didn't know to contact me until you told him."

"I assumed you would want him to know, and that you among all of us would have the most reason to want to attend this meeting."

"I do at that."

Despite Quon Ma's attempt to trap Willham, the guy seemed legitimate. Instead of lying and saying he'd spoken with Penzak or Ryzkhov, he'd let Amocacci handle it personally as they had agreed should always happen. Amocacci always called the meetings, and he was the sole person to contact each of them in turn. None of them talked to each other outside the official circle. The only reason Ma had even attempted to contact Willham directly was because of Pei's death.

"Naturally, he thought I was dead," Ma said. "So he wouldn't have tried to contact me unless you told him."

"Correct. Which is the *only* reason I told him."

"The situation has changed," Ma said. "We may no longer be able to follow the letter of the protocols we put in place. Especially not now that someone within our own ranks may be working with our enemies."

"I have the feeling we'll be able to expose the evil bastard behind all this turmoil that's been created for

us. And when I do, I will personally take great pleasure in watching his hide being stripped off him a little at a time."

"You mean *after* I'm finished with him," Ma said.

"Of course, of course."

"I look forward to seeing you, my friend."

"My sentiments, as well. And I'm glad my assumptions were correct about you. Your loss would have been
felt for a very long time to come."

"Thank you," Ma said and then he hung up.

The MSS specialist turned to his men and said, "Get
prepared. We're going to the meeting place. I think I've
found our assassin."

As soon as he received the call from Gastone Amocacci,
Lev Penzak put into motion the preparations he'd made.
The very fact that Amocacci's intent was to release the
name of the *true* traitor among them made Penzak nervous. Their situation was precarious enough without
publicly revealing the single individual among them
who had allegedly masterminded this entire affair. Of
course, he was pretty confident he knew who the traitor
was already. He and Ryzkhov had agreed that Willham
was the obvious choice. He was the only one who knew
the identity of the contact that Amocacci had been dealing with, a contact Amocacci now planned to reveal to
the rest of them.

Could Willham really act so surprised? Penzak
highly doubted it, and Ryzkhov had agreed. There was
no other choice but to attend the meeting, but Penzak
didn't plan to attend it alone. He knew that Amocacci
would bring guns, and there was no way he planned to
be left without any sort of escape plan. If Amocacci or

any of the others turned their people loose on him, or each other for that matter, Penzak planned to be ready. Yes, it was entirely possible that the foothills of the Strandzha would run red with blood.

But there was no way Lev Penzak would allow any of it to be his own.

AS SOON AS Willham had finished his call with Quon Ma, he picked up the phone and dialed Savitch, who answered on the second ring.

"I've been sitting around here waiting on you for hours!" Savitch told him. "When are you going to come up with some new money? I can't retire on the small change I've made."

"Just shut up and listen, you dumb arse!" Willham barked. He didn't wait for Savitch to protest. "They've called a meeting of the Council."

"And you're planning to go?"

"Yes," Willham replied. "So are you."

"I don't think so."

"I don't care what you think, you're bloody well going to go. But we can't be seen together, so you'll have to find your own way there."

"And once I'm there, just what exactly is it you expect me to do?"

"You said you wanted to make money?"

"Yeah."

"Well, then, today is your day because Amocacci has plenty of it at his estate in the Strandzha. You got something to write with?" When Savitch confirmed he did, Willham gave him the exact coordinates of the meeting place. "I want you to make sure there's a clear escape path for us."

"How do you suggest I do that?"

"There should be a flight out of Istanbul tonight, a charter that can take you to Malko Tarnovo. That's a major city near Amocacci's residence. Once you're there, I want you to arrange for some sort of transportation. You'll need a utility vehicle of some kind, something that can handle rough terrain. We'll use that to get back to Malko Tarnovo, and it should be large enough to haul a whole lot of cash."

"What about Amocacci and your other pals, eh? They aren't just going to let you walk away from this with all of that money."

"You're the one who's supposed to have all the connections. Get help from Wehr, if necessary. I don't care if you decide to hire a bloody fucking army. Just get it done and be ready for me because I'll probably be coming out of there like my ass is on fire."

"What about our plans in the U.S.?"

"What about them? It'll happen just as scheduled. Stop worrying about the stupid shit I've already handled and start worrying about how we're going to save our arses when this thing blows wide open."

"Do they know it's you?"

"Not yet," Hurley Willham replied with a maniacal laugh. "But they will. They will know *very* soon."

Istanbul, Turkey

"LOOKS LIKE THE ball's in play, Sarge," Grimaldi said as he entered the small briefing room. "We just got confirmation that a charter for Malko Tarnovo left twenty minutes ago."

"And Amocacci—" Bolan looking up from a scaled-down version of Serif's terrain map he'd been committing to memory "—was on board?"

"The one and only."

Bolan nodded. "Excellent. We leave in two hours."

"You don't want to get going right away?"

Bolan shook his head. "No, we need to wait for all the pieces to fall into place. I want to make sure before I go in that everyone is present and accounted for. I'll only get one chance at this, and we can't afford stragglers. Too much is at stake."

Grimaldi nodded and then sat at the table. "Mind if I ask you a question?"

Bolan gave the pilot his full attention. "Shoot."

"Do you *really* think letting Serif tag along is such a good idea? I mean...she has no field training. She's hardly equipped for this kind of mission. I'd think you'd want to go it alone so you can move fast and improvise if need be without adding an innocent factor to the equation."

"I'd like to be able to do this one alone, Jack," Bolan said. "But the fact is I gave my word. I can't go back on it."

"Even if it means she could get killed?"

"She's a big girl," Bolan said. "She knows what she's getting herself into. And besides, as she pointed out during the briefing, she's earned a right to see this through. Without her insight we would never have gotten this far. I don't think it's asking too much to let her be a part of it. She's promised to knuckle under and do as she's told."

"And you believe her?"

"No," Bolan said with a knowing smile, "but I've already accounted for that."

Malko Tarnovo, Turkey

WHILE TURKEY WASN'T where General Mikhail Ryzkhov would have preferred to reside, he had to admit it beat some of the other places in which he'd lived throughout his career in the GRU. The fact of the matter was that he would have preferred to return to Russia. However, his commission had come with a price since his family was from a lesser house. It was almost as if the days of czars and royalty had returned to Mother Russia, and Ryzkhov had grown rather sick of the whole idea.

No matter what else might have been going on, this wasn't the worse assignment in the world. At least it had been going smoothly until Amocacci called the meeting. As per protocol, Ryzkhov hadn't contacted any of the others. He'd also been very surprised to hear that Quon Ma was still alive, after all. So Amocacci's assassination attempt had failed. Except that he knew it wasn't Amocacci who'd pulled the strings.

Why none of them had simply been honest from the beginning and realized that Hurley Willham had been manipulating the whole situation from the start was anybody's guess. Frankly, as he sat there and drank, General Ryzkhov wondered why he'd put up with *any* of them this long. He had to admit he liked Quon Ma. Part of him had been very glad that Ma had managed to survive the attempt on his life, although that complicated matters now.

It had originally been agreed among them that Amocacci should be the one to go if it turned out the job on Ma had been botched. Instead the Italian had somehow managed to turn the tables on the lot of them. His ingenuity surprised Ryzkhov in a number of ways, and he'd begun to wonder if they hadn't made a mistake. After all, it was Willham who had cooked up the entire scheme from the beginning. Willham had been the one to accuse Ma of leaking Council secrets to their enemies, and Willham had been the one to hire his guy to dupe Amocacci into taking out the contract on Quon Ma.

What nonsense!

No, the more Ryzkhov thought about it, the more incompetent the entire lot seemed to him. It was probably time to cut their losses, and when he'd consulted with his people in the GRU they'd been in consensus. The thing was, each of the other men had probably called on his own resources for protection. That meant Ryzkhov could only win this game by employing superior numbers.

He supposed he could implement a full-strength unit, including a tank and possibly a couple of armored vehicles, but that didn't make much sense. He had a squad of Spetsnaz at his disposal and he saw little reason *not* to use their distinct talents to get the job done. More than likely, his former colleagues would have little more than thugs in place to cover their escape and nothing more. Ryzkhov would have to see to it that they didn't escape, and he would have to ensure the elimination of their personnel.

Ryzkhov considered for a moment if it would be better to try to take them individually, since the Council members were the high-value assets. He dismissed the idea after about three rounds of vodka. Too risky without a high enough return on investment. The best way would still be to wait until they were together in one place. Ryzkhov could then excuse himself and let his men come in to take care of business.

"How will we get in ahead of them, Comrade General?" asked Captain Sergev, the head of the Spetsnaz commando team.

Ryzkhov had summoned the man to his quarters, which occupied a small, nondescript building in a downtown section of the city. The buildings here were older but the population in the area sparse, so it had become the perfect place from which Ryzkhov could operate in relative obscurity. It was also convenient when he had to travel for meetings. The best part about the location was that nobody knew about it, not even the other members on the Council. They all assumed that he maintained a place in the Turkish capital of Ankara, and that he had a small base of operations out of Kirklareli. Ryzkhov had never seen any reason to refute their assumptions, seeing that it gave him a somewhat tactical edge.

"There's a special entrance to the underground facility off this access road," Ryzkhov said as they bent over a map of the area. It was a special map that the GRU officer had made not too long after their first meeting. "But that's the one used by all of us. What I need you to do is to come through the house and take that access down to those chambers. As soon as the job is done, you can escort me out the same way. The others won't know there's a problem until it's much too late."

"Yes, sir. We'll not fail you."

"See that you don't, Comrade Captain," Ryzkhov replied, dismissing him. "For the sake of your own life as well as mine."

Now Ryzkhov felt a headache coming on and a chill in his body. He didn't want to resort to this, but he was desperate. He didn't see any other answers to the problem at hand. His former associates had become quarrelsome. They couldn't be trusted, and Ryzkhov considered the irony of it. Here they had assembled with the purpose of tearing apart the U.S. military intelligence community. And indeed, maybe they still had a chance to do that. But Ryzkhov knew if nothing else he would need to be ready in case one of them attempted to perpetrate the ultimate betrayal.

To hear Amocacci talk, it was as if he already knew who among them was the traitor. For all Ryzkhov knew, it might still be Amocacci. Somehow, he didn't think so. He was still playing the odds that it was actually Willham, since the British SIS case officer had seemed to have his finger on this thing from the start. Unfortunately, Ryzkhov couldn't deal with maybes. He had to be sure that he didn't do something to expose his own ass and create a loss from which the GRU might not be able to recover.

So since he couldn't be sure, he'd take out the entire body and start anew. Perhaps he could find a group among his own kind that would be trustworthy enough to handle the operation they had planned from the beginning. That thought gave him even more of a headache. The ball had already been put into motion on that count, and Ryzkhov hoped he lived long enough to see the aftermath of their months of planning.

Realizing that he'd consumed quite a bit of vodka, and that he would need a clear head when his men acted, Ryzkhov stopped drinking and put the partially empty bottle in his desk drawer. It would be time to leave soon.

When the deed had been done, surely he could return to finish what he'd begun.

WHEN DEREK SAVITCH arrived in Malko Tarnovo, he realized very little time remained before all of the vehicle rental places closed up shop for the night. If he failed in this one mission, he knew Willham would never trust him with another job. The arrangement he'd made with Wehr to assassinate Quon Ma had failed. Savitch knew he couldn't allow a repeat performance like that. He wasn't afraid of Willham as much as he was if he ended up stranded in this godforsaken shit hole without any funds to get out.

He'd have to worry about the authorities detaining him; sooner or later the Canadian government would get wind of his plight and they would send someone to retrieve him. While his countrymen were much more civilized than most, the fact remained that prison was prison. Savitch couldn't afford that. Not only did he want a comfortable life, he wanted one where he could get the very best specialists in his country to treat his condition.

Not that Savitch had much loyalty to Canada anyway. In actuality, he'd been born in Argentina to parents who were missionaries. But because his parents were both Canadian citizens, Savitch had been declared a citizen of Canada despite the actual location of his birth. Not that it mattered, since he'd spent most of the first fifteen years of his life traveling all over the world with his parents, who spent their entire life scraping to get by—sometimes he could remember going a couple of days without much to eat.

When he'd finally made it into law school, it was

the happiest day of the young Derek Savitch's life. He'd earned his degree in about two-thirds the time it had taken most other students, primarily because while they were out pissing off and not studying, he was hitting the books every spare moment. It had taken time to rise through the ranks until he'd reached the grand and elevated post as an attorney for various government operations.

Eventually it paid off. But then the disease had struck him and hard. The rapid weight gain caused his wife to leave him, and his savings began to dwindle while he traveled to various countries and sought the help of specialists. They'd given him medication that had kept him from dying, but hadn't done a damn thing for him insofar as his overall health was concerned. He still had the thyroid disease, and he was willing to work with experimental therapies to attempt to resolve the problem.

So whatever happened now, he knew he couldn't screw this up. It would be his last chance to set things straight and get control of his life. He was smarter than all of these people combined, even smarter than Willham. Once the job was done and he had Amocacci's money, Savitch planned to make sure Willham understood that.

For when it was over, he planned to kill Hurley Willham with his bare hands.

CHAPTER TWENTY-THREE

It was nearly 0400 when the chopper crested the Yildiz Mountains and swung low off a peak to descend toward the foothills.

Jack Grimaldi piloted the Huey YH-40 with the skill and grace that had earned him the premier spot as Stony Man's chief pilot.

One of his passengers, the smallest of the pair, was more anxious than the other. In fact, Mack Bolan didn't feel anxiety—he considered it a stimulus that prepared him for whatever he might encounter. The adrenaline rush made him ready to handle whatever problems the enemy might throw his way. There was nothing to worry about.

But Alara Serif had never been in this type of situation before, and Bolan had to wonder if he'd made a mistake in his decision to take her along.

Bolan didn't let it worry him. If she followed him out of the bird without hesitation, then she'd be fine and would make an able companion. If she froze, Bolan would simply send Grimaldi on his way with her and call for the extraction when appropriate.

The Executioner double-checked his harness and then tapped the top of his helmet to indicate Serif should prepare to follow him down before he kicked out and away from the Huey.

Bolan descended the thick, nylon line with the practiced ease of an expert. That's because he was—he was equally comfortable jumping out of an airplane with a shoot at low altitude, or performing HALO jumps and plummeting at great speeds from heights of thirty-thousand feet. Equally, Bolan could jump from a chopper ten or twenty yards above the ground, just as he did now, and start taking out the enemy on his way down.

Fortunately there was no enemy here to engage him, so Bolan could concentrate fully on ensuring Serif got down in one piece.

The young woman had a faltering moment coming out of the chopper, but once she got clear she descended at just the right speed and tilt. Of course, Bolan was on the belay line the entire time and could have stopped her in a moment if she encountered trouble. Still, she performed admirably for it being her first time with very little chance to practice.

When her feet were on the ground, Bolan disconnected her carabiner and then flashed a blue laser light twice at the cockpit. The chopper lifted away, and soon the only sound was the wind whipping down the hills. The breeze had definitely picked up some but it was more than bearable. They were in the peak of the summer months but at this elevation there was still a chill to the predawn air.

Bolan got Serif's harness disconnected, then the pair set off down the rocky, uneven terrain. They had to proceed at a snail's pace while they waited for their eyes to adjust. As they progressed, they got more comfortable, and the Executioner started to pick up speed. They were still a good distance away. Bolan had predicted that all the players in the game would arrive by the time they reached the makeshift fortress; then he could take out the entire retinue in one fell swoop.

As they traversed the tricky ground of the foothills, Bolan kept turning it over in his mind. He knew there would be resistance, but he had no idea what those numbers looked like. Certainly he would expect Quon Ma to have a decent-sized force of his specially trained MSS agents in place. Amocacci wouldn't bring anyone, since he wasn't intelligent enough to think that this meeting was for anything other than the purpose of reuniting the group in its goals of disrupting U.S. military intelligence. Finally, Willham would probably put Savitch to work for him in some way, if for nothing else than to provide a fast way out of any situation that went wrong.

As to the rest, Bolan could not predict. Especially since he didn't know who "the rest" were or their capabilities and resources. As was typically the game, he would simply have to play it by ear and hope for the best.

"Hope for the best?" Serif had said when he'd voice his concerns.

"You can't plan for all eventualities in a scenario like this," Bolan had told her. "In fact, it's impossible to predict where things will go in *any* situation. Sometimes you just have to toss caution to the wind. Being adaptable to change and improvising when the situation doesn't go your way are two of the techniques I've used on more than one occasion."

Serif hadn't looked convinced, but then, it didn't matter—Bolan didn't have to sell her on his plan. All he had to do was to convince her he had the situation well in hand. That wasn't hard to convey since it was the truth.

THE SUN HADN'T even risen over the peaks of the Strandzha when the last of the attendees arrived. That turned out to be Lev Penzak, and when he stepped off the elevator he was dressed in very odd clothes.

"Good morning, Penzak," Ryzkhov said. "You're dressed in traveling clothes. Are you taking a trip?"

"Good morning, Comrade General." Penzak sat and said, "I have disturbing news. I've been recalled to Jerusalem. I'm leaving by midday."

"That *is* most disturbing," Ryzkhov said.

"Did Mossad give any reason for this sudden change?"

Penzak shrugged. "I don't know. The director is usually not forthcoming about the reasons for a recall until the agent returns."

"What do you think it means?" Willham asked.

"It varies from agent to agent, and situation to situation," Penzak said. "In some cases I've seen agents relieved and they take…early retirement. Other times, they've merely been reassigned. I cannot possibly know until I get back. I suspect I'm probably being reassigned."

"Well, it should not matter after today," Amocacci said. "Now that you're all present, shall we begin?"

"Yes," Ma said. "I would be most anxious to get to the heart of this matter you called so urgent."

"I think I speak for all of us, Quon, when I say how very glad I am to see you alive." When Ma sat in stony silence with only a curt nod as acknowledgment, Amocacci decided it was better to move forward. "As I told each of you, I suspect that we've all been manipulated by an outsider. This particular individual has penetrated our group in a very insidious way.

"Frankly, when this man first approached me anonymously I was convinced that he was an agent planted by subterfuge to penetrate the organization. It was only after I looked into his credentials that I thought he might become a significant resource. As such, I enlisted him in our plans to not only provide security for our group but to assist in our plans for the operation in America."

"Yes, yes, Gastone," Ryzkhov said, looking at his watch. "We know all that. Tell us the part we *don't* know. For example, the identity of this anonymous entity that was clever enough to fool all of us and to manipulate us into thinking that Quon Ma had committed a breach of trust."

"What are you talking about?" Ma asked. "Don't you already *know* who he is?"

"No," Ryzkhov said, looking at his watch again. "Why would you think I should know?"

Willham blinked. "Because you said Gastone gave you the name of this man."

"I never said anything of the sort," Ma replied slowly. Then he looked at Willham and added, "Except to *you*. You were the only one I told, and you told me that you'd not spoken with the others. So apparently you lied to me."

Willham looked like the cat caught with the canary at first, but he quickly recovered. "That's a ridiculous accusation!"

"Not ridiculous. It's the truth and you know it to be so. The fact is Gastone never gave me any name. I planted the idea in your mind because I wanted to see if when we gathered anybody else would make that claim. But they have not. And do you know why, you scum-sucking bottom feeder?" Ma's face reddened and veins started to bulge visibly in his neck. "Because they are not murderous traitors like you! You ordered this outsider to have me killed. But the difference between what you did and what I do now, the difference between us really on any level, is that you have failed and I will *succeed*!"

Quon Ma jumped to his feet and withdrew a concealed pistol, leveled it on Willham's chest and squeezed the trigger twice. Both rounds from the 9 mm pistol smashed through Willham's chest wall and exploded his heart and lungs. Ma finished the execution with a single shot to the head. The echoes died out in the room even as Willham's body slumped out of the chair with enough force to tip it onto its side and send both crashing to the ground.

The others sat stunned but nobody made an aggressive move. Ma's eyes moved to lock glances with each of them, the smoking pistol still held firmly in his grasp. It seemed abundantly clear that Ma was considering his next option and whether it was better to just kill all of them rather than take his chances one of them might come back to try again for him later.

Amocacci knew what Ma was thinking. The guy could not be sure if all of them hadn't colluded in the assassination attempt. There was little reason he had to trust any of them, frankly, since they had all been complicit in the affair on one level or another. But Amocacci hoped that maybe Ma's thirst for vengeance was satiated and they could get back to the job at hand, the thing they had all worked so long that it would be a shame not to see it through to its epic conclusion.

"Justice has been done," Amocacci said. "And now,

if you would please sit down, I can explain the rest of the story."

"I'm not sure that we have time to hear it," Penzak said. "And even if we did, I don't know that it would matter at this point. Willham is dead and therefore no longer a threat."

"I would tend to agree," Ryzkhov said. "With Willham gone, the rest of this doesn't matter."

"But I think it *does* matter to Quon Ma," Amocacci replied.

As Ma slowly took his seat, keeping his pistol close at hand in case anyone decided to try something foolish, he said, "Don't pretend to know me, Gastone. I'm still not sure you didn't have something to do with the attempt on me, too."

"I did, Quon," Amocacci replied, putting the deepest and gravest tone of regret possible in his voice. "But unfortunately, it was because I was manipulated in much the same way that Willham manipulated you. The man who ordered the actual assassination goes by the name of Derek Savitch. He apparently has something to do with Canadian intelligence, and he was assigned to oversee the contract to assassinate you. Fortunately, the assassin did not succeed and I was approached by an agent in the NSA who Savitch attempted to recruit. That man saved my organization, uncovered the plot to make it look as if you, Quon, had sent men to retaliate against my business interests. He was also the one who suggested we have this meeting to resolve the entire misunderstanding."

"You mean there is *another* outsider who knows about the Council?" Penzak demanded, climbing to his feet. "You're a damned old fool! I'm leaving!"

The doors that led from Amocacci's residence to the meeting room opened and a single man burst into the room. He had a pistol in his hand and he exchanged glances with each of the men in turn before his eyes finally came to settle on the deceased form of his boss.

Ma raised the pistol. "I assume *you* are Derek Savitch?"

"I...I don't know what's happen—"

Ma's aim was so accurate that his first round ended up going through the mouth of Derek Savitch and blowing his brains out the back of his head. His entire body snap-jerked with the impact and his finger coiled reflexively on the trigger of the pistol he'd been holding. The round ended up striking Ma in the chest and the Chinese MSS agent shouted with a mixture of surprise and pain. He looked down and saw the hole in his chest, clearly surprised by its appearance but not really acting as if he was in pain. Then blood began to spread out from the hole to soak his clothes and his breathing became erratic. A moment later the pistol fell from his grasp and he collapsed face-first to the floor.

"I'm afraid that this has not ended as I'd hoped," Amocacci said in a quavering voice.

"I'm leaving!" Penzak said with a curse. "Allying myself with any of you was the worst mistake of my career."

"It may well be the last," Ryzkhov muttered.

"What? What are you talking about?"

"At any moment my men will be coming through those doors." He pointed to the entrance Savitch had used. "There won't be any discussion. Their orders are to shoot anyone who is left alive that's not me."

"That's just great. So you have doomed us all!"

Amocacci put his head in his hands as he sat at the table. It had all gone so terribly wrong and he knew he had nobody to blame. The Council of Luminárii had dissolved itself by its own acts of avarice and self-indulgence. All he'd built up to work to his advantage now seemed to be unraveling at the seams like a ratty garment. Amocacci knew without a doubt, even as he heard the first reports from autofire somewhere above, that he'd once more let someone manipulate and betray him.

As SOON AS Mack Bolan saw the uniformed men in commando dress, he went into action. There were perhaps half a dozen of them and they were moving in staggered formation toward the entrance to the main house of Amocacci's estate.

Bolan got behind the largest rock he could find, engaged the burst-mode of the selector switch on his M-4 and sighted the first target. The night-vision device lit up the several figures that approached the house on a very direct course, not as if they were moving in to protect the place but more like an assault team. Their movements were precise and calculated, and Bolan realized where he'd seen that kind of formation before.

It was as if he were watching ghosts from his past. Those were Spetsnaz tactics if he'd ever seen them! Bolan reacquired the sight picture and squeezed the trigger. The weapon kicked twice as both rounds rocked on their ballistic trajectory with deadly accurate results. The rounds smashed open the man's skull and twisted his body at a gross angle. A moment later he toppled to the hard, unyielding ground.

A similar fate awaited the second commando, this one dropped by a double-tap to the chest that left a pair of holes in his chest and pummeled open the air-filled pockets of the chest cavity and chest wall. Ribs cracked, lungs collapsed and blood spewed from the man's mouth. He crumpled to the ground in very similar fashion to his partner who had preceded him in death.

Realizing they were taking fire from a sniper of considerable marksmanship, the squad leader ordered his surviving team members to spread out and find cover. Before they could do whatever grisly task they'd been sent to accomplish, they would have to fight Bolan in a battle to the death.

Unfortunately it became suddenly apparent that Bolan wasn't their only problem.

CHAPTER TWENTY-FOUR

A screaming horde suddenly appeared from the copse that stood between the foothills and the house, running parallel to Bolan and Serif's position among the rocks. They were armed with a variety of automatic weapons, some machine pistols but a larger number of full-assault rifles. Bolan could no longer determine if the new arrivals were house staff assigned to protect the estate or perhaps a different faction brought in to represent one of the other council leaders. In any case, it didn't matter because all of the entities joined in the battle begun by Bolan.

Some of the combatants fought against each other while others made a point of engaging Bolan's position.

There had to be at least a dozen, maybe more, and if he didn't handle them quickly they would overrun his current position. Bolan dropped the magazine and loaded a fresh one. He fired for effect, triggering short bursts and interlocking his fields of fire as much as possible. There wouldn't be any way to pin them down, although he'd managed to get them in a bit of a cross fire with the other group and that was helping to narrow the odds considerably.

Light had broken and Bolan could now make out his targets. In a short time he wouldn't need the special sights. He put another gunner in the crosshairs and triggered a short burst. One round cut through the man's throat and tore out a sizeable chunk of flesh. The second round hit him dead-on in the forehead and took the fight right out of him. Bolan dropped another of the newcomers with a cutting burst to the abdomen.

While the Executioner was making his shots count, the opportunities weren't coming fast enough. He'd take down one here and one there, then he'd have to grab the shelter of the rock as a fresh salvo of hot lead burned the air around him. The ricochets were also something of concern since the terrain around them was littered with boulders and stones.

"Let's move!" Bolan said. "It's now a free-for-all."

"What?"

"Kill or be killed."

"I'd rather not fall into that latter camp," Serif said.

Bolan was amused that the woman was using her wit to cope with the stress, but he didn't have time or the inclination to repost. If they didn't get out of the hostilities quickly, Serif's wit wouldn't matter because the mission would be over and they could count themselves as just two more casualties in the fray.

Bolan grabbed Serif's hand and directed her to climb the jumble of rocks behind her. Bullets whined around their heads and fragments zipped past from ricochets off the unyielding rocks. While the aim of their assailants was nothing short of abysmal, they had sheer volume on their side.

"You got to give them an A for effort," Bolan remarked.

Serif cried out suddenly, then lost her footing and fell. Bolan knew immediately from the odd angle at which she struck the ground that she'd probably turned her ankle. It really didn't come as much of a surprise to him. She'd had a considerable amount of trouble getting down the rugged terrain, Bolan on a couple of occasions having to provide her with significant help.

Bolan shone a flashlight onto her leg and found it wedged in the rocks. The soldier ran his hands over her leg, looking for a break, but he didn't find one. "Okay, you haven't broken your leg. Can you stand?"

"I think so," she said, scrambling to her feet. She put pressure on the right foot without complaint, but as soon as she tried to step on her left she went down and let out another cry of pain.

"You sprained your ankle," Bolan said.

"Or broke it."

"Don't be a defeatist."

Before Serif could concoct a biting, smart-aleck retort, the situation got desperate. Two men came around the rocks on the left front flank and leveled their weapons in Bolan's direction. He could now see they were Asian, and he realized that it was probably the little band Quon Ma had brought along in case things went south. Apparently that time had come and especially for Bolan and Serif.

The Executioner pressed forward in his defense, undaunted, protecting their position with a steady, accurate volley of bursts from the M-4. The 5.56 mm rounds shredded a path through the bellies of the two terrorist gunners, demonstrating the reactionary forces at play in the combat-hardened reflexes of the Executioner. The men seemed to dance like puppets under Bolan's unerring accuracy, and the rounds they had triggered didn't come close to Bolan or Serif.

Before the bodies hit the ground, Bolan had Serif on

her feet with one arm around her waist and the opposite holding her arm around his neck. They tried retreating up the rocky incline, but the terrain was simply too awkward. Bolan set her down and considered alternatives. He couldn't call Grimaldi in to extract them, not in that hot of an LZ. Not to mention, the Stony Man ace would have to fight the prevailing down drafts, all the while keeping the chopper under control as Bolan attempted to extricate.

Bolan handed his M-4 to Serif and said, "You know how to use that?"

She nodded.

"Good. Point it at anything that moves. I'll be back."

"Where are you going?"

"To draw the heat off your back."

Bolan burst from the rocks with Beretta 93-R in hand. He triggered a couple of shots on the run as he moved off their position at an angle and headed for an open area he'd spotted earlier when coming down the rocky hill. Light had now begun to spill over the peaks as the sun climbed higher into the sky. Bolan eyed his previous position, watching to see if anyone made for it. Apparently it had been too dark or their position too obscured for the gunners to see Serif, because none headed in that direction.

The various factions fighting one another realized they had a common enemy who'd been picking them off one by one. With only a few enemies left, Bolan figured it might be time to create a diversion to see just how resolved his foes were in protecting their position as best possible. The heavily armed men continued to press forward, moving on Bolan's position with less hesitancy and increased courage.

It was at this point Bolan decided to bring in the heavy guns. The Executioner reached to his harness strap and came away with an M-67 HE grenade. Bolan ducked behind the concealment of the rocks and remained in a crouch as he changed positions, moving behind an adjoining bolder about fifteen yards to his right. He didn't expect to toss the grenade into the midst of the crew but rather thought he'd catch their attention by offering no resistance whatsoever.

It took almost a minute before three of the men approached and peered around the edge of Bolan's boulder. Meanwhile he'd been holding the spoon against the body with the pin drawn. As soon as he heard the first tumble of rocks crunching beneath boots, Bolan let the thing fly and counted a cook-off interval. At the last moment he tossed the grenade gently over the boulder and it came down between the enemy gunners just a moment before exploding. One man's head was completely separated from its owner's body while a second was instantly blinded by the hot flash that scalded his eyes and face. The last man stared in shock at his arm, which had been separated from the shoulder socket and lay several feet from him as he stared at it.

Bolan swung around the opposite side of the rocks and came up on the right flank of the two survivors waiting in the wings to draw him out. They looked surprised when Bolan appeared on a rock right over their heads. They were on their bellies and tried to bring weapons to bear but Bolan wasn't having any of it. The Executioner cut them down with short bursts to the head.

As the sounds of battle died quickly in the crisp, morning air, Bolan's ears picked up what sounded like the roar of a vehicle engine. He quickly sprinted in the direction of the sound and rounded the corner of a massive rock in time to see three men rocket out of the clearing in an open-topped Range Rover. Bolan didn't recognize the man in the passenger seat or the man in the back seat, but he definitely recognized the driver. Amocacci was attempting to escape, and there was no way Bolan could permit that.

The soldier whipped out his radio. "Striker to Eagle. Come in, Eagle!"

"Eagle, here," came Grimaldi's reply.

"Come down on this signal. Our friends are trying to escape by vehicle, and we can't have that."

"Roger that, Striker. I'm on my way!"

Bolan clicked off and raced back to the position to find Alara Serif waiting patiently for him. Her face was smudged with dirt but it did nothing to rip the fire and verve from those smoldering dark eyes. More than ever, she seemed intent on seeing the situation through. Despite her pain, she indicated she would walk with Bolan's assistance.

Toward the last thirty yards or so to the LZ, Bolan had to pick her up and toss her lithe form over his shoulder as a matter of expediency.

Once they were up in the air, it didn't take Bolan and Grimaldi long to spot the Range Rover's plume of dust. Bolan couldn't help but wonder what had transpired. He didn't recognize either of the men who accompanied Amocacci, who was fighting desperately to keep the vehicle under control despite the unwieldy terrain. He'd not seen Quon Ma; he assumed the guy was dead. He also hadn't seen Derek Savitch.

Bolan gestured at the Rover as soon as he spotted

it, and Grimaldi nodded at Bolan's hand signals. The chopper came down low and hovered over the bouncing vehicle. Amocacci jerked the wheel back and forth, trying his best to evade, but at one point he nearly tossed one of his passengers out and flipped the vehicle. It was when he slowed considerably and Grimaldi slowed to match speed that Bolan saw his opportunity.

The Executioner planted both feet on the skids of the Huey and timed his jump so that he landed on the rear deck plate of the Rover. Amocacci jammed on the brakes and tried to send Bolan flying, but the soldier had anticipated that move and managed to get a hand on the roll bar. When the vehicle suddenly slowed from Amocacci's move, Bolan simply rolled over the bar to displace the motion and came down with both feet flat on the seat.

The guy in the back and to the soldier's left tried to stab him in the gut with a knife. Bolan blocked the attack by hammering the man's wrist with his left fist. He then wrapped the crook of his left arm around the roll bar and jumped while using the bar for leverage. He managed to get his thighs locked around the smaller man's neck and squeezed, pinning the guy to the seat.

The comparatively older man in the front passenger seat—who had been an observer to this point with the obvious belief his compatriot could handle Bolan—reached beneath his jacket pocket and withdrew a wicked-looking pistol. He leveled it at Bolan and started to squeeze the trigger. The soldier did something completely unexpected, lashing out with a rock-hard punch to the back of Amocacci's head. The blow jarred the man with enough force that he nearly lost consciousness for a moment and his foot tromped the gas pedal.

The sudden acceleration caused the gunman's shot to go wide, missing Bolan by a considerable margin.

It was the delay Bolan needed to draw his Desert Eagle. The pistol gleamed with silvery menace in the morning light. The front passenger looked surprised as the barrel of the .44 Magnum pistol wavered only a moment in front of his face. Bolan squeezed the trigger and the man's head blew open like a melon under a sledgehammer, the heavy-grain bullet entering his skull with such force the normally closed container could not cope and responded in the only natural way possible under such circumstances.

Bolan's legs started to cramp and he eased up the pressure, the knife-wielder no longer fighting and obviously unconscious. Somehow, Amocacci had managed to remain conscious. He started to come around and tried to get the vehicle under control. Bolan put the warm barrel against Amocacci's head.

"Stop now!"

Amocacci started to slow as if he planned to comply, but at the last minute he jerked the wheel hard left. The sudden turned sent Bolan's top-heavy arm flying and it struck the roll bar, knocking his pistol out of his grip in the process.

Amocacci bailed from the Rover while it was still in motion and Bolan suddenly realized why. Looming straight ahead was the lip of a precipice. The soldier scrambled to the edge of the Rover and leaped out before the vehicle went over the edge and disappeared from view.

Sweat now poured from Bolan's forehead and he breathed hard with the exertion of battle. He heard a sound and looked up in time to see Amocacci swing-

ing a heavy tree branch in his direction. Bolan rolled
from the blow and it glanced off his left shoulder; fortunately not the one that had been winged. But it wasn't
for lack of trying on Amocacci's part as he attempted
to get inside the Executioner's guard. Bolan ducked
under one last mighty swing and moved in and took
Amocacci to the ground with a midsection tackle. The
Italian squeezed from Bolan's attempted hold, which
fell short of the waist and instead degraded to a loose
capture of the ankles.

Amocacci had been trained in the finer points of
hand-to-hand combat, but years of soft living had left
him less than proficient. Still, he seemed pretty able
and probably tough enough to take a beating. He managed to wriggle free by driving a boot into Bolan's
cheek that split the skin just below the Executioner's
eye. Bolan and Amocacci got to their feet simultaneously. Bolan kept his guard up and parried each attack Amocacci threw at him. He deflected numerous
punches and kicks, but he knew he outclassed Amocacci
in both experience and weight.

When the opening finally came, Bolan took full advantage of it. Amocacci managed to land a hammer
blow on Bolan's wounded shoulder and when the soldier stepped back in pain, Amocacci seized the moment
and produced a boot knife. He rushed for the kill, but
what he hadn't planned on was Bolan's deception that
Amocacci's blow to his wounded shoulder actually did
him more damage than it had.

Amocacci looked surprised, then, when he drove
the knife toward Bolan's gut and suddenly his opponent seemed to erupt into action. Bolan pivoted side-
ways to present a narrow target and so that he could

deflect the knife with his right hand, shuffling to get on the outside of Amocacci's guard. Bolan grabbed his opponent's wrist and pulled tight as he drove an elbow downward and connected with the meaty part of the arm at the elbow joint. The blow numbed the hand holding the knife and it sprang from Amocacci's useless grip.

Bolan swept the Italian's leg from under him while pulling in the reverse direction he had before to take the guy off balance. Bolan then came down on top of Amocacci's chest with his knee and drove a ridge-hand blow into his adversary's throat. The blow fractured the voice box and Amocacci let out a gurgle and crackling noise. Less than a minute later, he lay utterly still and his breathing stopped.

Bolan, soaked in sweat and his body aching, retrieved his Desert Eagle just as Grimaldi set the chopper down less than twenty yards from his position. Bolan waved at Grimaldi to hang tight and then rushed to the precipice. He stopped and carefully peered over the side only to find the vehicle had merely dropped into a very large depression.

And he heard the only survivor of the Council of Luminárii moan.

CHAPTER TWENTY-FIVE

Tyndall Air Force Base, Florida

Heinrich Wehr sat and studied the fighter jets that sat on the tarmac and gleamed in the midafternoon sun.

The fighters were F-22 Raptors, the latest class of stealth air superiority fighters. There wasn't anything Wehr didn't know about these modern marvels. The specifications had come easily enough to him through his various connections within the DIA. Alongside those fighters were the variant future jets based on the original Lockheed Martin design. The F-35B Lightning II fighter was the most advanced aircraft ever to take to the skies, developed to take on a number of roles, including reconnaissance missions, air-to-surface first-strike capabilities and air-to-air defense. It could travel at Mach 1.6, exceed more than a thousand nautical miles on its own internal fuel capacity and had max-out at nearly 9 g.

It was this marvel of avionics that had been brought to Wehr's attention and the reason he'd gone to Savitch with the idea. The entire thing had been a setup, of course, and he'd managed to get them to let him on the inside of their plans. It was when Quon Ma had been snooping in affairs that didn't concern him that Wehr realized the need for the man to die. He'd manipulated the situation exactly as planned but managed to keep the rest of the Council of Luminárii members restless. He'd done it all—from the provision of manpower to disrupting the operations of the American military officer named Stone to engineering the kidnapping of Alara Serif.

Wehr had even convinced Amocacci of the need to seek vengeance on the U.S. after the death of his family. Unfortunately it wasn't U.S. special operatives who had actually been responsible for their deaths. Once more, that had been the handiwork of Heinrich Wehr and his men. It was the British SIS agent who'd proved the most difficult to control. Instead of keeping Willham on a tight leash, Wehr had sent Savitch directly to him without Savitch even knowing he was behind it. Wehr had then arranged for Savitch to hire him to do the hit on Quon Ma, a hit that he'd botched because he'd been sloppy.

As good fortune had it, Willham had been more than kind enough to take the heat for that entire situation, and he'd played perfectly into Wehr's hand by letting the control over Savitch go to his head. Wehr had been disgusted by the complete lack of vision on the part of the other members of the Council. Not a single one of them had been able to realize their full potential, and now they were dead. Not a single one of those pathetic bastards had been able to understand the importance of this operation. The American military intelligence groups weren't a threat because they conducted random operations here or there where a few noncombatant casualties occurred. Such were acceptable losses in any military action, regardless if it was peacetime or war. Where the U.S. military intelligence was dangerous was in their protection of military technologies that made them unaccountable to anyone else.

No nation, no world government and no treaty organization could stop the United States. It continued to develop its weapons in secret and to manipulate the rest of the world into disarming while it continued building its military industrial complex. It was the greatest war machine of hypocrisy the world had ever seen, and it was the military intelligence people who continued to perpetuate the myth. They were the propaganda arm that was answerable to no one. They did not recognize any other authority, whether that was mandated by human life or by a higher power.

Wehr didn't necessarily believe in a divine creator, but he sure as hell didn't believe that it was the place of any nation to rule the destiny of others. Wehr had spent his entire life growing up in the EU. He'd moved from one country to another and seen the terrible, destructive forces at work in the United States. There was no accountability here, no means of recompense when America interfered with the sovereignty of other nations while proclaiming in a single loud voice how much they cherished liberty above all else.

Their activities throughout the world spoke of another agenda, an agenda that wasn't uncommon to empires that had come to rule in the past. No, America was perhaps the greatest deterrent to a free world, and it was the U.S. military intelligence channels that kept their activities hidden from the rest of the world. And until somebody revealed that on a global scale, nothing would change. America would continue to build new fighter jets and new oceangoing behemoths they could distribute throughout the world. Before long, no country could be safe from the monsters in the American war machine. And Heinrich Wehr could no longer stand by and watch it happen.

Wehr would be a council of one! And he would shed light into the dark heart of America and expose her shame for all the world to see.

"THERE'S NO DOUBT about it," Bolan told Price and Brognola over the conference line as the plane touched down. "Penzak wasn't the only surviving member of the Council. There's one more, apparently, and he's the one who masterminded this entire plot."

"And you say you don't have an identity on him?" Price asked.

"We may have been able to get the information on his travels into and out of Turkey that fits the same time window as the assassination attempt on Quon Ma," Bolan replied. "Penzak wasn't initially cooperative with us, but once I applied some pressure he seemed quite anxious to come around to my way of thinking."

"There are times when we're quite glad you can be so persuasive, Striker," Brognola said. "So what're your thoughts about this guy?"

"His real name is Heinrich Wehr. He's never been a major player in the game. He began life mostly as a small-time hit man for a rather large criminal enterprise in Germany. Essentially this was a group that ran some major action in some of the smaller countries that make up the European Union. Baltic States and such. Small potatoes."

"So how did he end up with a group like the Council without any sort of ties to the intelligence community?" Price inquired.

"Apparently he got wrapped up in political assassination. That put some legs under him and when he happened to come across some confidential documents after the accidental assassination of a CIA agent operating right in Germany, he went off the deep end. He used the information to get to others and that's when the blackmail started. He formed the Council to act as a shadow agency so he could make his own plans."

"You think he's orchestrated all the other recent events?"

Bolan nodded. "It explains how some of the security controls put in place on our military intelligence community were so easily compromised. If it wasn't somebody he could bribe, then it was someone he'd manipulate. If he couldn't manipulate them, he'd threaten them."

"And it explains how he was able to put the team together in Colorado that managed to crack our signals intelligence."

"Right. Once he knew how to work the flaws in the system, he could replicate that throughout every intelligence agency that had any connection to American military intelligence. He also assassinated a courier used quite often by agencies throughout the regions in Turkey."

"So what makes you think Tyndall Air Force Base is his intended target?" Brognola inquired.

"It only makes sense, Hal," Bolan said. "You'll recall that when all of this started, the trail led us there. I think it was the plan all the time. But when I almost had it figured out down in Guatemala, Wehr did what he does best and put up a bunch of smoke and mirrors to distract us. Plus, Penzak seemed pretty insistent that's where we needed to look. I just didn't want to put the whole base on high alert because of the potential fallout. Not to mention it's going to make my job that much harder if things get hot and the press starts crawling over the base looking for answers. A few newsworthy shots of yours truly and the whole thing could blow up in our faces."

"Not to mention how it might alert Wehr that you're on to him," Price added.

"We don't want that. Especially in light of the recent deaths of our servicemen," Brognola said. "We're still trying to sort out that whole mess with the government in Guatemala while keeping it quiet. The families are asking a lot of questions and we don't know how much longer we can hold them off."

Bolan shook his head at the two faces peering back at him on the small computer monitor, part of the communications package aboard the jet. "Our government could try the truth once in a while. They died in action attempting to defend their country. People can be pretty understanding if they think they're getting the straight story."

"Well, politics won't necessarily permit us to go there," Price said, although there wasn't a hint of malice in her voice.

Bolan knew that it wasn't either Brognola or Price's idea to cope with the death of American military personnel in such a fashion. People just wanted to be informed when it came to their loved ones, and they could better accept the death of a loved on defending his or her country and being a hero than some glad-handing or cockamamie story that didn't explain a thing.

"I know," Bolan said. "Let's forget about that. The

important thing now is to locate Wehr and neutralize whatever he has planned."

"Any ideas on how to do that?" Brognola asked.

"Penzak said Wehr plans to do something spectacular," Bolan said. "Those were his words, not mine, and apparently he basically quoted Wehr in saying it. The Council put the location and other stuff together but only Wehr had the actual plan."

"Well, there are any number of spectacular things a maniac like that might come up with to do on a military base," Price said. "He might explode a bomb in a barracks building or he might charge an AP security gate with explosives strapped to his chest."

"I don't think so," Bolan said. "It's just not big enough."

"It would be big enough to the media," Price reminded him.

"Wehr doesn't care about the media," Bolan replied. "He's a fanatic, and the only thing fanatics typically concern themselves with is creating as much wanton destruction as possible. They want to kill lots of people, destroy...*something*. Make a statement."

"A mass shooting spree?"

Bolan shook his head. "Wouldn't be anything as mundane or obvious as that. You have to remember that getting the credentials for base access would be child's play for Wehr. But getting something like weapons or explosives onto the base, that's something else entirely."

"You think he'll use whatever's available to him?" Price asked.

"Exactly."

As the aircraft rolled to a stop, Grimaldi's voice broke in. "Sorry to cut into your chat here, folks, but

I was listening to the conversation and something just occurred to me."

"We're all ears, Jack," Price replied. "Lay it on us."

"Well, if memory serves correctly, there's supposed to be a demonstration this morning of the new F-35B Lightning II airspace superiority fighters delivered to Tyndall. It might be that Wehr has something planned for that. There are supposed to be a lot of dignitaries for the initial demonstration, not to mention it's a PR extravaganza. Air shows are highly popular in Florida and this one promises to be a doozy."

"That's it!" Bolan said. "There's no doubt in my mind that's the mark. Wehr wouldn't be able to pass it up. It plays right into his wheelhouse. It was clear that he'd all but brainwashed Amocacci into taking the role he did with the Council, and there's evidence to support his antiwar machine doctrine."

"Okay, Striker," Brognola said. "We'll leave this in your capable hands. Be careful and don't take any chances. The President has authorized whatever action is necessary to neutralize this individual."

"Understood," Bolan said. "Out."

Bolan killed the connection and levered his big frame out of the seat. He donned a web belt that had been hanging from a nearby seat and then grabbed an MP5K from the onboard armory.

Bolan made it to the hatchway just as Grimaldi got it opened up and the stairs lowered.

"Want me to tag along?"

The Executioner shook his head. "Not this time, Jack. I'm going this one alone."

"I understand."

"Take a rest. You've earned it."

"So have you."

"Not yet," Bolan replied grimly as he descended the steps.

The government sedan he'd requested waited just off the tarmac. It was a new Dodge Charger with a couple of special modifications. One included bulletproof glass and the other was a reinforced body to withstand rolls. Bolan laid the MP5K on the seat next to him and cranked the engine. He dropped the selector into gear and tromped the accelerator, heading directly for the flight line where he recalled the fighters were parked. He couldn't be sure if Wehr had something planned for after the fighters were in the air or if he'd arranged a ground show.

Whatever it was, though, Mack Bolan intended to make sure it never came off.

BOLAN HAD SPENT more than thirty minutes driving up and down the flight line looking for anything unusual. A small crowd of civilians had begun to gather behind the barricades, but most of the military dignitaries hadn't yet arrived. Bolan checked his watch again. More than an hour remained until showtime and he wondered if he'd showed up too early. His plan had been to see if he could flush Wehr into the open, but now he was beginning to wonder if he'd been duped.

Bolan was about to leave the area to go check out some of the other flight lines when he spotted a technician walking toward the aircraft. Then the technician did something completely out of character. He walked directly behind one of the aircraft and straight into a path line that under live conditions would have gotten him sucked right into the engine. Any *real* technician or mechanic would never have done that if for no other reason than out of sheer habit.

Bolan stepped on the accelerator and rocketed toward the technician's position. The man turned toward him at the sound of roaring engine, then started to race for a massive repair hangar about fifty yards away. The Executioner tried to coax more speed from the powerful engine, but he knew he wouldn't make it to the hangar before Wehr made it inside.

Bolan grabbed up the MP5 on the passenger seat, jacked the charging handle to the rear and stuck the subgun out the window, triggering a burst that diverted Wehr from his initial goal of getting inside the hangar. He tried to hit the man in the legs, cut out any chance of his escape, but Wehr juked to the left at the last moment and Bolan missed. The Executioner nearly lost control of his vehicle but managed to keep it aright as he adjusted direction for another shot.

Wehr suddenly cut left again and ducked between a pair of fifty-five-gallon drums. Bolan tromped on the brakes, suddenly aware that those drums looked out of place in their present location. Smoke rolled up from the tires as rubber melted into the pavement. The Executioner managed to get the vehicle stopped. Through the haze of gray-blue smoke he saw Wehr reach into one of the drums and withdraw a long, cylindrical object.

Bolan recognized it immediately: rocket launcher!

He no longer wondered what Wehr had in store relative to his demonstration, but he also knew the guy would change his plans in a moment if it meant the possibility of escape. Brognola's words echoed in Bolan's ears as he vaulted the center console, opened the passenger-side door of the Dodge, and went EVA.

He managed to clear the vehicle by about ten or twelve yards before he felt the whoosh of heat and flame that seemed to consume the air around him. Bolan smelled the singed hair on his arms, felt the crispy curl of the hair on his head and hands just before he realized the flames had ignited his fire-resistant blacksuit. Bolan dropped and began to roll on his back to put out the flames while he beat at a patch just inside his right thigh.

Bolan finally rolled to his feet and whirled in time to see Wehr load a second RPG. Instead of firing at Bolan, though, he turned and began to run in the direction of the flight line and the F-35B fighters parked there. More of concern, however, were the unsuspecting bystanders and citizens just standing around. It was another sunny day in Florida, and a chance to see some exciting aeronautics of the most advanced fighter jet in the world was not to be missed. Little did they suspect that a maniac named Heinrich Wehr had planned to turn it into more like a Fourth of July celebration by creating some of his own fireworks.

The Executioner wouldn't allow it to happen.

Bolan went after Wehr, wisps of smoke still emanating from his charred clothing as he hammered the pavement for all he was worth. Blood pumped through his strong legs and his lungs burned with the already humid morning air.

Bolan rounded the corner of another hangar building that opened onto the flight line and watched as Wehr came to a halt and aimed the RPG at one of the F-35B Lightning II aircraft. Bolan snap-aimed the MP5 and yanked on the trigger, but nothing happened. The subgun had jammed, probably taking damage in the fall after the explosion. Bolan dropped the weapon and clawed at the military holster on his hip. He cleared the .44 Magnum Desert Eagle.

The Executioner sighted and squeezed the trigger. The heavy slug punched through the center body of the RPG and it shattered in Wehr's hand, becoming utterly worthless in a moment. Unfortunately, while the bullet went through the fragile plastic and thin metal of the launcher, it missed Wehr's head entirely. The impact had apparently dazed him, though, because he hesitated for a moment or two. Then he seemed to regain his senses, turned to see Bolan now on approach and immediately took off again.

Bolan saw the guy heading directly for the crowd of civilians, but at the last second he seemed to veer off.

The Executioner let out a massive breath of relief, thankful he wouldn't be forced into a hostage situation. The foot chase continued up the long tarmac; it looked as if Wehr was determined to reach another hangar building.

Before Bolan could wave them off, a pair of security police vehicles rushed toward Wehr on an intercept course. One of them squealed to a halt just in front of him. The driver jumped out and reached for his pistol. He'd just cleared it from his holster when Wehr slammed into him full-force, punching him in the throat with his right hand as he grabbed the AP's pistol with his left. The kid's head was slammed against the metal roof and then Wehr raised the pistol and shot the officer in the face.

Bolan clenched his teeth as he watched the carnage unfold. The man's partner, a woman, was out of the passenger side of the vehicle and had her gun drawn with admirable speed. Unfortunately the only shot she managed to get off went right over Wehr's head as he ducked into the vehicle and shot the officer in the belly low enough that the vest wouldn't protect her.

Wehr put the AP vehicle in gear and started off when the second squad came up and rammed him in the side, attempting to put him into a spin that would cause his vehicle to either stop or flip onto its side. Wehr managed to gain control of the car while simultaneously sticking the pistol out the window and triggering one successive shot after another at the other car.

Bolan reached Wehr's commandeered vehicle just as the tires were smoking and he attempted to get away. The Executioner raised his pistol and blew two holes in the passenger-side window before throwing his entire body through it, arms extended directly in front of him. The maneuver surprised Wehr and his head rocked against the B-post of the vehicle as Bolan's fist connected with his jaw.

The Executioner wasn't finished—not by a long shot.

As Wehr fumbled for his weapon, and as the images of the young man and woman who'd just been killed in cold blood rushed through his mind, Bolan pointed the .44 Magnum directly under Wehr's chin and squeezed the trigger. The top of the man's head exploded and the roof turned a splotchy gray-red color, splattering both top and side window with a gory spray of blood and brain matter. The vehicle was now slowing, the driver no longer alive to demand acceleration.

Bolan dropped his pistol and twisted his body so that he could reach the brake pedal with his left hand. He slammed the palm of his hand against the pedal and then put the gearshift in Park. The heat blasted off the tarmac and sweat ran down his forehead and stung his eyes. With one last effort, Bolan turned the ignition off and fought the urge to pass out. Only his stinging eyes and his sides, which hurt with the exertion and impact of the battle, kept him conscious.

Two officers helped extricate Bolan from the vehicle as additional squads and an ambulance arrived. They immediately began to block off the scene, but nobody asked Bolan questions. In the utter pandemonium he was able to slip away.

Bolan hadn't gotten more than fifty or sixty yards from the scene when Grimaldi rolled up in another sedan. "Hey, there, buddy. Need a lift?"

* * * * *

Don Pendleton's Mack Bolan®

Insurrection

**Jihadists are one strike from turning
Nigeria into a mass grave...**

A jihadist bomb brings down a massive church
in Ibadan, forcing Catholic bishops straight into
Nigeria's most fearsome terrorist group. This
bloodbath is only the beginning of a reign of
terror linked to al Qaeda. Mack Bolan sets out to
hunt the leader down...

Yet the moment Bolan hits Nigerian soil, his
identity is compromised. With the death toll rising,
Bolan will have to play one last gamble to restore
the region's rightful government—and send this
unholy gang of jihadists into fiery oblivion.

Available March 2015 wherever books and ebooks are sold.

Don Pendleton
MIND BOMB

A drug that creates homicidal maniacs must be stopped...

Following a series of suicide bombings along the US–Mexico border, the relatives of a dead female bomber attack Able Team. Clearly these bombings are far more than random killings. Searching for an answer, Stony Man discovers someone is controlling these people's minds with a drug that gives them the urge to kill and then renders them catatonic or dead. While Able Team follows leads in the US, Phoenix Force heads to investigate similar bombings in the Middle East. With numerous civilians already infected, they must eliminate the source before the body count of unwilling sacrifices mounts.

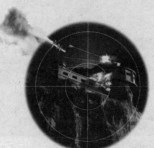

STONY MAN®

Available February 2015
wherever books and ebooks are sold.

The Executioner®

Don Pendleton's

PERILOUS CARGO

**Ruthless killers race to find a
stolen warhead…**

The Himalayas become a deadly hunting zone when a
nuclear warhead is stolen. Knowing the incident could start
World War III, the President sends Mack Bolan and a CIA
operative to retrieve the weapon.

Bolan and his ally are up against cunning assassins and
several local warlords. These competing parties are
determined to reach the weapon first—no matter how many
witnesses they eliminate. With the harsh mountain terrain
working against them, the Executioner will need to rely on
his wits to win this race…because coming in second is not
an option.

**GOLD
EAGLE**®

*Available March 2015,
wherever books and ebooks are sold.*

GEX436R

James Axler
Outlanders®

TERMINAL WHITE

The old order has a new plan to enslave humanity

The Cerberus rebels remain vigilant, defending mankind's sovereignty against the alien forces. Now a dark and deadly intelligence plots to eradicate what it means to be human: free will.

In the northern wilderness, an experimental testing ground—where computers have replaced independent choice—is turning citizens into docile, obedient sheep. The brainchild of a dedicated Magistrate of the old order, Terminal White promises to achieve the subjugation of the human race. As the Cerberus warriors infiltrate and get trapped in this mechanized web, humanity's only salvation may be lost in a blinding white doom.

Available February 2015

Or order your copy now by sending your name, address, zip or postal code, along with a check or money order (please do not send cash) for $6.99 for each book ordered ($7.99 in Canada), plus 75¢ postage and handling ($1.00 in Canada), payable to Gold Eagle Books, to:

In the U.S.	In Canada
Gold Eagle Books	Gold Eagle Books
3010 Walden Avenue	P.O. Box 636
P.O. Box 9077	Fort Erie, Ontario
Buffalo, NY 14269-9077	L2A 5X3

Please specify book title with your order.
Canadian residents add applicable federal and provincial taxes.

GOLD EAGLE®

JAMES AXLER

DEATH LANDS®

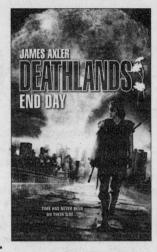

END DAY

Time has never been on their side...

On the heels of Magus, a Deathlands nemesis, Ryan and his companions find themselves in a place more foreign than any they've encountered before. After unwittingly slipping through a time hole, the group lands in twentieth-century New York City, getting their first glimpse of predark civilization—and they're not sure they like it. Only Mildred and Doc can appreciate this strange metropolis, but time for reminiscing is cut short. Armageddon is just seventy-two hours away, and Magus will stop at nothing to ensure Ryan and his team are destroyed on Nuke Day. As the clock ticks down, the city becomes a deadly maze. The companions are desperate to find their way back to Deathlands...but not before they trap Magus in New York forever.

Available March 2015 wherever books and ebooks are sold.